KNOCK KNOCK

KNOCK KNOCK
a Life

Suzanne McNear

THE PERMANENT PRESS
Sag Harbor, NY 11963

For information, address:
   The Permanent Press
   4170 Noyac Road
   Sag Harbor, NY 11963
   www.thepermanentpress.com

Library of Congress Cataloging-in-Publication Data

McNear, Suzanne –
   Knock knock / Suzanne McNear.
         p. cm.
   ISBN 978-1-57962-286-2
      1. Women—United States—History—20th century—Fiction.
   2. Self-realization in women—Fiction. 3. Autobiographical fiction.
   I. Title.

PS3563.C38845K66 2012
813'.54—dc23   2012029102

Printed in the United States of America

To my family

ACKNOWLEDGMENTS

My thanks to Lysbet Rogers, Lily Tuck, Glynn Woolfenden, my friends at Ashawagh Hall, most especially Laura Stein, Susie Schlesinger for the cabin at her ranch, and my editors Judy and Marty Shepard.

It's brief and bright, dear children; bright and brief.
Delight's the lightning; the long thunder's grief.

—JOHN FREDERICK NIMS, "Day of Our Years"

Even before she is born March Rivers hears all about it. She rocks down there in that dark warm river, listens to the music, the enchanting soap operas, bits of chatter, and tells herself, oh you're going to love it out there. Life. Yes you are, March. I promise you anything, but I give you a fox trot, ten toes, a dab of Arpège. I send you on your way, and all you do is wave and say hello to the world. There there. Head up. Shoulders back. Never fear. Say, Hello, my name is March Rivers. What is yours? What is your hobby? I am fine. Fine thank you. How do you do? Laugh and the world laughs with you. Squeeze a little around your eye until something happens. Thus, a wink. Indicating, this is all in fun. Now, a smile, and there you are. Splendid. Remember, being alone is scary, and you only live once. God bless America, and God bless you.

And so March enters. Small, but tough. Very red, very fierce. Soaked, but a miracle, nevertheless. Born early at hot dawn with the sun just looping its way over the choppy Lake Michigan sea, the temperature on the bank building already pushing eighty, and the Saturday night music playing on. What we have here is a four-pound tomato, a real survivor. It is 1934. Not the best of times; still, Ivan Bunin has been awarded the Nobel Prize for Literature and Helen Moody is the Wimbledon champion; Brokers Tip has won the Derby; Sally Rand is a star. And it's going to be a beautiful day! A lovely day. Seventy-nine, clear as a bell. Out on Main Street people will move right along, hum a tune, keep the beat, dream new dreams, praise summer skies. On this summer morning, hardly a cloud in sight.

March Rivers, growing up in the Rivers family in La Rue, Wisconsin, on the stony western shores of Lake Michigan. In a world of dust motes, lilacs, pheasant feathers, smoldering coal clinkers, linens and silver, frozen windowpanes. An old, dark prairie house. The garden with sweet peas, bleeding hearts, a thousand lilies of the valley, an apple tree, a weeping willow. Next door, another prairie house; this house also belonging to the Rivers, the grandparent Rivers. Bumpa, a distinguished man who uses oxygen for his emphysema, and Nana, a small pink puffy woman with airs: jewels, party dresses, tiny golf clubs, sporty shoes. Her son has married, but it seems that she will not let him go. His wife, March's mother, will—perhaps rightly so—resent this woman, and the feeling will be reciprocated, even after the move to the new house twenty years later.

The new house beside the lighthouse. Where the foghorn will blow. Where at night the beam swings above sloping lawns, past pine trees and the beach, out over the water.

Through the years the son, March's father, will continue to stop by what is known as the other house each evening on his way home from the office. For a proper visit. Even after his own father is safely interred in the cemetery on the hill; during the years when his mother continues to tend her garden, pack for the move to Blue Lake in the summer, order new butter plates—Singapore bird with the charming pale blue background. Until March is in her senior year in college when she will receive a mink stole, her inheritance, along with the promise of a heart-shaped pin with an arrow of rubies which will be kept for her until her wedding day. The stole will be worn over her pajamas in the winter of 1956 as she types her collection of stories for her senior thesis at Vassar, the mink heads quivering against her shoulder. The heart-shaped pin will be lost on a snowy evening in New York, after a party at which March will have consumed too much champagne, and learned from the husband of a famous opera star that he practiced walking in water, like a racehorse, for his health.

Within this family March is briefly cushioned from the world in a pink bassinet with a lace canopy, and a nursemaid to watch over her, but almost from the beginning she is perceived to be a problem. She is described as a difficult baby and is returned to the hospital. Oh, you would not stop crying, her mother will say one day, laughing. We sent you back. Home again, she continues to exhaust everyone. Later she displays a temper, later still, a tendency to run away. She wears a perpetual scowl. Nevertheless, she looks like a Rivers. She has the nose, the high forehead, the legs (stocky, or as she insists years later, plow, plow legs!), and even the eyes: eyes so blue, and round as ping pong balls.

The christening picture taken by Herman Studios is framed, and a copy is put in the family album, a photograph glued in there with generations of other wobble-neck bald monkeys. Nodding at the age of seven weeks above the same fragile dress with the lace trim once worn by March's great grandmother, grandmother, mother, four uncles, three aunts, a brother a year older than March, and later a sister. Through it all it remains a beautiful dress to be passed from one to another in a long line of Episcopalians who support the church, but tend to be somewhat vague about what's in it for them.

Is there life after death? March's father asks. We don't know, but there is consolation in this: nobody escapes. He names Alfred Lord Tennyson, Stephen Vincent Benét, Richard Halliburton, Ernest Hemingway. Important men who have died. Or will. Still, he frowns when he says this. March's mother smiles and says there will be no whoop de doo in the sky. When I'm old, she cries. Shoot me!

As for the christening dress. You don't find lace like that anymore. You don't find that kind of workmanship, that attention to detail. No, you certainly don't.

Trotting down Rivers Avenue at the age of one year, minus one month—there goes the little Rivers child in her birthday suit again—the urge to keep going may have been strong, but March's luck was limited, and she was returned to the house by a great aunt who had bad lungs and white gloves. And you'll have them too someday, the aunt assured her. For she was a Rivers. Being a part of such a family ought to be considered a privilege! Ought to encourage good behavior, a head held high.

Once English, Scotch, Welsh, French, Czech, German, Swedish, the Rivers, like many other families in La Rue, like their friends, are now true Midwesterners. Manufacturers. Makers of tractors, automobile parts, radiators and wax, marine equipment and malted milk products. Shiny lake-fed men and women. People whose forefathers cleared and settled the land, built their city around them. Polite, proud, conservative people who do not dwell upon the past. For the most part they do not keep trunks in the attic, hang family portraits, prop historic documents on mantelpieces. There are tales perhaps, but few storytellers to spread them out. Businessmen instead of poets. Family trees never drawn.

People caught on holidays and wedding days, baptisms and birthdays, in photographs pasted with black sticky edges onto the pages of leather-bound albums, or hurrying about in home movies shown in darkened rooms with the projector light blazing, the whirring sound of the film turning, someone calling out, There I am! See me!

The Family. Standing around their great stone fireplaces, seated at long dining room tables, on lawns, on docks, on the steps of summerhouses. Bodies in costumes. Silk prints flapping over white shoes, straw hats, stiffened linens, summer wind and summer ribbons, flopping furs, hunting jackets, high cuts, knickers, ruffles, starched cuffs, a face peeking out from the center of an old soft lacy valentine. Generations of people firmly opposed to but not immune to exotic fantasies, excessive drinking, madness.

Midwesterners whose state flag is the symbol of mining and shipping on a blue field, whose bird is the robin, whose tree is the sugar maple, whose motto is Forward! And Bucky Badger says, *If you want to be a Badger, just come along with me, by the bright shining light, by the light of the moon.*

❦

WE ARE at war, March's father said, or cried out. We are at war! On that Sunday morning March and her father were leaving his office where she often accompanied him on Sundays. She heard the excitement in his voice, remembered for many years the way he threw up his arms and took a flying leap down the steps. We are at war!

For March the war meant a much more interesting world. She trudged around the neighborhood collecting paper for the paper drives, fat bundles of newspapers tied and hauled to the Willow

School. She pasted stamps into a savings bond book, planted a victory garden, occasionally accompanied the neighborhood air raid warden on his walk down Rivers Avenue. On the other side of town, in a meat locker, there was half of a half of a cow, frozen solid! What this had to do with the war effort, she was uncertain. There was tinfoil to collect, and March delivered foil balls made from cigarette packages to the Tin Foil Committee. She and her war club, the Busy Bees, knitted ugly washcloths they sent on to the knitting committee, where the motto was Purl Harder. She roamed the neighborhood for news, and in her notebook recorded what people were up to, what they said they hoped for: the end of this war, money, a new mangle, better health than last year. And what they were scared to death of: polio, Hitler, the Japanese. Nips, Mrs. Sidenspiller called the Japanese. They will put a sword through you, she told March. Through your abdomen!

Prowling through backyards she checked out laundry on the lines, stopped on front porches, looked into windows or sat in kitchens drinking Dr. Pepper, eating soda crackers taken from pretty green tins, and small stale chocolates long hidden in red heart-shaped boxes. These were the houses in which, for the most part, the members of her own family did not express interest, but the houses and the people in them, the talk of Midway, Guadalcanal, the iron lung, bad weather was always of interest to March, and made up for the difficulties of her life in her own house.

On a winter Saturday she presented herself as your neighbor cleaning houses to earn money for the war effort, for our boys in the Pacific. She carried a dust mop and a pail full of supplies she had smuggled from the Rivers pantry, and on Lake Avenue, and Rivers Avenue, and Main Street, and Ninth Street, the Christian Science reader, the man with beet-sized tumors in his cheeks, a Baptist minister's wife rumored to weigh five hundred pounds and keep chocolates under her mattress, and Mr. Eye Eye, rumored to be a spy, all consented to her services. Clean away, they told her, and March, dusting and sweeping—poking her head into closets—remembered for years ugly brown flowered wallpaper, the smell of iodine, cigar smoke, mothballs, the large bottle of Prince Matchabelli perfume she dipped her finger into, a playroom floor littered with broken toys.

Because she did not appear to be seeing much or hearing much, because she was small for her age and rarely said anything, people failed to notice, or perhaps to care, that she was busy inhaling their amazing lives. They sank so cozily into her own life and stayed on, accompanying her and comforting her, long after she had left, long after they were gone: Mr. Eye Eye who presented her with pens decorated with fat glass stones, Arthur Schroeder who read in the window across from her own, late into the night, next to the reading lamp that shone near his narrow bald head, Harry Morris with his yard full of plumbing supplies and his lady friend who came in her leopard coat to walk to lunch with him on Sundays, Hatsie Armstrong with the photograph of her student, the movie actor Fredric March, on her piano. With deep affection, he had written.

An April morning. March, out and about, keeps her eyes half shut, allowing the world around her to shimmer and quiver. The street becomes a river running in sun and shadow. She becomes a magician. A magician with certain physical deformities, a leg she lets swing out, head and arms that hang down about her knees. She stumbles along.

Cutting through the park, heading down Lake Avenue, lurching and sliding, turning the street into a hall of mirrors, she suddenly bangs into someone. What had looked like a blue and silver and pink dancing bear coming down the grand staircase of a castle becomes her grandmother. Nana. Nana mailing a letter at the box on the corner. Nana in a flowery dress, with her pink hair and many jewels glittering, had been standing there wondering who that poor dear child was, that poor little crippled thing coming down the street so slowly, so painfully, never dreaming that it might be her own granddaughter.

March Rivers! For shame! March examines her tennis shoes and nods.

Yes. She is a thoroughly bad human being. Frequently whacked on the bottom with a vicious hairbrush, a fancy silver hairbrush with a monogram, and sent off to her room on the top floor of the gloomy old house, she does her best to raise support from the neighbors. Up there with her mess of tears, her streaky face, and her throat all sore from crying and shouting, she opens her window and cries, You should know what is going on in this house. A person's life is being ruined. A person is being murdered. The pigeons under the eaves coo, the starlings pick off red berries in the trees and splatter the sidewalk with pits.

Listen. MARCH RIVERS!

She feels the angry mother's angry heat rising, up the stairs, around the landing, into her bedroom. She is so anxious that while she is waiting to go down there, she scratches the skin on her arms and soon looks as though she has been attacked by a cat.

For years and years when someone calls her by her full name she feels how small she is, how insignificant and powerless. Her name, her full name, becomes the sound she least likes to hear. Her fierce declarations, her taunts to her parents, saying to her father, oh you brave little fellow, you think you should be king, saying to her mother, to hell forever on the wings of dead birds; these many threats surprise her. And delight her. They seem to spring from her quite without notice, pleasing her with their cleverness. This word factory is a gift from who knows where, but ultimately, of course, the words lead to the humiliating need to apologize. I am sorry. I am very sorry. But she is not.

Again, MARCH RIVERS!

She descends. Slowly. One step at a time to the front hall where she sees her mother's gloves and pocketbook on the hall table. She hears her mother in the kitchen, feels her mother's rage seeping from under the kitchen door. She waits. She opens the kitchen door, peers in, pretends that she has only a head, and it is now in the doorway, but the rest of her body is traveling directly around to the kitchen window, and leaning in, and very quietly GRABBING HER MOTHER AROUND HER NECK. SCARING HER TO DEATH! A throttle would do this woman good.

Her mother is doing something at the sink, and she is still wearing her hat. A very beautiful hat with bluebirds on it, and green leaves, and soft pink flower buds and fascinating bent twigs. March has noted that her mother, entering the house from an errand or one of her many meetings, has no time to remove her hat before she is at it again.

At the house. At her lifetime work of keeping it all together. Keeping it up. Her mother has help, but there is never enough help. Never the right kind. Down in the laundry room one morning, Birdie the laundress screams for Jesus and has to be driven home by the police. In the pantry one fall afternoon, Lorraine, who has been making applesauce, kisses the man putting on the storm windows, and in the spring says she and her Leroy will be opening a bar and grill in Alaska. The help. Nightmares all, her mother says, attacking with venom the silver, the linens, the dangling blobs on the dining room chandelier.

On this day her mother in her hat and pearls, her navy blue suit, which for all March knows she wears to bed at night, is rubbing at a spot on what looks like a tablecloth, really going at it. Scrub scrub. Suddenly she turns. Her hands pull at her pearls, twirl them around her throat, surely not intending to choke herself? She is not smiling. She is so strong, so clean, so well ironed, so straight in the spine, and she has perfect skin and red movie-star lips. Only her eyes are small and steamy. Her eyes look like the murderer's eyes in the *True Detective* magazines March collects.

When I call you. Her mother takes hold of her arm and shakes it, and March nearly loses her nerve. But she does not lose it completely.

What you want? Go to hell, angry lady.

A mistake. Within hours March is on her way to Colorado, on a business trip with her father. She is to be taken away to see what can be done with her.

At the Northwestern station she stands with her small suitcase, beside her father, and worries that Mr. Brown, in his brown felt hat, with his back turned, will slip on the wet cobblestones, and failing to catch himself, land at her side. Down there on the pavement he will look up and say, March Rivers, why are you waiting for the train?

You should be in school. But then, why was Mr. Brown waiting for the train to Chicago. Was it possible that he was going to see his lady friend. A woman who might be discussed with voices lowered, almost whispered, yet excited. A woman who could cause a small flutter among her mother's friends. So and so had heard. Someone had said. Frank Brown was seen in Chicago. At the Cape Cod Room. With a blonde! Oh yes. And then, of course, sympathy would be expressed for his wife, our dear Gloria who was known to be a good sport, a trooper. Poor Gloria. March would sit on the hall stairs and peer through the banister rails and listen.

Mr. Brown who used to duck his head and smile like a helpless, pink infant when he said hello, his smile so hopeful, who in old age would marry his nurse, news that would surprise March, even in her own middle age, because she could not imagine him without Gloria, dead though she was, and so felt the kind of mild disbelief that comes when life impinges on childhood memories.

SHUG IS dead, her father said. Boarding trains, overseeing the salesmen for his father's company, he traveled from La Rue to Chicago, from Chicago to Denver, from Chicago to Tennessee and Georgia, or north to Montreal, visiting men named Hap, or Jack, or Faxon, or Mr. St. Mar, or Sugar from a town near Memphis who drove his car into a truck one night. Shug is dead, and so they would drive to Tennessee in the spring to have Tennessee ham with Shug's wife. Later it was Noel. Noel a friend who caught pneumonia after a night in his car during a snowstorm.

A salesman, her father wept. He should have been more. He would have been more! Her father would drive miles down snowy roads that morning to deliver whatever consolation he could think of to the wife. To Katherine. Then he would fly to Mexico with March's mother who refused to put off their departure.

Katherine was one of her mother's closest friends, but her mother remained firm about the plan. We are going to Mexico. At noon. Today. And they went to Mexico.

March reviewed the names of the men who worked for her father so often they might have been working for her. Good men, her father often remarked, getting ready for another trip. He would press the formidable locks on his brown leather suitcase.

For many years she pictured this suitcase filled with clothes, but also dollar bills, so that whenever her father needed money he had only to dip his paws into the pale linen pockets. She imagined the suitcase bulging, and one day splitting open, the bills blowing above the station platform, caught in a sudden storm, becoming great soaking wads to be scooped up and stuffed back into the suitcase. She imagined her father with his money drying on the bed in a hotel room somewhere. He would be sitting quietly in an armchair, drinking a sweet, green drink. A generous, kind, thoughtful man who might have been relieved to spend time away from March's mother.

AT NIGHT, the self-appointed family guardian of the very family she hoped to escape from, March would listen for an intruder, creep downstairs to check the locks on the doors, read by the light the street lamp threw on her bedroom wall, watch at her window. The year before she was born Dillinger had come from Chicago and taken one of her father's friends from the bank and tied him to a tree; and there was the possibility of being kidnapped by the man who had taken Susan Degnan from her bed in Chicago. Susan Degnan's body parts had been found in a sewer. A little girl. Someone six. The announcer on the radio said the murderer was headed toward La Rue.

In bed, one hand covering her mouth to prevent poison from being spooned in while she slept, if she should sleep, it occurred to her that she would die someday. She would disappear, and it would be as though she had never existed. The possibility of not existing shocked her. Why had she not thought of this before. But the alternative, of living forever, made her shudder and huddle deeper under her comforter. The thought of this life going on, and on, and on.

SHE RAKES leaves, starts the bonfires, pokes for the chestnuts and potatoes, watches the apples and tomatoes cooking in the kitchen, the mason jars bubbling, snow clouds coming over the open fields at the edge of town. She swears she can smell the snow before it comes. Often sick with asthma she plays one man Parcheesi and listens to the soap operas. *Aunt Jenny's Real Life Stories, Ma Perkins, The Romance of Helen Trent, Our Gal Sunday*, humming the theme song she knows by heart, *From this valley they say you are going, we will miss your bright eyes and sweet smile, for they say you are taking the sunshine, that has brightened our pathway a while.*

Face pressed to a winter windowpane she listens to the sound of shovels scraping the sidewalk in the early morning dark, listens to car engines whining, to country music on her radio, to the advertisement for Zymol Trokeys, throat lozenges for farmers. Her older brother and younger sister come and go, though except for an occasional squabble with her brother, they hardly seem to live in the same house. Years later she wants to ask, where were you? Then? And where was I? Lost. Hibernating. Like a rabbit under a rug.

She stores the smells, the sounds, the comforting sense that the seasons are dependable, that there is a promise of good to come. The snow covers the cars on Rivers Avenue, ice walls build up along the lake shore, the ruts in the roads freeze. Then the ice breaks, sap flows, the river out near the dam runs again. The wild flowers come up in the ditches along the straight flat blacktopped highways.

At the Woman's Club winter costume dance March moves inside layers of cotton wrapped around her head and body, and the pine branches that stick out of the cotton, and tinsel and ornaments that dangle from the branches. She is a Christmas tree. It is hard to move, hard to breathe or see. She walks in a circle waiting for some boy to take hold of one of her branches and dance with her. She waits to win a can of Planters Cocktail Peanuts for being the most original. But why, she wonders, did the simplicity and ease of coming as a gypsy, a ballerina, a queen never occur to her. She peers around the room. Such ideas have occurred to more than a dozen other girls. They are all in gold, and silver, breathing without distress.

On a spring Sunday she is confirmed. There are nine people in her class and she is in the middle row of boys and girls kneeling at the altar rail. She is frowning. She wants the Bishop to take his time. He appears to be in a hurry, and this is an important occasion. Also, she is extremely anxious because under her white dress which is too tight, she is wearing a garter belt to hold up her stockings. Will people in the congregation see and mention this to each other? In case they are thinking about this she turns around and sticks out her tongue. Now the Bishop pauses. Think only of God, March thinks. She smiles. She aches to be blessed. And to be loved. Then it is over. A touch, and the sign of the cross, and a slap on the cheek for being a Christian isn't easy. The class rises, and fills the aisles, a shower of moths.

◈

THE BOMB has been dropped. Truman is President instead of Dewey, thus a morning of surprise and deep disappointment in the Rivers house. Last night, her parents say. Last night when we went to bed, we thought. We thought . . .

The All American Girls Baseball League, of which March is a dedicated fan, will exist for a few more years, but the era of the husky women in their uniforms, playing under the lights is, essentially, over. Farewell then to the Belles, the Peaches, the Daisies, the Comets.

March's grandfather's company receives the Navy E for its war production effort, and the family drives to Detroit in the new blue Oldsmobile. They sit on folding chairs in the hot sun and clap. On another day, some years later, her father receives an answer from his letter to Admiral Husband E. Kimmel, commander of the Pacific Fleet on December 7th. Husband Kimmel got a bad deal, her father believes. He was made a scapegoat for Pearl Harbor. The admiral appreciates her father's support, and his letter is framed and hung on the wall in the house at Blue Lake where March and her family spend a month in the summer, every summer, in the house built by her grandfather. March is the only member of the family who finds the admiral's name worthy of extended attention. What *were* his parents thinking?

At the Venetian Theater there is music, a starry sky, swans and giant columns, a portico, what is often described as a Renaissance Palace. Certainly a wondrous world, and movie stars to care about. Gregory Peck in *Twelve O'Clock High*, Cary Grant in *I Was a Male War Bride*, Betsy Drake in *Every Girl Should Be Married, Take Me Out to the Ball Game* with Esther Williams and Frank Sinatra. Wonderful, comforting, heartbreaking stories.

The televised hearings between Whittaker Chambers and Alger Hiss begin. William Faulkner wins the Nobel Prize, though March, absorbed in her own life, does not take note of these events. In preparation for the fall she reads *A Tale of Two Cities* by Charles Dickens and *Vanity Fair* by William Makepeace Thackeray, whose name she mumbles under her breath with relish. Makepeace. Makepeace. Her own middle name is Weed.

When the summer is over she will be sent off to boarding school in Connecticut, wherever that may be. For the moment there is swimming in icy Lake Michigan, in the pool at the high school with an island in the center and lights shining on summer nights. There is Mrs. Johnson's pool that is solemn, splendid, remote. So impressive from a distance, it is even more imposing up close, with silver dollars to dive for at the deep end, limes in the filter, once, a small blue mouse.

The pool, designed by Frank Lloyd Wright, belongs to a friend of her mother's, an actress, who continues to speak with a thrilling movie star accent; calling out, "Dahling," squealing with joy, fluffing up her red hair, so glad to be alive! Mrs. J. with her emerald and diamond rings and the hairdresser from Chicago, Mr. Reynard Arnaud, who arranges his beauty parlor in a bedroom off the pool so that March's mother and her friends may spend a number of summer days having their hair done, drinking gin and tonics, eating miniature sandwiches, chinning, as they say. March dives for silver dollars, practices sitting on the pool bottom.

Imagine a mouse in the filter, her mother says, after March reports this. A blue mouse in Frank Lloyd Wright's filter. In the filter of Mrs. J! Life is full of small dramas.

Her mother will sometimes tell the story about going to a party at the La Rue Country Club where Frank Lloyd Wright was to be the guest of honor. According to her mother Mr. Wright noticed her turning to look at him as she entered the club. Why is that b-i-t-c-h (she spells the word out) staring at me? She had just turned to look at his cape, she claims. How often do you see a man in a cape in La Rue? March does not know exactly why, but she knows that her mother often invents such stories.

She has begun to recognize her mother's need to be the star, the beauty at the ball, the woman in the ice blue dress with the sapphires at her neck. Still, her mother was not like Mrs. J. She was not boisterous or exuberant. In her self-consciousness there was a bit of doubt, the fear of not quite succeeding at the art of presenting herself as easily as someone like Mrs. J. or several of her other friends—women who appeared to be so optimistic. Sturdy, jovial women. March who certainly did not know how to present herself saw in her mother someone unsure of herself when out in the world. Someone on the rampage within the fortress of her own castle, hesitant when she crossed the moat.

Late August. March and her friends sit in the waves at the edge of Lake Michigan, singing songs from *Your Hit Parade. Lavender blue dilly, dilly*, they croon. *Again, this couldn't happen again. This is that once in a lifetime, this is the thrill divine.* On Friday nights they walk to the high school gym. March stands where the metal folding chairs meet the wall under the basketball net. Colored lights spin, couples bend and sway like beach grass, dance cheek to cheek. She smiles and scowls, and smiles again. (Life is nothing but an aching jaw.) But she knows the words and hums along. *Pack up all my care and woe, Here I go, Singing low, Bye bye Blackbird. Where somebody waits for me, Sugar's sweet, So is she, Bye bye Blackbird.*

The summer world. Books, inky fingers, stories, what? The drive-in movie south of town, the A&W, the Dairy Queen, fireworks over the lake, the Fourth of July parade with six marching bands, Bunny Hill waving like a fancy fool from one of the floats, fur monkeys on sticks, Brownie Brown's Troop of Stars, Brownie with her enormous white teeth, twirling her baton and dropping it, barely pausing as she scoops it up again, flings it high again. The heavy sweet smell of grass after a sudden storm, the empty taste of the house when it has been closed while they are at Blue Lake during August, the milkman's horse clomping up the street, the smack of a baseball, lawn mowers crossing the long backyards, pausing at the turns, a screen door opening, the twang of the lazy spring, the door almost closing, but not quite. Close the door! The flies will get in!

Time to put the past away. A drawer full of tinny bracelets, a dead gardenia, snapshots, junk. The Memory Book. This is like an autobiography, a record of your years; and it can be whatever you want it to be. March's book is full of matchbook covers and movie stubs and other stuff she has glued in. Pages of notes, answers to questions posed by the people who had designed the book; first kiss they teased, first dance, favorite song. Many hints, truths and untruths in March's book, because you never know when someone is going to look through a record of your life and wonder how it was for you.

Smile, her father suggests. They are in the garden taking pictures of March to prove that she is pretty. To smile is to engage the world in a way that will mean success, her father reminds her. Happiness. Happy days. People like people who are cheerful. People who smile.

Just be yourself.

Why would she want to do that?

Beauty comes from within, her father says. The most beautiful woman he had ever known came to a bad end. She grew up right here in La Rue, and when she was seventeen someone came along and took her to the World's Fair in Chicago. She never came back, but ten years later there was a picture of her in the *La Rue Journal*. She had been shot in a bar in Texas. He would not have recognized her without her name. Rayette Sweeny.

They spend a summer afternoon in the garden. March in a new yellow latex bathing suit, in a plaid skirt and a pale blue angora sweater, in blue jeans; leaning back off the swing so that her hair might appear to be blowing, in the apple tree, peeking through the leaves. The heat is terrible, but she knows the look she is aiming for.

Head a little more this way. I only have your ear, her father says. Smile.

It is five o'clock. The end of summer. Almost Labor Day. In two weeks she will board the Commodore Vanderbilt for New York, then the train to Hartford.

Her life in La Rue is over. A new world. A new beginning. She must succeed. Failure is out of the question. She pokes her head through the soft green leaves. She hears the band practice beginning. The bell on the ice cream truck sounds on Rivers Avenue. She rubs her eyes, takes the small hand mirror from her pocket. Too much sun. Eyes the color of plums now. Rayette, she thinks. Rayette Sweeny.

⊙∭⊙

MARCH LAY in the infirmary under a green blanket, and watched the Connecticut sunlight come and go over the green walls, and prayed. She was sick with asthma, frightened and exhausted. And she had only been here for two months. Let me be calm, she prayed. Let me be liked. Let my brain grow. Let me catch up.

She did not belong. She would never know enough, never understand the girls who seemed to be so comfortable, so knowing. Girls who drank black coffee, who wore sheared raccoon coats when the weather turned, who did not shave their legs, but poured hot wax on them, whose rooms then smelled of burned hair. Girls who wore scarab bracelets, and scarves from St. Paul's, or Groton, or Princeton, whose handwriting curled up into fat rounded letters. Girls who talked about boys they knew; but also about money, and houses that had indoor swimming pools and riding rings. L.'s family had the historic house on the Hudson, and someone in her family had signed the Declaration of Independence. D.'s grandmother entertained the Duke and Duchess of Windsor when they were in New York and they, the Duke and Duchess, had no money. Not a penny. G.'s father

⊷ 24 ⊷

lived in Hollywood and ran a movie studio. S.'s father was a famous race car driver. M.'s father was a sugar king in Cuba. R's mother would marry Clark Gable. Such information made March dizzy and fat. She ate and ate, and wheezed.

Their world was as foreign to her as the Latin verbs she studied. But the desire to be a good student was as strong as her desire to decode this new world. She felt like a hungry animal determined to burrow its way under the house and into the kitchen, into the sugar canisters and down the hall, up the stairs to the bedrooms, the way a raccoon had done at home. And what happened to the raccoon? Her father shot it.

Girls talked about trips to Paris and London and Havana. They talked about where to shop in New York. About the coming out parties they would have, about the Met, a museum, and also a holiday dance. And Sara Jane who would not be coming back. Sara Jane was pregnant. How could she be? How do you think? It was not ignorance that made March question, but disbelief. Pregnancy in someone like herself seemed daring beyond what she had ever considered. And the Sound? Marjorie's father had drowned in the Sound. It's over there somewhere. Off of Greenwich. Water. It's just water. Nothing.

She did not know about Jane Austen? That was not possible. And the sisters? The Brontës. Emily and Charlotte? No, she had not known about them. Or Shakespeare. Or William Butler Yeats with a long A, or Keats with a long E. Nor could she understand *Paradise Lost*. She could not. Or do the math. Or the French. But, she would. She would find a way. She put on her glasses and burrowed under her sheets with a flashlight. She studied. She smiled and smiled. She listened. She observed.

In a letter to her parents. April 1st. I am reading *The Mill on the Floss*. I am a prefect, which means that when I come back next fall I will wear a black robe for chapel. The minister comes from New York. He is extremely good looking. I do not have to take math anymore. A good thing. I don't know what they are talking about. I am taking advanced history with the seniors instead. We had a dance with a boys' school. We wore the ugly blue dresses and black velvet jackets and did not dance close to each other. Everyone here has divorced parents. (It was unclear to her whether she meant this as a compliment to her own parents, or a criticism of them.)

Another year. January 20th. I am on the honor roll. I am very good at Latin, and next year I will be in the hardest English class. The teacher is old and coughs all the time, until she can hardly breathe, but she is the best teacher here. I am writing poetry. I am reading Willa Cather and Joseph Conrad, but I will probably write poetry instead of novels. Diana has loaned me her horse to ride. He is small so there is not far to fall, if I fall.

June 1st. Her birthday. Three years, then, success, of a sort. Honors in history and English, banishment of the Midwestern accent (why do you talk that funny way, March), a scarab bracelet on her wrist, Arpège behind her ears, and on a spring weekend, a whiskey sour in one hand, a Chesterfield in the other. But a price had been paid. She had become someone else, but she had no idea who that person was. She was a cheery bit of fluff bouncing in the spring breeze. She had no center, no anchor.

On graduation day, holding a copy of *Lord Weary's Castle* in her arms as though it were a good luck charm, she explained to her parents that Robert Lowell was the person she most admired. Her parents stood on the green lawn in Connecticut and nodded and smiled. She had been a source of discomfort to them for so many years, a chubby troublemaker loved by her father, an annoyance to her mother; but she had accomplished more than they had hoped. She would go to Vassar in the fall, and room with Judy from Pittsburgh with whom they had just had lunch at the pretty little inn. The father was in steel, March's father noted. The mother seemed nervous, perhaps she was ill? Still, all in all, a pleasant couple.

❦

VASSAR GIRLS were said to wear black, to go out with older men, to spend their time in New York. All three possibilities appealed to March. She imagined herself in beautiful, severe clothes, black clothes, an unlit cigarette in one hand, a book in the other, on the train to the city, a boy settling into the seat next to her, nodding, smiling. Would you care for a light?

She did not have time to go to New York and she did not know quite where to go the few times she did venture forth. She did not meet older men. She did not meet any men with the exception of a few blind dates who expected her to drink, to kiss, to allow them to rock her very substantial breasts back and forth. All of this made her anxious. Also, she had no gift for small talk. She never had, but this seemed to matter more now.

Judy from Pittsburgh left after two months to marry her Pittsburgh boyfriend, and March had the room to herself. She studied, and sometimes went away on weekends with girls in her house who lived in New Canaan, or Far Hills or Short Hills. One place looked like another. She traveled in other people's cars, in taxis, on trains at Christmas, and counted on nothing but Grand Central Station remaining at a fixed point as she went back and forth between the East and the Midwest.

She continued to explain where she was from. La Rue? Is that in Michigan? No, Wisconsin. Near Minneapolis? No, nearer Chicago.

She wrote to her father. Why do people think Midwesterners are foreign? We are the heart of America, her father wrote. We are the roots. The producers. Once, some years ago, at a dinner in New York, I found myself the only businessman, the only manufacturer, in a group of ten, perhaps twelve other men. All of them spoke as though life away from Wall Street did not exist, and yet, I said to myself, and yet, where would they be without us. Without men such as myself there would be no Wall Street.

Occasionally March said she was from some place people would recognize. Milwaukee or Chicago. Or she might say she was from Peoria. Or Butternut, Wisconsin, or Cable. And sometimes when people asked if La Rue was in Illinois, she would say no, North Dakota.

In the fall of her sophomore year she spent a weekend in New York, and there in a living room overlooking the East River she drank Dubonnet and watched rain falling on the terrace on one side of the French doors; and on the other, lamp lights on the blue and cream of the oriental rug, on the dim twinkle of crystal and jade, on gold bracelets, on heads bent toward paintings from another century. Missy, one of her roommates, had brought her here, to her aunt's, for a lunch, and March was excited by the people and the conversation. She had never thought old people could look so well, so lovely and so young, could find so much to talk about. How was it possible for all of these people to look so much alike. Their bones were so fine and the men were so tall. So handsome. The women seemed to have extremely long necks. They were unusually thin. They had perfect hair.

She listened to the talk of books, art, music, London, the President. How did they find the time to know, to keep up, she wondered. They seemed to have access to a network that kept them informed without, apparently, wearing them out. Matisse, Stravinsky, José Quintero, Elizabeth and Philip, Dwight Eisenhower. Dwight, as though they knew him. The White House is looking a dash shabby.

The words floated delicately, twirled upon ribbons of smoke, touched the rims of glasses, fell, drowned, rose, paused before a quick flame, disappeared between the folds of a brilliant white handkerchief. A man next to March touched her arm. I say, is it true that you New York girls always carry your contraceptives in your pocketbooks? Your diaphragms? Hmmm?

Darling, are we eighteen or twenty? the aunt asked a man with the face of a hawk.

We are eighteen today, The Hawk said.

March felt the hand of the aunt's son touch the base of her spine and move slowly up to her neck. She swallowed. The aunt, seeing, paused, and raised an eyebrow. When March went into an enormous bedroom and stood at the mirror combing her hair, the aunt followed her into the room and asked where she was from. La Rue, March replied.

Moments later, seated at the long dining room table, the aunt raised her breasts and her glass. All of our guests today are from foreign countries, she said.

March found this world desirable, this world so many of her boarding school and college friends came from, but she did not know what to do with it. Partially excluded from it, she wanted to interrupt it. Offended by eastern exclusivity, sensing she did not belong, she wished not only to belong but to offend as well. She was, she understood, expected to be amenable, gracious. She wished instead to step on this world's well-protected toes.

❧

SHE STUDIED philosophy and English Lit and Drama and grew thin. She wrote for the newspaper and volunteered in the children's ward at the local hospital. In the summer after her junior year she went with two friends to the University of Wisconsin for summer school, and met a boy in her writing class who wrote romantic stories he read to her as they floated in inner tubes and drank beer on Lake Mendota. Jamie Lord. March found him breathtakingly handsome, she swore she had driven her borrowed car into a tree when she first saw him; but their plan to go to India faded with the summer. On a winter night, years later, sometime after Jamie's third divorce, he took March to dinner and they laughed about that summer, about the visiting writer, Mari Sandoz, who had always called on him to read first. Mr. Lord will read today, Miss Sandoz would croon, would swoon, March used to say. He was still good looking, tan from a stay in Zihuatanejo, philosophical about his marriages; the last wife had found someone else, no regrets, he was taking a year off to think, perhaps he would write that novel, the one he had never had time for, not like March whose stories he said he had read and loved. He was on his way out West, but soon he would get to it. They walked through town in the snow for a while and planned another dinner. Two months later he died of a heart attack.

❧

BY THE time she was a senior March lived with four roommates on a corridor that included a living room, and her own very small room, a room she treasured. There she read, smoked, typed, surrounded herself with heaps of books whose authors gave her a sense of entitlement, courage, such hope for a future she could not yet imagine. She was fiercely proud of her collection: Kierkegaard, Nietzsche, Spinoza, Kant, Wittgenstein, James Joyce, Flaubert, Walser, Eliot, Tolstoy, Mann, Fitzgerald, Hemingway, Faulkner, Tennessee Williams, O'Neill, dozens of books she had gathered over four years. She liked to say they rose up like small towers overlooking a Syrian plain.

With her books beside her she wrote a paper for her philosophy seminar, another for her drama seminar on the work of Tennessee Williams, and finally she scrambled to finish a collection of short stories for her thesis professor. She was exhilarated and uneasy about what she would do next. She drank too much coffee. Her heart raced and her hands shook. Then it was spring and she reported an epiphany.

I had a vision, she told her roommates. It was May already, the year rushing to a finale, but she had been stunned by this magical moment. Something amazing happened, she explained. I was walking home from my philosophy seminar last night. The lights were on in the buildings around the quad, the dogwoods were in bloom. The air was so still. And all of a sudden. All of a sudden, I knew what my life was to be! I reached up and shook a branch, and the petals fell, and I said, right there, out loud, I know. I know. I am a prophet. I will tell the world.

The roommates sighed. March. Oh, please. Tell what?

They were sprawled on a sagging couch, or lying flat on their backs on a tufted blue rug, while Lucy packed her perfect clothes into her perfect small suitcase for the weekend at Princeton. What are you talking about, March? You say the craziest things sometimes.

Missy who was marrying Squish from Yale instead of the guitar player from their Wisconsin summer—because her family had sent a detective after that one, and because she was pregnant—thought March would be better off if she stopped daydreaming and made a plan.

Now listen, Missy drawled. I really do think you all have to make some kind of plan for the rest of your days, and I do think it would be better if you just stopped talking about tree blossoms, and dreams, and going to bed with that crazy drama teacher you go on and on about.

Marriage, Missy offered. There are worse things. You can't spend your whole life daydreaming. You'll end up being some awful man's secretary. You know that's what happens. She dangled the Phi Beta Kappa key she'd had since her junior year and raised an eyebrow. Trust me.

I just had this feeling I had something to say, March said. I was seized by this. It was amazing and I believed it.

She had spent most of the last term in her small, cluttered room reading until late into the night, in her nightgown, the mink stole with the heads and tails of the dead animals dripping over her shoulders. It was the stole left by Nana and sent on by an aunt who had hopes of March wearing it to New Haven or to Princeton where she herself had enjoyed many a tea dance. March patted the small heads, and read and wrote, and came out now and then for classes, for drying silverware in the kitchen which was the penalty for coming in late at night from a movie, or for a room that had not passed inspection. She went to dinner at the local diner with Leonard Kestenbaum, who taught the drama seminar, who fed both of them liver, bacon, mashed potatoes and banana cream pie, and talked about Gertrude Stein. March picked at her food and wondered what Leonard would be like in bed.

When the weather turned warm, she put the mink away, adopted a stray puppy she named Nietzsche who ate her typewriter ribbons, then part of her typewriter. She tried to think of a topic for her orals. These were important, including work from *Beowulf* to Virginia Woolf, but instead of staying for review sessions she made several trips to New York, to the theater cubicle at the Public Library where she surrounded herself with folders of Tennessee Williams press clippings, where she went twice to the Theater de Lys to see *The Three Penny Opera*, so highly recommended by Leonard Kestenbaum.

One night on a blind date in New York she went to the Monkey Bar where she hoped to lay the groundwork for an affair, and instead drank too many martinis. She was spending the night at Missy's apartment on Sutton Place, and after the doorman let her in she took the elevator to the wrong floor. The door was unlocked, and the apartment looked familiar, so she wandered into what she thought would be her room, and found a strange couple sleeping, snoring. Dead to the world, fortunately.

You're lucky you weren't shot, Missy said. March agreed.

On the afternoon of her orals, her mind was a blank. She sat before Mr. Smith, the thesis professor, and who was, she thought, possibly headed for some kind of breakdown, and a very old woman whose field was Chaucer. Mr. Smith looked out the window and lit a cigarette with trembling hands. The Chaucer professor demanded to know what March was talking about. Get to the point, she wheezed. How does that relate. March struggled on. Eliot. Spenser. Milton. Eliot again. Fear made her sleepy. She began to recite from *The Four Quartets*. She yawned. The three of them paused and listened to rain falling.

TIME.

That was unusual, Mr. Smith said the next day. What happened?

March shook her head. I needed more time, I couldn't organize. It doesn't matter now.

That's not the point, he said. His hands shook. He was gray with exhaustion. He had a wife, children, classes, papers, a novel to finish.

What is? March asked.

I don't know. He touched her arm, as a kind of sad blessing, and she watched him hurry off. She had let him down. She had let herself down. She wasn't brainy like Missy. She was just . . . ? Desperate? Excited by learning? Nuts? About to have a heart attack? Probably all four.

She needed a plan, but she could not settle on one. When Ringling Bros. came to town she thought of joining the circus. She thought of buying a secondhand car and driving to California, or applying to graduate school, though her grades were nothing to brag about, and she had already been told she would need two foreign languages. Her roommates could not wait for the year to end. Missy was trying to find a merry widow that would partially conceal her bulging belly at the wedding they would all soon attend in New York. Margo was writing about Henry James, and planning a trip to Italy. Franny was getting ready to marry someone disgustingly rich, and was already concerned about his drinking and carousing. Libby was going to Rhode Island for the summer.

The lawn was littered with girls sunbathing, holding sun reflectors to their faces. They gathered on the lawn in front of Main, lounged on the library steps, sat in circles for classes taking place under the trees, shone their new engagement rings on the backs of their Bermuda shorts, idly tracing with the tips of long, perfectly shaped nails, invisible monograms that would soon appear on pale blue stationery, on bath towels, and sheets and knives and forks.

In another day parents would begin to arrive. Beneath her window two boys in Bermuda shorts were sitting on the hood of a convertible, and she could hear people calling to each other, and radios and record players playing, and down the hall Fred Astaire's voice rang out. *I'm putting on my top hat, tying up my white tie, brushin' off my tails.* There was a streak of sunlight on her desk, and she could see the shadows of the trees on the lawn, the lights beginning to go on in the houses on College Avenue. In another few minutes it would be time to go out for dinner, to some kind of class party.

She watched the cars coming through the front gate, the boys standing up in their convertibles, a Yale pennant flying from a bicycle. She had a wooden bulldog and a Princeton scarf she had bought at Fenn-Feinstein in New York to display on her dresser so that people would assume she had been to those places, and it seemed to her that these acquisitions had been adequate. Mostly, she thought how much she had loved this last year, the work, the solitude, this time of day when she would look up from her desk and watch for a while before she turned on her lamp and went back to work. It was a certain hour of the day in a place where, for the first time in her life, she felt at home.

❦

NEW YORK was full of classmates. To March they seemed settled, older, highly organized. She would sometimes move in with friends for a month, more often find a sublet for herself and stop in for friends' dinners of tuna fish casseroles, and soggy rolls, lettuce with thousand island dressing, ice cream and instant coffee. She would listen to their news: their engagements, their teaching jobs at their old private day schools, their nights at the opera or the theater with their parents. She would examine their baby blue stationery, and tour the apartments she had not seen before, apartments that all looked alike, that displayed ominous schedules for cleaning, cooking, shopping, on refrigerator doors. Tuesday, Betty clean refrigerator. Wednesday, Pam buy groceries. Loren cook dinner. Pam help with.

Late in the evening, over some terrible sticky liqueur, March would entertain with the stories of her travels, her jobs, her apartments.

She would tell how she was working for a producer with a wooden leg who had introduced her to Marilyn Monroe and Arthur Miller; how she had taken up riding in Central Park and been thrown from a horse and rescued by a man who had given her a pair of red shoes; how Missy's stepfather had invited her to lunch and suggested they go back to his apartment. The girls would laugh and say, Oh, March. You should write a book about it. You really should. Then March would nod and smile. Yes, she really should. She ought to do just that. Instead, she had her first affair.

On an afternoon in October she walked through the park with Libby after their lunch with Libby's cousin, who had outlined her life for them while they sat at the counter at Schrafft's. The cousin would marry someone named Teddoe in a few weeks, and would not sleep with him until after the wedding which would take place at St. James with the reception at the Colony Club. They would have Lester Lanin's orchestra. They would go to Bermuda, and then at last, they would move into their apartment. Her aunt, a decorator, was helping with the fabrics.

Fabrics? March chewed on her straw.

For the slipcovers, and the curtains, and the dust ruffles. Kelly green. To give it a zing. The cousin pulled on white gloves, waved good-bye, and headed for an appointment.

A zing.

What about you, March? Libby poked her and smiled. Tell all!
March wondered if she had guessed. Did she look suddenly
radiant? I'm having an affair. I have a lover.

A lover?

She had not said this aloud before. Yes.

You don't!

I do.

Oh my God.

Max. Someone so far from the world March was from, so unlike
the boys she had always known, her prize, her acquisition. He would
belong to her. She was stunned by her good fortune. He was from
New York. He was Jewish. The fact that he was Jewish was central
to her interest, her determination to find someone outside of the
narrow limits of her own world.

He was magnificent. A man in a formidable suit. Black. It seemed
black. It was not the suit boys from her world wore. Not gray flannel.
And a white shirt. Blazing white. Or blue. The blue of a Montana
sky. Montana blue, she would hum, though she had never been to
Montana. And glossy black hair. Not worn as short as boys she had
known forever, boys with their Protestant hair, their thin, pathetically
short, proper, stuffy, uninteresting hair, their thin wizened lips.

There were riding boots in Max's bedroom. A canvass was draped
over the chair in the living room, the work of a Chilean artist whose
paintings were in museums. What was it doing there. In his bedroom. Draped over the chair? On the table was *The Wall Street Journal*
which he clearly took seriously, which seemed to be imprinted on his
heart. She was terrified. Thrilled.

She was out of her league. This was something she recognized,
but fought against. March with the lifelong problem of smallness,
the Midwesterner adrift in the city, the orphan just now living five
flights above a fur shop with an aged neighbor named Valentine
Kay. Valentine who had arranged for them to have a roof garden by
removing flowers from the islands on Park Avenue. March in her tiny
apartment and Valentine with no hair, and hard of hearing, at the
end of the hall. Valentine who would hobble to March's door in the

evenings to have her dress buttoned up the back from the waist to the neck before she sallied forth to gather flowers; Valentine who had shown March her trick of opening the skylight above her bathtub to facilitate an occasional shower.

Yes, March was out of her league, but she would have him. Max whose reputation with women preceded him. According to Max's friend Jerome who had pursued March relentlessly, who had refused to introduce her to Max until she swore she was moving to San Francisco—according to Jerome, Max had been involved with a well-known movie star, then a model, then an actress and so on. Such a legacy. March was not deterred. Not at all. She was invigorated.

⊙≫≪⊙

LIBBY WANTED to know his name. Libby who seemed to know everyone.

Max Lowan.

Wall Street. At least the father.

Exactly.

Money.

Money. A lot of money. It's a little unnerving, In his parents' house in the country there is an honest-to-God butler. Who runs the bath water! Who tests it. Too hot? Too cold? I don't even like baths.

How old is he?

Twenty-nine.

Old.

Yes.

How did you meet him?

March told about the farewell party Jerome had given, and how she had introduced herself because she was afraid Max was about to leave, and she was running out of time.

I said I'd been waiting for the right person to start an affair with and he was the one. He wanted to know what the criteria were. I said, someone sophisticated, older, not too old, smart, good looking, maybe a little arrogant, a little self-centered, very sure of himself. And I thought he might be what I had always had in mind.

Then what?

He said, you're very daring, aren't you? I think he thought this was going to be fun. He wanted to know if this was my first time, my first affair, and I said it was. He asked me to meet him after the party at his apartment. Then, later, I lost the piece of paper with his address, and had to stop at the Whamburger to check the phone book, and when I finally got there I couldn't remember the floor. I knocked on the wrong door and found a woman who was wearing a nightgown and spoke French.

I was thinking about going home, but then I thought, no damn it, you are not going home. So I went back down to the lobby, to the desk where the night man was half asleep. I explained that I needed Max's apartment number. I said I had gone to the wrong floor and he—this old half-dead goat—made me stand there like a fool while he raised his condescending eyebrow, and arranged a kind of half-knowing smile, and finally gave me the number. I got back in the elevator and went on up. 10E, and the door was open!

And where was he?

In bed!

Oh my God. What did he say?

He said, Come on in. I thought you were lost.

And you didn't chicken out?

It was too late. Anyway, after twenty-three years.

What were you wearing?

The dress with the long sleeves.

The blue.

No, gray and green with the slit in the back.

From Bonwit's. Perfect. So? Then?

Then he told me to take off my clothes and I did, and he said, Well come on. Get in bed. He seemed very amused. So I got in bed. With him.

So what did he say. Then?

He said I had a good tan.

Oh my God, March. Did you go all the way?

No. Of course not. We just talked!

No!

No.

Oh my God! How was it? Are you sorry? Did it hurt? Was there blood all over the bed. Oh my God I would never. I'd be too embarrassed. What if you're . . . Jesus, March. You could be pregnant right now you know.

It was fine. No blood. Not thrilling but ok. But waking up in the morning. Having someone there. That is unbelievable. Even if you haven't really been asleep. You open your eyes, and you look over, and there! Right beside you. Is this absolutely fantastic, gorgeous man, this magnificent body, this amazingly beautiful man. Eyes, eyelashes, ears, nose, lips, legs, arms, everything else, and it's all yours. You can just lie there and drink it all in, and then you know, he opens his eyes and smiles. I was so happy I just wanted to shout and jump up and down on the bed. I wanted to pound on the ceiling and say, look what I have.

But you didn't.

Please.

Then what? In the morning? What did you do then?

We got up. He said he didn't like making love in the morning. So we got up and after a while we had breakfast. Eggs. Soft-boiled. Enough to make you sick. I guess that's what men eat. He read *The Wall Street Journal*. And I picked at this mushy little egg. We were sitting at this table a waiter had wheeled in because there is a restaurant or something somewhere in the building. It's like a hotel. I don't know. He read his paper, and then he said that if we were going to continue this relationship. This relationship! That I would have to get a diaphragm.

God. What did you say?

What could I say? He just picked up the phone and made an appointment for me with some fancy doctor on Park Avenue. That afternoon I went over to this man's office, and got the damn thing, and got this long lecture on wearing it, and not coming in and crying about being pregnant. Then I went out and met Max, and we had dinner, and went back to his apartment, and went to bed again, and this morning the eggs again.

Oh, March. Dear, dear, wonderful March. Maybe he'll marry you!

⟨∾⟩

MARCH DID not tell Libby the rest of the story. The ending. She had waited for the end, from the beginning, and half looked forward to it, an event that would make her more interesting. Worldly. Tragic. But the end did not make her look or feel interesting. Instead, she felt confused and desperate. The suffering she had looked forward to was more terrible than anything she had imagined, and she could not believe that it was happening, and she could not let go.

It was the party in Harlem that sounded the alarm for her. They had gone to a dance there because, according to Max, it was the thing to do. To go to Harlem, and to ask people you met in Harlem for dinner at the restaurant in Max's building. They did this again and again. March could tell the women excited him. And so on this night when Max was over there in a corner, dancing with a woman whose neck he appeared to be devouring, March found herself dancing with a man whose last name was Rivers, and maybe they could get together, get something going, he said. You know what I mean? March thought she did know. She listened to the music blasting—Charlie Mingus and "Lovebird," and the Haiti song. The room was so dark she could barely see. It was filled with smoke and bodies bending and incense burning. March thought we will never get out of here.

They were high up in the back of a building that looked from the street like an abandoned fortress, and beyond the rooms where the walls were only rough plaster, and where rows of beads hung between the arches, there were empty corridors, and wide concrete stairwells and light bulbs dangling. March could only think that she was tired, and she would like to go home, but in fact she had no home.

Home. Where was that. A hotel. Not Max's apartment, but the Barbizon Hotel for Women. She had taken a room there on the day she had come home to her sublet, and found a woman, and a baby, and a room full of baby furniture. The man who had let the apartment had failed to mention certain details. Like this is my apartment, the woman said. This is his little bundle.

She was not sure where her record player was. Her beautiful black hat was gone, and she had left her records at the Chinese laundry. All she had was her typewriter and her clothes, and her room, but it was not her room. It could have been any room, and she was ashamed to be there so often. To be there on the bed waiting for Max to call.

Waiting for Max who had not asked her to move in with him. Waiting for the next day to begin. Waiting for the desk to answer when she called for messages, for the elevator, for a tuna salad and coffee to go, for the elevator again. I have nothing, she thought. I am disappearing. I am a shadow. When I am with Max I smile, and read *The Wall Street Journal*, and talk about the curious implications of Sputnik, and the Dow Jones and Bernard Baruch. What do I care about Bernard Baruch. What do I care about the stock market or outer space. I care about Max. That is all I care about.

Driving home from Harlem, through empty rainy streets in the early hours of the morning Max said, I saw you dancing with that good-looking guy. Maybe he'll be your next.

Next what?

Lover. Max was smiling.

Was he mad? It had never occurred to her that he would expect her to have another. Who did he think she was.

You never know, March said. You just never know. And then. After a moment. What would happen if I were pregnant?

Are you?

No. But . . .

Cuba, Max said, making a fast right and sliding into his parking garage.

Cuba?

Cuba.

Right.

I've been thinking, March said at dinner after a week when Max had been in London, supposedly learning about his father's investment banking firm. I've been thinking about our relationship and I see now that there were certain things wrong from the beginning. But I've changed and I think that we. We could begin again! And this time. You see I no longer need you and I think we could just be friends. We could have a drink. Laugh about old times. Go to a movie.

Max put his hand over hers and smiled. March. Don't. Nothing lasts forever.

She was running out of money. She looked pale, as though, she thought, she'd been sick for months. She was working at an ad agency, but in the evening she was often in the bookstore at the Barbizon where she wondered if the woman in charge was beginning to suspect she was not actually engaged. The ring on her finger was a fraud. Where was this fiancé March had mentioned. She had told the woman about Max, told her too much, probably, but she was happier in the bookstore than in her room, and now the woman had begun to make remarks. How's your lovely Jew? the woman said. Sick-a-bed?

But if she went away and came back, tan all over. Then? Possibly? There was that line of Max's. Nothing lasts forever. But what did that prove. Zero. She hated him. Though when he called late one night and asked if she could come over, she surprised him by arriving with nothing on at all but panties under her white cotton coat. Poor Max, she had said. I am always startling you.

In truth, Max never looked startled. He looked somewhat preoccupied, and sometimes when the phone rang he looked excited. But who was calling?

On summer evenings after work, March would walk past townhouses on the side streets and see cooks standing in kitchen windows, a family gathered, a man and woman talking, children being fed, a dog looking out, all that she had made fun of and now wanted so desperately. If I had a tan, March thought. If I started over, all that could happen for me.

MAYBE YOU'RE ONE OF THOSE PEOPLE WHO WILL NEVER MARRY.

March lay back in her chair and pretended to examine her toes, but she had stopped breathing. She had gone to Wisconsin to visit her parents at Blue Lake, and there had been bad omens from the beginning. But this? This body blow?

She had flown up from La Rue with a fool in a model airplane. Her parents had driven up the day before, and they had made the arrangement for her.

Joel Pots will bring you up.

He's crazy, March said.

Don't be silly. He's been flying for years. You're safer in the air than you are in your own bathroom. They were safer in the air. They were safe anywhere. They had known Joel Pots since he was born. They knew his father and his grandfather. Both dead, March pointed out. Heart attacks. But don't worry about me. They did not.

Here come the clouds, Joel Pots announced when they were above Milwaukee. Peachy keeno. Now we see some real weather! He turned from the cockpit and leered at March and his friend, who got out a deck of cards and told March they were playing gin rummy.

Potso, the card player said. Potso, does this remind you of the good old days or does it not?

If we are not over the Dells right now, Pots announced. If we are not over the Dells we are ding dong daddies. I see nottin' and nottin' sees me.

March wanted to know if Pots had a compass or whatever and the friend said Pots flew by the seat of his pants. And gin again, March baby.

Hang on to your overcoats, Pots shouted.

Another hour and they hit some kind of roller coaster and came out through the clouds to see a man snipping water lilies in Rivers' Bay. That's a no no, Pots called, and dropped the plane down so that March could see the fuzz in the man's ears quiver. Then they did what Pots called a fast, hi Daddy, over his own house and headed for the airfield.

Some circus up there, eh kiddo, Pots said when they were on the ground.

Laugh a minute, March said.

Your daughter's a hot rummy player, the card shark said. March and her parents and Pots and his friend stood around in the sun, and looked at the plane and thanked each other, and looked pleased that March had been a success up there. One hell of a gin player, all right. Absolutely.

Stick with me, kiddo, and you'll get used to anything, Pots said, winking at March's father.

He's crazy, March told her parents as they walked to the car.

You just don't fly very often, her father said. If you flew you'd get used to it.

To crashing.

Flying. Her father squeezed her arm to indicate this was a joke, and March smiled.

The next day was overcast, and March was left to read in front of the fire, and contemplate the whitecaps, while the rest of them played golf. Her parents, and her brother, and a girl he was crazy about, and her sister, and a pitiful giggling friend went off every morning, and came back for lunch, and ran through their chip shots and putts, and played bridge and gin rummy, and told March she ought to play golf. She had been good at that once. She should take it up again.

March swam and read *An American Tragedy*, and thought about that old oar hitting *her* head out there on that black lake. At the end of the week she developed an eye infection that made it impossible for her to read.

I wish you would stop looking like that, her mother said.

Like what?

You cast gloom. Life is what you make of it. You ought to play golf.

It's difficult to play golf when you can't see, March reminded her.

You could make an effort.

I'm in the hands of the Blue Lake Drug Store, for what that's worth.

You could put some clothes on.

How would clothes improve my eyes?

You have been in that bathing suit and that sweater, or that black outfit for a week. It's depressing

Being blind is depressing.

You're not blind.

Her father asked about her plans for the future, and March decided to be brave and sound as though she knew what she was up to. I may be going to California, she confided.

Why would you be going to California?

Oh there are opportunities in the West. In New York everything is settled, but I see a wide open future in the West.

You're sounding a little like an earlier period in our history. What exactly do you have in mind? What sort of job? Do you intend to have a career?

A career? Was he crazy. Not exactly a career right now, March said. That might be premature. I'm thinking more of something in export-import, or marine biology or outdoor furniture. Possibly something in the movies. Or forestry. It's all there. I'm mulling over the possibilities.

I see, her father said. How are your finances? When March failed to answer he said he thought it might be wise for her to refrain from any new plans until she had given more thought to all of this. Whatever happened to that boy you were seeing? he wondered. Max someone.

Oh Max. Yes. Old Max.

You know we had trouble reaching you, her father said. For a long time you were not home at night. Or in the morning. That was disturbing.

Yes. Well I was working in the theater. A production. Nights. And mornings. I was helping with a Noel Coward revival. Arthur Miller's sister was in it. He and Marilyn Monroe would come to rehearsals.

Who would not be impressed with that bit, March thought. The play had closed after a few weeks, but Marilyn Monroe? Wasn't that something?

Her father was not biting. Are you interested in marrying this boy? Max.

Arthur Miller and Marilyn Monroe, March said. She always wore a scarf and dark glasses, even when we were sitting in the dark.

What is your exact relationship with this young man? Is there any talk of marriage?

Marriage. Hmmm. I don't know about all that. I suppose some people do get married. If they can't work out another kind of life. I suppose they just give up. And get married. Max and I feel that rushing into something so permanent, something so settled, that seems to ruin people's lives, something that makes them so full of anxiety, and discontent, and fear and terrible distress. She paused for breath. It is a well-known fact that people who marry are often sorry.

One thing I am sure you have thought about. (A pause) Girls who are running around with someone. Girls like Lady Brett in *The Sun Also Rises*. Aren't the kind of girl nice boys marry.

March shivered. I thought you liked Hemingway. I thought you were crazy about Hemingway.

Lady Brett ended up a very unhappy and unpromising woman. In the end she was little more than a prostitute.

I always liked her.

The point is that you are not Lady Brett. You are March Rivers. Our daughter. The point is that we have all the confidence in the world in you, and we just want you to find what will be right for you. There is a time when you have to take very seriously what you will do with your life. It has also worried us that this young man you have been seeing is apparently Jewish. Your mother and I feel that could be difficult.

Difficult? For who? For whom? Difficult for them, maybe. His family would have a fit if he wanted to marry me so you should stop worrying. Besides it might be healthy for our family to branch out a little.

March had sometimes insisted they were Jewish too, describing how a long time ago one pink-cheeked great grandmother, and one dashing, dark-eyed, hot blooded, slim-hipped, tight-assed (she left that out) brilliant, long-suffering, gentle, brooding Jew rendezvoused in a country inn? In a French village? Not even a night, just a quick coupling in a darkened hallway, just a moment, hmmm? And didn't that explain her nose and her own self-deprecating sense of humor? Her gloom? And her mother's own brother? Uncle Ben. I spotted him years ago, she liked to say.

Her father stood up. We only want what is best for you.

∽⊗∽

It was toward the end of the second week that her mother made her announcement.

Maybe you're one of those people who will never marry.

Her mother had that skill. Suddenly slipping a piece of icy probability into a conversation. And she could be right. It would not have surprised March one bit if she were told tomorrow that she would go through life without finding anyone, that she would find someone, but that someone would not dream of having her.

Her mother's words had elasticity. And the weight of bowling balls. March sat in her bathing suit near the fireplace, and considered the puffed-up sofa where her mother sat in her pale blue cotton golf dress. March was interested in a tan, and a little peace of mind, but from the beginning she had seen that her mother was not enthusiastic about her breezy descriptions of life in New York, her bare feet, her so-called slouch, her two-piece bathing suit, her bikini that needed so much attention, either to keep the bottom on or the top yanked up.

After looking all over New York for something like it, she had found this amazing suit at the Bermuda Shop. Of all places. The stuffy little Bermuda shop. The saleswoman had told her that nobody wore two-piece bathing suits. Everyone is wearing a one piece, the woman insisted, and took March's choice and put it back in the drawer.

Not everyone. March extracted the suit from the drawer.

You'll see, the woman said. You will find that we are right about the current style.

The problem was, it was not easy to stay in the thing. She gave another hitch. Never Get Married? Couldn't her mother guess that she would throw her life over tomorrow if she could have what *she* had. Pretty furniture, clean clothes, golf balls, sheets, those pink blanket covers! Money! Couldn't her mother see that she would gladly give an arm and a leg for someone who would not be a creep, who would marry her, and save her from being a wanton woman. She saw that coming all right, and she still got chills when she thought of Max saying that the guy at the party in Harlem might be her next. She could already see herself in ten years. Staggering in and out of bars, dozens of lovers, a worn-out saggy body, abortions, cancer, syphilis, dyed stringy hair, bad teeth, fangy fingernails, pimples, puffy skin, a hideous purple dress, a chewed-up monkey fur around her shoulders. She sat there in the living room and saw March The Slut schlepping down Madison Avenue.

A west wind came up off the lake then, and blew the curtains into the room. Upstairs a door slammed. Beyond the windows the birch trees swayed, then it was still again. If you don't marry you'll have to think about what you will do, her mother said, lighting a cigarette. You're getting older now. It's your life. We can't live it for you.

Right. March swallowed, and smiled, and raised an eyebrow. Actually. I may be going to India.

Life is not one long picnic, her mother said.

March heard a boat coming up to the swimming dock, heard the waves begin to slap the shore and got up to see. A launch was being secured by a man in baggy shorts and a blue shirt with the sleeves fluttering above the elbows. He gave his hand to a woman in a bright print dress with white sweater and matching shoes.

The Placemans, March said. Jesus.

Their daughter is engaged, her mother said. Put on some clothes. She glared and slapped March hard on her bare shoulder.

March went out through the kitchen door, and along the stone path that ran behind the house to the boat dock where she kept her sailboat. Twinks, the Placemans' daughter, had a fascinating job in Washington. She worked for a congressman or senator, and was learning politics from the bottom-up. Learning all the tricks of the trade. And Twinks had a beau. Yes, a beau. A nice young man, cum laude from Princeton, now in law school, and the most attractive parents, from Philadelphia. The Placemans had met them when they were all in Washington. The father was a lawyer with a very prestigious firm in Philadelphia. Very possibly a candidate for the Supreme Court. And they played golf. Oh yes. And the son, the beau, was a champion skier. And there might just be an announcement soon. Wedding bells might well be ringing before the year ended. Oh to be young again. It made the Placemans' tiny hearts ache.

⚭

MARCH SHOVED off from the dock and headed out of the bay. What will happen, she thought. If nothing happens. What do people do with their lives. What am I doing wrong.

She moved toward the narrows, listening to the water hitting the boat, dragging one foot in the wake, keeping her face out of the shade of the sail and into the sun. She thought about Max, and reconstructed each scene again from the beginning: The first night, their first conversations, the glances, the jokes, the clothes she had worn, the first weekend in the country, the first lunch, the first time he had given her a present, a book on finance, the first time she had given him one, a new pipe, the second lunch, the third dinner. She made a mental chart that showed the significant changes in the relationship. She had once made a timetable to show the frequency of his calls at first, and noted the day when he had only called twice, then once, then not for two days. She had noted the beginning of certain fibs, lies actually, the beginning of long silences, the beginning of his being impatient, a little mean, short-tempered, bored, very bored, extremely impatient. Nothing lasts forever, March. You see? She did not see.

There was a not a cloud and barely a breeze, but northern lakes could be suddenly treacherous. Once, sailing with her father, she had tipped the boat, and her father had nearly drowned. She had socked him in the jaw, and grasped him around the chest the way the course she had taken had taught her, and she and her brother had kept him afloat until a fishing boat picked them up; but she remembered him lying on the dock later, seemingly dead, while a fisherman worked on him, while she prayed that he would live.

What would Max say if she was caught in a sudden storm and drowned? He would be very sorry. He would say, oh that fantastic body. Gone. So young. So interesting. So mysterious. Always reminded me of someone. Yes. Someone beautiful and amusing. Audrey Hepburn. Grace Kelly. Life is not worth living without her. But. Then. One morning: his hair slicked back, in that beautiful dark suit and that clean soft shirt and the perfect tie, the faintest touch of aftershave in the air, his blood beginning to rush because, yes, yes, pharmaceuticals were up! And Deedee or Yvonne or what's her name was suggesting a weekend in Barbados, and there was an auction at Sotheby's and life was worth living again! Finally, it would be time to go on breathing and drinking champagne, and eating melon, and rare cheeses and making love to other women. While March, of course, would lie at the bottom of Blue Lake.

No, the truth was, he would never hear. There would be a sudden storm, but by the time March was fished out of the lake and buried in the cemetery in La Rue, Max would be in London. And the news would never reach the *Times*. It would be in the *La Rue Journal*. There would be the depressing funeral. Mr. Placeman would be a pallbearer. And yet, twenty years later Max would say, I wonder whatever became of that, what was her name, that sweet young thing from wherever it was, somewhere in Wisconsin. He would be flying over the Midwest on his way to California, and he would turn to the man in the next seat and say, tell me the name of a city near Chicago. And the man, Mr. Placeman, would say, I happen to be from La Rue, myself. That's it. La Rue. Of course. Do you know someone I knew a long time ago. March. March Rivers! Alas, Mr. Placeman, would say. I did know her. A lovely young woman from a lovely family. She drowned twenty years ago in a sudden storm on Blue Lake, without a beau. Without a beau. It broke our hearts. Never married. Not like our Twinks who was one of her dearest friends, and married shortly thereafter. Married a fine young man. They live in San Francisco now. They have five children and they are all very happy. All of them. All the time. Poor March Rivers.

And Max would say, What? No beau. What a terrible tale. How awful. No. He would not say that. No. He would narrow his eyes and lean over and say in a loud whisper, No beau. Are you kidding. I knew her. I knew her well. I loved her. We fucked the daylights out of each other. She was the love of my life!

Maybe if I'd cared less, March thought. Had other things on my mind. Had a life. But just now on the calm surface of the lake, her mind was backtracking, well on its way up the Hudson River to the family country house where she and Max had been in May. They were walking back through the woods after Sunday lunch with Max's grandmother, and the talk of the weather, the flowers, the tapestries, cabinetmakers, good wood, lovely craftsmanship, Paris, that splendid apartment in the 16th. A lovely lunch, grand-mère.

Consommé, sesame toast, how it did crumble, and lamb something, and fresh asparagus, and yes, poached pears. The rich did love their poached pears. March too had begun to love the pears.

Heading back to Max's parents' house after the lunch, Max's arm through hers, and Max saying, What's on your mind, March? Nothing. Nothing much. Max was being especially concerned that day. It made her nervous. Her mind had become something like an overripe lemon. Squeeze it and no surprise. Squashy fruit, sour juice. Same desperate little question, does he care. DOES HE. CARE? Very little variation there in the warm spring days, and very little hope either.

Shoulders back, back straight, Max forever talking about her slump, telling her to stand up, her neck all stretched to hell and gone, hoping—you know—to make it seem like women in *Vogue*, women in *Harper's Bazaar*, women in love. Ten little fingernails perfectly shaped, clean, polished; likewise ten little toenails, and wouldn't all the old roommates smile. March who had always had so much trouble with emory boards.

Little tweed suit, blue cashmere sweater, matching the blue in the tweed, suit from New York, sweater from Ireland, March from La Rue, aka Milwaukee, and the hair a little askew, but what could be done under the circumstances. Walking along through the woods, home from grandmother's house to what, to the wolf, to the other house, to Max's house, to bed maybe! But not at all. What Max had in mind was a trip to a nearby junior college to see a girl he knew. Someone from London! Who so hated being trapped there, off in the country, who didn't give a bloody damn what the school said because next weekend she was going to that party in Washington. So there.

The girl, Tea, arrived at the gate, stuck out her pink tongue which was pinker than most, and fuller—somewhat like an all-day sucker—and ran it along her upper lip which was also very pink and chubby. She called him Max, darling. (March would never.) She wiggled her cute nose, and closed her eyes and tipped her head back and looked out from under eyelashes thick as currycombs. The tongue came out again, and March thought, so she is a spoiled child, and maybe dumb, but maybe she knows all she needs to know? March was spellbound. She stuck out her own tongue, but was not encouraged, her tongue being more like a tongue than a cherry lollipop, and now it encountered a bit of chapped lip, and she pulled it right back in there where it belonged. Does he care. Yawn. Yawn.

They drove away from the school gates, waving good-bye, good-bye, and over the river and through the woods in the Jaguar; Max (darling) rubbing his throat and neck. The shirt open at the neck to accommodate the blue ascot (the ascot that March finds so splendid, so truly sophisticated), one arm out there in the wind, one hand on the wheel, not a word, but a sudden low groan, almost a moan from his gut, his groin? A low hum. Surely Max did not have her problem. Moaning over his troubled thoughts for hours. Was his mind on her now, or on what's her name? The charmer with the tongue?

Goddamn kike, a man shouted from another car Max had come close to clipping at the turn, and March felt sick.

She reached out and put her hand on his arm, and just settled it there without a word. March felt sick. To use that word. To call Max a kike. Maybe that rude man, that little, fat, suburban WASP would end up in a ditch. Her hand rested on Max's arm for a minute, then she began to gently rub his shoulder and his neck, her hand working itself nicely inside the open shirt and down against his chest, awkward but interesting. For March this was somewhat new, this reaching out instead of waiting for him. This gamble.

Out of the car, and up the steps, up the staircase and into the bedroom, and shut the door; onto the bed where March dared to take over, to make love to her lover, to do what she had not had the nerve to do before. To seduce him. Carefully, slowly she removes her own clothes; carefully, methodically she begins to remove his. To undress him, her lover, one shoe at a time, one sock, then the other, the shirt and the soft leather belt, the trousers, now the shorts— Turnbull & Asser—and she smiles, thinking what Turnbull & Asser would say now. Change from a pocket hits the carpet, never mind. The watch drops to the floor. The crystal shatters. Never mind. May the coins scatter. May time stop. Far away, a phone is ringing, the sun is low in the sky, falling on Max's throat where she can touch the pulse, a shadow on his cheekbone, a warm breeze on her hand where she lets it rest for a moment on his hip, before she slides her hands beneath him and begins to make love to him, to devour him, her lover. Her lover's body, her map of the world.

Later Max asked her a question. March could not say. She shook her head. She did not know anything. She shivered and Max pulled the blanket over them and they lay there in their own dead sea while he told her a story about childhood, the first time he heard that, the first time some boy had called him a kike, and she lying there in his arms thought that this story and his telling of it was his gift to her. A lover's gift. What more could one ask for. To love someone. To be loved.

The wind came up then. The boat heeled. March came back from Max's bedroom, let out the sail, fixed her attention on the water. Heading in she saw the Placemans and her parents emerging from the boathouse. Watching from the dock. Waving and waving. Calling.

Ahoy there! Ahoy! Hard to the lee, Mr. Placeman shouted. March slipped past the dock, jibed, and headed in again. She slid up to the dock, and Mr. Placeman caught her and leapt to secure the boat. Ahoy!

✧❦✧

In September March received two dozen roses from Max. She did not see him or hear from him again. She went to La Rue for Christmas, and in January moved to San Francisco where she shared a house with three other girls, found an editorial job with the Bay Area Council, found Warren Wright, became pregnant, became engaged, flew home to La Rue to wait for Warren and the wedding.

᠁

If, she had thought after she had known Warren for a while, *if* I should become pregnant, if by some chance. Perhaps all for the best? Salvation from slutdom? Once pregnant, very definitely pregnant, she had of course had doubts. As had Warren.

Married! She could still see Warren on Telegraph Hill, a rainy Friday, on the corner of Union and Greenwich. They stood facing each other and Warren the raconteur, the daredevil, died a quick death. The dashing, free soul who had stories to tell about Warren in the war in Nevada, watching the bomb, love, Warren the chef knocking his hibachi off his windowsill on Telegraph Hill and watching with amazement as it traveled along with four lamb chops through the Volkswagen sun roof of one Carleton Leon, the Chinese laundry man, who decided not to sue, because as Warren and his lawyer pointed out in court, they were friends, neighbors, part of a small world, and Carleton agreeing, they were indeed. Warren dressed as William Tell driving home from a costume ball, hitting a telephone pole, the smashed apple on his head causing the assumption of a serious brain injury instead of a shattered hip. Will Private Wright ever walk again, observers at the military hospital inquired as Warren was wheeled out of the amphitheater and the doors closed. But of course Private Wright did walk again, albeit with a limp and pain that grew more severe over the years.

And yet, Warren, her husband-to-be, was resourceful. He called March to say there was a man in Zihuatanejo. Very gifted. Does movie stars. Hacienda by the sea. March could hear coins going into a pay phone. She hung up.

A better idea. A doctor in San Francisco, very social, helps all the debutantes. You go in there, March, and talk about your family. Talk about my family. No. Don't talk about my family. Just say someone from very old California. Around since the Gold Rush. grain king, ships from Maine. Guy is nuts about all that stuff. You say you need some way out. Besides the Golden Gate Bridge. Leave him openers.

They rehearsed. Warren was the doctor. March was March. They did the scene over and over until Warren said she had it down. He bought a pair of crutches from a hospital supply store. You need a crippled look. The guy loves losers. We can sell these back. We'll say you had a fast recovery.

I feel like a nut, March complained. I don't look like a cripple. He'll know I'm a fake.

And don't forget the gloves. Wear gloves. The guy is a big snob. Shit, March said. Gloves and crutches.

You're having a baby the fancy doctor said. He seemed pleased. I'll kill myself, March pleaded. I'll jump.

No, you won't. You'll get married. He kissed her on the cheek and shook her glove. Congratulations. I'm looking forward to the wedding!

OK OK, Warren said. Let's not rush. We'll get engaged. Big Dot has a ring. She got it from the Shah.

The ring was produced and March wore it with relief and a sense of history, though Warren's mother said she didn't know where Warren got that idea about the Shah. She had lived in Persia when her father was the envoy at the time of the *old* Shah, and her ring. *Her ring.* But this particular ring. Whatever, March thought. Whatever. This rather large woman whose grand youth had given way to a kimono at dinner, who talked with tears in her eyes of meeting Warren's father on the Panama Canal trip. We were young and gay. She sighed. March sighed. The next day she flew home to La Rue.

❦

IN LA RUE her presence was unnecessary, a fact for which she was thankful. She could barely keep her eyes open and she was busy consuming soda crackers for morning sickness. The star of the show was out.

Her mother went about with pencils sticking out of her pockets and telephone cords looped around her neck. She asked March to make a hair appointment, to stop picking nervously at the carved figures on her desk. Then she went off to make notes, to check wedding presents and write a description of each in a wedding book. She put down a small black mark for anyone who had sent a lemon.

What constitutes a lemon?

Something like this plate. March picked up a gold plate and found a small knife at the end of a chain.

I have never in my life seen so much silver, one of her mother's friends said.

Do you realize what your mother has done in three weeks?

Three weeks!

They came, the jolly busy friends, to help unpack and place the presents on tables covered with white cloths and satin ribbons.

Her mother had accomplished a lot in three weeks. Yes, she had. Nobody asked why the hurry, and it was this silence, this deception on her part that March did not dwell on then; this slithering around the truth that would mark her life for years to come; this refusal to say, I have done the unthinkable. She could not say it. They could not say it.

Those wineglasses will break, her mother said, moving them next to a silver coffeepot. March backed away. The room reminded her of an operating room.

Would you believe this vase from Edna Rutherford? I think she's losing her buttons.

Losing. Lost. You ought to see her bright red hair, and she has lunch at the hotel every Friday with the man who makes lampshades.

Harold Gossage. Harold Gossage is a fairy.

Yes but his lampshades are very nice. And he makes his own potato chips!

※

On the morning of Warren's arrival March was up early, eating crackers, thumbing through mail on the desk, looking at a note from

Max's mother. Max was in France. She knew he would be sorry to miss the wedding. I'll bet, March thought. All torn to pieces. She sniffed the heavy notepaper for some old taste of him, but there was nothing.

A lopsided sun was coming through the mist on Lake Michigan, a rabbit sat on the frozen lawn that dropped off to brambles and beach grass, and out on the horizon a tanker was moving south. She looked into the dining room where silver shone on the table, and flowers floated in a bowl, and the heavy dusty rose color of the curtains gave to the room a soft pink light.

In the garage she settled into her father's car and headed up the drive. The car was huge, dark, soft. She turned on the radio and pushed the window buttons so that all the windows went down at once. She drove past the lighthouse, along the lake, into La Rue and out again, past the edge of town, past the shopping centers, past farms and through another town that was nothing more than a store and a train station with the windows boarded up, and grass growing over the tracks. She stopped at the crossroads near the highway exit, parked near gas pumps now overgrown with weeds, turned off the ignition and waited for Warren and his friends to arrive.

She watched a pheasant in the stubbled field beyond, a woman opening the door to the roadhouse across the way. Old March Rivers is getting married, she thought. Twenty-five, feeling one hundred, but listen, here in a new red coat, no longer standing on some flat patch of earth, waiting, hoping, reaching out to life, making so many leaps and stumbles, a thousand strange pluckings, attempting always to find what might help her to make sense of her life. Boarding school, college, New York, San Francisco, but here she was. If people had now and then told her she looked lost, and they were right—a lost soul a boy she had known had called her—so, so what did he know. Little guy who drank too much. Here she was at the finish line.

She was almost asleep on the hood of the car when she heard honking, saw the white rental car come down the exit ramp and into the parking lot in front of the roadhouse. Then the car swerved, and reversed and crossed the road to where she waited.

Rabbit. Baby. March. Darling. Sweetheart. We made it. We're here. In the old Midwest! In the cornfields! Those are cornfields? And cows. Thousands of cows, March. Little black and white jobs. Very sweet. Millions of them. Dear dear March. Very flat here. No?

Six of them stumbling out of the car, stretching and rubbing their eyes in the sunlight, shaking themselves, laughing. For one wild moment March knew she was going to jump into her father's car and beat it. Who were these people. Why did they look so awful.

You wouldn't have liked that plane trip, March. Not at all. We came down in every town in the country. Omaha. We've been to Omaha. Oh! Oh Ma Ha! They were all laughing.

We got lost. Right after O'Hare. Right in O'Hare. Couldn't get out. Not possible. We rented this. This car. And we got lost and then we got lost again. We went to Weekoogan. Waukegan. And Zion. We've been to Zion. That's where we've been. And Kenosha. To a cheese farm. A regular farm with cheese. Everything grown right there. On the premises! March, dearest. I think we might have a little drink. One little drink to celebrate the whatever? The nuptials. The sweet nuptials!

March nodded. She knew. They had fallen into Warren's plan to fly out of San Francisco on the red eye. (Cheaper, March. And probably very dramatic seeing the country at that hour. Sunrise, fields of grain, amber waves and all?)

I'll get away now, before it's too late, March thought. This is all a terrible mistake. By midnight I could be in Nebraska. I could be in Tennessee. I could be dead. Or drunk as a skunk up the road at the Mosquito Inn. Get me out of here.

Then she welcomed them to the Midwest, kissed Warren and got into her car with him and led the way into La Rue. It's going to be some week, Warren said. I never thought I'd see this. Never thought I'd see myself in Wisconsin with the boys. Reaching out, he patted March's stomach. How's you know who? I hope we make it, he announced a few seconds later. Then he fell asleep beside her.

THEY'RE ALL certainly large, March's mother said. Why does Warren keep calling you Rabbit? What about the one who shakes?

I'd like to have time to sit down and discuss your financial program with Warren, her father said.

I think we're in business, Warren told March. Though we may not live to see it. In case you didn't know, you do have money. It's just not exactly available. At the moment.

They stood in the minister's office.

Do you mind if I smoke, Warren said.

I do, Father Sanders said. We're here to discuss the rest of your life. I'm about to say a prayer.

Warren was filling the cuff of his gray flannels with ashes and the room was filling with smoke. Sorry, Warren said. No ashtray. He smiled, and held the cigarette butt in his fingers.

Father Sanders coughed. Was Warren confirmed?

Not exactly.

Had he received instruction. In this church?

Not exactly. I went to a Catholic school for a while. I had a little place I used to pray when I was six or seven. I made it myself! In my bedroom. Of course I was pretty small. But I'm not a Catholic. I'm open as far as religion is concerned.

But you are baptized. The Episcopal church requires that.

That old guy gave me the death watch feeling, Warren said later. Baptized. Christ, I almost blew it!

Does Warren have diabetes? March's mother wanted to know.

Why should he have diabetes?

Sometime during the night he drank three quarts of ginger ale. The bottles are in his room.

I think he just gets thirsty, March said. He gets hot and thirsty.

What is he giving you for a wedding present?

March had no idea. She suspected the answer was nothing, but she would never say that.

You have the silver mugs for him, her mother reminded her. They're in a box on the dresser in your room.

Right.

March forgot about the silver mugs until the last minute; then grabbing a box from her bed she took it to the church and gave it to Warren while they waited. He opened it and inside was a cookie jar. Very sweet, darling, Warren said. I know I'll learn to love it. Don't say anything, March warned. The mugs are in my bedroom. I think they're drinking mugs. With glass bottoms. So you can see if someone is coming to kill you.

What is all this business about presents. Your mother started in on this yesterday, hinting. Darkly. I think she suspects.

She says it's the thing. There are certain traditions. You give me something. I give you something. I give the bridesmaids presents. You give the boys presents.

She's all atwitter, March. I can see that. But I can tell you right now we'll be lucky to get through a week in Mexico. Then he poked her. I'm on! And he disappeared down a corridor that led to the front of the chapel.

I will, Warren said.

I will, March said. I will. I will. I will.

Very well then. God the Father, God the Son, God the Holy Ghost, bless, preserve, and keep you and fill you with all spiritual benediction and grace, and so on unto death. Forever and ever and ever.

Warren closed his eyes and smiled. And that's enough of the kissing, Father Sanders said, and sliced them apart with a long, veiny finger, or maybe it was one of the fine, silver butter knives, of which March and Warren now had sixteen.

It was a cold dark night in the church in La Rue. The service was brief, and they should take longer March thought, as she had so many years before when she had been confirmed, and the grand event seemed to have flown right past her. From the corner of her eye she saw her father in black and white, her mother in pale blue. What she had looked forward to for years was standing at the entrance to the chapel with her father and coming slowly, majestically down the aisle on his arm. Her mother alone for a moment, and someone waiting there for her. So this is what she had dreamed of: flowers, music, candlelight, white streamers, the old deaf sister in the choir loft thumping out the notes, four hundred guests leaning over the edges of the pews that faced the aisle, thinking probably, how dare she, but then again this is the event of the year and so be it, and March the impostor, moving along in her white white dress, nodding and smiling at the blur of faces.

March Rivers Wright. Be careful what you wish for, she thought. Then it was on to the reception.

The minister's son, now a minister himself, kissed March on the cheek and shook Warren's hand with enthusiasm. God bless, he kept saying, and March thought about the weekend with this cheerful son in some upstate New York college town where she had spent two days and nights drinking warm beer and necking, until, at last, on Sunday afternoon she had sunk onto the hairy green train seat, and all the way to Poughkeepsie sipped warm orange drinks through lips that felt as though they had been permanently bruised.

Thank God for the canopy, a woman leaving the church said.

You don't have a wedding in November without one, March heard her mother say.

How could you do all this in no time, someone said. Truly. Amazing. In a thousand years. Never. I couldn't have done it.

Now it's legal, a fat man whispered.

Ha Ha. I bet you're preggers, her friend Sam whispered.

Who are all these people, Warren wanted to know. They stood in the receiving line at the La Rue Country Club and shook hands, and danced, and had dinner, and danced, and cut the cake. Warren said it was a splendid party. He wanted to know the names of all the pretty girls. He wanted to dance with all of them. He wanted to dance with her mother who was so alarming, and one of the bridesmaids who was so adorable. It was a splendid event. The ushers, his boys, were having a splendid time. One of them, the one who ran the industrial film company Warren worked for, the one Warren referred to as Fig

Leaf, was pursuing March's sister. Fig Leaf was married and old, at least forty, with dyed black hair. Her sister was fifteen.

Fig Leaf makes me nervous, March said. Where is his wife?

I think she's a dancer somewhere. Las Vegas, maybe.

I wouldn't mention that.

What about these Dells, a couple from California wanted to know. We saw signs for days. Four hundred miles. Three hundred miles. Ten. Five. Nothing.

We've never been east of the Rockies.

We've never been west of the Hudson.

Look here, March. My schedule says there is a breakfast tomorrow and a lunch. We may be here for the holidays!

We're starting the press at midnight, March. The editor is taking us down to the paper. For the wedding picture!

Lovely people here. There's a party after this you know.

March threw her bouquet over the balcony, and watched an usher and one of her bridesmaids on the far side of the room, and thought yes that was something she would miss. Meeting someone, watching someone watching you, the lovely ache of hoping something was about to begin. Summer nights when the wind came up, or a Christmas snow falling and a fire burning. All that was over now, but a small price to pay.

Do you know all these people, March? Warren wanted to know.

All these people. She had grown up beside these bright expectant faces, the twang of their greetings, the hum of their voices raised, their hymns that would stay with her through the years.

> VAR SI TY - VAR - SI - TY U - RAH - RAH - WIS - CON - SIN
> HAIL TO THEE WE SING
> HAIL TO THEE OUR AL MA MA TER
> U RAHHHH RAHHH

From the balcony off the dressing room where she had gone to change she could see their outstretched arms, their heads thrown back. She could remember the names of many, and the faces of those whose names she had forgotten, but what was imprinted on her memory for good was the place, the town itself: the angle of the streets, the curve of the shoreline against Lake Michigan, the habits and customs of generations of men who talked about the company, the lake, the club, the Community Chest, the hospital, the University, the men who set the tone in the town and their wives who were all bound to a way of life she was leaving behind; but one that was, after all, the geography of her childhood, one that would stay with her as surely as the lines on the palms of her hands.

CALIFORNIA, HERE we come, Warren had chanted, but three weeks after Mexico, two weeks after settling into their apartment in San Francisco forever, they were packing their bags for the move to Chicago. For Warren this was supposed to be a step up in the business world. A promotion, he said. More or less. Fig Leaf who ran the film company out of MGM in Los Angeles, where March and Warren had just been for a weekend, had decided to open a Chicago office, and Warren was his man.

Chicago, March said. What are you talking about? Maybe she was not hearing correctly. It was midafternoon. She was busy in the kitchen, cooking again. Trying to get her rum pie out, trying to get her ham in. Working over some dusty mint leaves that were boiling in a little pan of water. Maybe Warren was sick. He looked sick. He looked terrible. His eyes were closed and he was just standing there, leaning against the kitchen wall.

Chicago!

Figs is closing the office here.

You're kidding. We just left. We said good-bye. Give us a call when you're out here. Now we're showing up again.

It's supposed to be a good deal. Of course if that office closes too. Warren made a loud popping sound with his tongue.

What was that for?

Kiss of death. The thing could fall apart in a minute.

The wedding presents were shipped yesterday, her mother said on the phone that night. She sounded as though this change in plans was March's way of ruining her life. All that silver. All that china. All those brandy snifters. Rattling around in some moving van, and for what. To turn around and rattle back. Everyone knew that everyone in La Rue wanted to live in San Francisco; some people for a few months, some just before they died, some right away, for life.

Of course Warren could quit, March said. He could look for something else. In San Francisco.

Her father did not see that at all. This is an opportunity and I'm sure Warren will give it his best. And I'm sure you will. *March?* You're part of the team now.

The team.

It could be a good deal, Warren said several times. But you never know about Fig Leaf.

He's slippery, March said. He's the kind of person who's always putting some deal together, some hot company, then getting out before it falls apart. Also. When he was after my sister at the wedding, it made me nervous.

It probably made Figs nervous, Warren said.

Let's be optimistic. I'll have the whole Midwest, Warren said, looking doubtful about what that might include.

The whole Midwest. As far as Warren knew that was La Rue, and a night in Chicago after the wedding, a morning spent wandering around the river that ran through the city, a walk along streets behind the river where men slept in front of grated windows. Warren had wanted to see the Loop and Michigan Avenue, but March found that for all her talk about La Rue being just outside of Chicago, having spent half her life changing trains there, when it came time for her to lead a sightseeing tour she had not been able to find much at all. I think the Loop is right around here somewhere. And this is, well, this is a railroad yard. She was not exactly sure what the Loop was. That afternoon they had taken a helicopter to the airport and put the problem of Chicago behind them. Finissimo, Warren said as they rose above the city and headed toward Mexico and the Pacific.

But this time. This time they were really going to get to know the place. Warren said, This time I want to see all the old famous hangouts. Gangster haunts. Dillinger. Bugs Moran. Sam Golf Bags Hunt. Did I ever tell you that story about the golf bag? A silver dollar, March, for the first person to locate the sight of the St. Valentine's Day Massacre!

A passionate sightseer and crime buff, Warren now spent hours marking red X's on a map of Chicago he had picked up at a second-hand bookstore. And March said this time she would show him the city. She certainly did know it. She had friends there from school, aunts and uncles who lived in the suburbs, friends of her parents, friends of friends from New York, Boston, Atlanta, all over.

Actually, she didn't know anyone in Chicago that she could think of at the moment. The people she talked about were people whose names had more or less stuck in her head, people she had imagined from other people's conversations and adopted as her own. Scott Osterwinder from Lake Forest, Rags Pole whose father had gone to prison, old Chicky Moss from Winnetka who was supposed to be in the CIA, and Tricks West who had been thrown out of Yale. Walter French who had already published a novel. These people were so real to her that it was hard for her to remember that she had never met them.

I'll call up people when we get settled, March said. She did the packing, and hauled Warren's belongings to the curb. His books on crime, twenty-five travel posters, fifteen small pillows he had collected for his sofa, several boxes of wedding presents, a painting of Telegraph Hill, a totem pole with many initials carved by classmates at Berkeley, three avocado plants growing in instant mashed potato boxes.

Warren was out saying good-bye to the city, to the boys, to the old hangouts, to the owner of the corner grocery who had given them a farewell lunch, to an old girlfriend. At six o'clock when he was ready to pack the car it was raining, and they were due at his parents' house in Woodside for a Christmas Eve dinner.

Nothing to it, Warren said, tossing whatever March had lugged to the curb into the trunk and onto the backseat. March said they would have to take everything out and start over. They weren't going all the way across the country like this.

Warren said this was the way people traveled. He lit a cigarette and considered. If the car doesn't break down we're golden. We could have problems. Keep your fingers crossed.

He stuffed the many colored pillows into the empty spaces and talked about how painful these last days had been for him. Saying good-bye. He had never lived anywhere else. San Francisco. His hometown. Now he was pulling up stakes after twenty-eight years. Christ, March. I'm the first to go.

How could any of the boys go somewhere, March wanted to know. Warren was the only one who had a real job. The boys had jobs of a sort. They had investments, or land or real estate. Mostly, they seemed to have lunches and cocktails.

That's true, Warren said. I'm the only one. The only one who's out taking a chance on life. He looked pleased. But I'll miss them.

Twenty-four hours later San Francisco was part of history, their history. This is it, March, Warren announced. America. He turned on the radio and lit a cigar.

They drove south to Bakersfield, stopping for the night at an inn where they were the only people in the dining room, and in the morning they headed for Las Vegas. Warren called out the towns and points of interest like a tour guide. Tehachapi. Barstow. The Mojave Desert. Death Valley. Lowest point in North America. 125 degrees in summer. Last chapter of Frank Norris' novel. What was the name. Something *McTeague*. *McTeague: A Story of San Francisco*. And he was born in Chi, March. Our new hometown. Old Frank Norris. Great man. Died after they took out his appendix. Great book. And you won't believe Vegas.

March did not. Now and then she stopped feeding money into slot machines long enough to put in a call to her parents; to say, Merry Christmas; Merry Christmas from March in Las Vegas; how was Christmas, there? What did you do? (Without me?)

She had never been away from home on Christmas, and the one she had just spent with Warren was not like any Christmas she had ever imagined. They had called on ancient San Francisco aunts who called her Marble, who talked about copper and ships coming from

Maine. Did Marble know about the *Mary Wright* that had sunk? Did she know about Captain John? No. Oh dear. Well, another time. When would the wedding be? Had she been through the Panama Canal? No? Oh dear. And there was the business of choosing a fountain pen from Aunt Emma's collection. Aunt Emma resided on an immense Spanish bed in an apartment at the top of the Mark Hopkins, and after receiving the fountain pen, March said she thought Warren should probably stop hoping for his ship to come in anytime soon.

Visiting the aunts had been almost funny, but Christmas Eve with Warren's parents had started with a long cocktail hour around the pool, and before dinner began Warren and his father had argued, and started to fight, to tackle each other, while March watched, horrified, and Big Dot kept saying, please, please. So there had not been a dinner, and she and Warren had gone to a neighbor's for the night. The neighbors had not seemed surprised. Oh come right in. How about a glass of champagne. Of course the next morning they had gone back to the house so that Warren could pick up his Christmas check.

⟨৸⟩

It was the twenty-eighth of December before March was able to get a call through to La Rue. Merry Christmas, Merry Christmas, she shouted.

Hello. Hello? March, is that you? Who is calling? She heard her mother's voice.

We're in Las Vegas. In a casino. She could think of nothing more, and they were a little slow because it turned out that it was two in the morning in La Rue. It's another world out here, March said. You never know what time it is.

Have a good trip. Drive carefully. Good-bye. Good-bye.

They had managed without her. They had not sounded lonely or abandoned at all. They had sounded tired.

This could be the place to try a new life, March said that night. I think we might be more comfortable right here. In Las Vegas. There was nothing familiar about it, nothing that seemed real. Not a soul they knew. She liked it.

But Warren knew all about people who stayed on. You see them by the side of the road. Trying to sell their cars. Trying to unload watches, rings, clothes, suitcases, a dog, a bird. Anything.

And Las Vegas was nothing compared to the Hoover Dam. The Hoover will blow your mind, March. You go right down inside the little jobbie and hear the water going over you. Thousands of tons of water going right over the sweet head.

You are now inside the dam, the guide shouted the next afternoon. Thousands of tons of water are now going over you.

And over the rabbit, Warren whispered. He patted March's belly.

March wanted to get out of there, but Warren was busy talking and making friends, getting information on driving conditions, hearing all about a road that was not marked out on their map, making notes on a shortcut suggested by a man who got in the elevator with them.

Here's a little secret I don't mind sharing. Only the natives use it. You won't have traffic. Believe you me! Warren believed him.

Three hours later Warren looked at March. This may be it. The end.

March looked out and saw nothing at all but land, ditches, the chalky road, sky, bumps, potholes. The sun shone. The whole world was flat, white, empty.

You don't know the West, but people get lost out here, March. Months later someone finds a car in a ditch. A steering wheel. Shattered glass, and springs poking through the holes in the seats. Grass growing out of the tires.

Warren chain-smoked his Lucky Strikes, fiddled with the radio, and barreled ahead; chin on the steering wheel and shoulders hunched, eyes hidden behind large black plastic glasses he was forever stocking up on in drugstores and gas stations. The glasses all looked the same. They had the same gold and black price mark on one lens, and were snapped, or cracked, or lost within days. Warren said the lost ones were stolen. People were always stealing things from him. Cars, television sets, glasses, cigarette lighters, cigarettes, money, his mystery stories, his socks. If thieves had never got hold of his socks he would now have approximately two hundred pairs. Small black jobbies. Thirteen to a bag at the surplus store on Market Street.

March was hungry. She was always hungry. And always tired. But Warren said hunger was only one of their problems. They were both going to die of hunger and thirst and every other thing that people died of out here. They were going to run out of gas, and be eaten by coyotes. All because of the little bastard in the elevator inside the dam.

I should have known. I should have seen it for what it was. A setup. He's following us right now. You wait, March. Just wait. It's all a matter of time. In about five minutes a car will come out of nowhere and block the road, and he'll take our money and shoot us and leave us for the coyotes. You'll see something coming up behind us, and then you'll see something blocking us, and then you'll see our elevator friend. Hello from the Hoover. Then bang, bang. Good-bye you. Good-bye me. Good-bye to the rabbit. Good-bye Chi Town.

If we're shot we won't have to worry about the future. That's all I think about. And I wish you'd stop calling it Chi Town. It's like saying Frisco.

Good-bye, March. Good-bye. Good night. Fuck us all. Amen.

Warren put his foot on the floor, and the car shook, and dust flew. The toaster fell off the pile of boxes in the backseat and landed at March's feet. Minutes later they curved to the left and came out onto the highway their own map had outlined. Warren slowed down; fiddled with the radio which suddenly worked again, smiled, wiped his forehead and began to sing. *I want to go back to my little grass shack in Kalikua Hawaii. Where the humuhumuunukunukuapua goes swimming by.*

They crossed from Nevada into Arizona, then New Mexico, Texas and Louisiana. Tonight New Orleans, Warren announced. Have dinner, celebrate the new year, then shoot straight up the middle.

The middle of what?

America.

By noon the next day, Warren, full of oysters, black-eyed peas, eggnog, hush puppies, March full of oyster crackers, they were on their way across Lake Pontchartrain.

And now, Mississippi and the northlands. Warren tapped the wheel and sang. *Oh when the saints, oh when the saints.* Some life they have there, March. Some life. I could stand it. *Oh Lord I want to be in that number!*

Tennessee and Missouri, and suddenly, March!

March had been asleep.

Out there. Que pasa?

Snow.

Snow!

Snow.

Christ.

March thought of being stuck somewhere, never having to arrive, retreating into a future that would set her free, free from the family she could not let go of, from motherhood, from the terrible permanency of marriage, free from the sinking realization that had been with her even in Mexico, that she did not want this life, and there was absolutely nothing she could do about it.

Bundled in the California clothes they began to wear in extra layers to offset the failing heater, and the draft coming in from somewhere behind them, Warren pointed out that March must have known this would happen. She must have remembered in some off-beat corner of her interesting mind that it did snow out here. Every winter. It got cold, froze, little droplets fell, normal people put on boots, gloves, scarves, heavy coats, did not feign surprise when something like this happened. In January.

March looked at Warren, and felt sorry for him. He would never belong here in the Midwest. He was a Californian, and after his years of an easy life in San Francisco he was as desperate as she was. He had no clothes, and not much money, and he was afraid. He sang, he teased, he made up stories, but she knew. She felt the stubborn rock of her stomach, felt it growing more like a football, more emphatic, more permanent each day, and longed for the snow to bury them.

On they went, hour after hour, listening to the radio, half listening, thinking of what lay ahead, when suddenly they looked at each other.

March!

I know. March smiled.

There was organ music, and names were read, and then more organ music, and thank you to casts of hundreds, and heartbreaking farewells. They were listening to the wrap-up of years of radio soap operas, the programs of childhood, with names as real to them as their own childhood friends.

Please don't leave me, a woman would cry. I need to leave you, a man would say. This life for us is over. I love you with all my heart my darling, but we cannot go on. Then sirens and screams.

Our plane is going down, a woman would shout. And the man would say, We are going down together, my darling. Me and you.

Terrible grammar, March complained.

But Warren would not hear of any fault. This is history, March. The wrap-up of the soaps! The end of the era. The coming of a new age. Farewell to the fifties.

For March, and for Warren, radio soap operas had been part of what you did when you had measles, or chicken pox or asthma. You got to lie in bed and listen to a favorite program, a new one every fifteen minutes. And even when you had missed weeks or months, you could go back and find you hadn't missed much after all.

Warren knew the names of all the old actors, and he remembered the scenes, moments from yesterday, from the fifties, the forties, the thirties. The terrible things that had happened to people over the years. The trials, tribulations, deaths, births, tears, fresh starts. And now they were listening to the end. Planes crashed, rivers flooded, fevers led to comas, guns were fired, night fell, sirens whined, wedding bells rang, a lost lover knocked in the dark, confessions were made, disaster beckoned.

Sometimes they sound like us. March said.

Stella Dallas!

Helen Trent!

Ma Perkins!

Our Gal Sunday.

Can a little girl from a mining town in the West find happiness with England's richest, most handsome lord. Lord *Hen*-ry Brinthrope? They laughed, and then the theme song "Red River Valley" was played, and they both joined in. *From this valley they say you are going, we will miss your bright eyes and sweet smile, for they say you are taking the sunshine, that has brightened our pathways awhile.*

Missouri was behind them, and the next day they drove through Illinois and around Chicago, following a snow plow north toward La Rue, home until they found an apartment.

And the Governor welcomes us, March!

They had crossed the Wisconsin state line. A new year. A new life.

Shoulders back, Warren announced. Head up, stomach in, a belated Merry Christmas and a H.P. New Year! We'll manage, March. He reached for her hand and squeezed it.

❧

ANOTHER YEAR. Another year. They flew by so quickly.

❧

SINCE LATE fall March had been thinking, brooding. Emerging like Snow White from a troubled sleep, and yet this fall had been like the others. Every day like every day, except for an incident with Lovely Blades, an acquaintance, not even a true friend, just someone.

Fall for March was a time for planting. A time for conception and the beginning, yet again, of the birth process. After the birth of Littlemarch, then Alden, the next two pregnancies had ended prematurely, but March had announced this fall as in other falls, Here I am again. Pregnant. As usual. Hungry, dizzy, sleepy.

Like a cow. Like a sow. Like a garden. Putting in bulbs before frost, for fruit in the spring. Like a garden.

Like a Catholic, her mother said.

Like the *seasons*.

Dead silence at the other end of the phone.

Then, from March, every year the ritual repeats itself, as surely as the turning over of the seasons.

And just about as mindlessly, her mother added.

What is this about a garden, her father wanted to know. If I were you I would try to think of myself as a mother with two lovely daughters. It seems to me that you owe it to yourself and to the rest of your family to stay well. To stay alive!

I want to stay alive.

You have a wonderful life ahead of you.

I read that. Everywhere.

In the clean clean library in the house in La Rue the telephone clicked and in the dirty little kitchen in the apartment on Barry Avenue in Chicago March rocked on her heels and thought, well these events aren't planned. These things happen. I am as surprised as anyone. It may be fate, or some amazing blessing, or the crack of doom, but it is not as though I deliberately set it up this way. It was something. Something to do.

And on the bus someone would offer you a seat. Please, missy, please take this!

March thought about the matter of life happening to her, of another year being settled. Then, on the way home from an afternoon meeting, she had been out there raising money again, for homeless children, for a hospital, for some man running for office, for muscular dystrophy, for the Vassar scholarship committee, for old folks, for the Crusade of Mercy, for the Junior League, who could keep track? On the way home, something was said.

She had just prepared five pounds of a peanut butter and chutney mixture which would be used on Triscuits at a cocktail party to announce plans to raise money for a new wing on the rehabilitation clinic, and she was thinking about peanut butter and chutney. One of three, against twenty-five others, she had held out for bacon wrapped around Waverly crackers and broiled and served hot. Now, she suddenly turned to Lovely Blades who was driving her home, and said she thought that peanut butter and chutney was a lousy idea.

It'll stick to people's teeth. It's going to get up on the roofs of their mouths and stay there. People will choke to death instead of giving money. Also. I've had that about five times recently. People don't seem to realize the cat's out of the bag as far as peanut butter and chutney are concerned.

Lovely said she could care less, and they went on in silence while March tried to get the conversation going again. Do you think people will come. To the party?

No, Lovely said, and went on with her driving.

March tried to think of more topics. She was always trying to think of topics, even in taxis. It was her obligation to the world. So. Here we are in April, she would say. Snow in April. I never. Who would have dreamed of thunder in December. Imagine. Have you ever known a hotter June. How many days has it been? That's Chicago for you. Who was interested in talk about the weather? Well, bank tellers, for one. She had picked this up from them. Quite a storm, wasn't it? Mmmmm.

Here we go, March said to Lovely. Fall again.

I always fall in love in the fall, Lovely said. She drove with one hand on the steering wheel and one foot under her, easily, as though she had spent all the years of her life, since birth, in this car.

Fall's all right, but I don't like winter, March said. Winter's terrible. People go inside. There's no one to talk to.

Lovely smiled. It's cozy in winter. Warm in front of the fire. People coming by. We look at pictures of places we'll go someday. Islands. Deserts. We listen to music, read aloud sometimes. Joyce. Dickens. Yeats. We lie there and drink wine and fuck a little, smoke, whatever.

March could not believe her ears. You do? Oh that's nice. We read a lot too. We have a fireplace. A fire. A fire is nice. Warm. She could not take her eyes off of Lovely. She had known Lovely Blades in college, but she had not seen much of her since, and she was something all right. She was all brown and slim, and her hair was the color of white wine, or wheat blowing, or sand on river bottoms, or sun or something. She was barefoot! She was running around barefoot, in the city, to a meeting. She must have worn shoes to the meeting and taken them off in the car?

March spent so much time getting ready to go places, she was always late. She wore dresses, or suits, and leather shoes, little pumps, and she carried a leather pocketbook that matched the shoes, and she wore a gold pin, and if she was going down town she wore gloves. She no longer wore hats. Hats were out now, but she always had her hair done at the beauty shop on Oak Street, even when she couldn't afford it, even when she sometimes wondered if it was worth it to spend two hours and eight dollars to look nice when you knew that it would all be blown to bits in two days. I go through cans of hair spray like it's going out of style, she would tell her friends.

How could Lovely just say that, about in front of the fire? Just drop that into the conversation. Lovely's husband Jeremy was all gold and sandy too. She thought about the two of them in front of the fire. Then she removed Lovely and put herself right there on the hearth and said, I am crazy about you Jeremy, and Jeremy smiled and flashed his beautiful white teeth and bit her lip. You, March, are my great love, he whispered.

What a lazy, sleepy day, Lovely said. She stopped at a light, and leaned back and stretched and yawned. Jeremy and I took the children to the zoo last night. We climbed the fence and danced. The children were in their pajamas and we were just being foolish. There was a harvest moon and we thought it was a perfect time. The seals barked. Then we went home and got up at dawn and had breakfast on the beach. The sun came up very slowly, and we took off our shoes and ran in the waves. The water was still warm. Andy Warhol has been staying with us. I think he makes us a little crazy.

The artist! Andy Warhol!

The zoo, the beach, Andy Warhol, reading Joyce. How could people do all that. Live like that. No shoes. Like a movie. Like some fairy tale. March wanted to say something about her own life. Make it sound more interesting. Give it a lively tone. What could she say?

When I was at Vassar we read *Finnegan's Wake*. We had a professor. Leonard Kestenbaum. We had our seminar, at night, in his apartment.

Lenny. I was in love with him, Lovely said. He had very hairy nostrils.

Leonard Kestenbaum! Was he in love with you?

I guess. He talked about it enough, but I think he just liked sex.

How did you meet. Did you take a course from him?

I think I just bumped into him one day.

Really. Something snapped in March's head. Her old life shot up through her. Leonard Kestenbaum, James Joyce, bare feet, NoDoz, black coffee, dirty sneakers, blue jeans, William Faulkner, sex, love, art, life!

She wanted to say that she too wanted to read aloud, dance in the moonlight, talk about writers, about ideas. Since she had been married, living in Chicago, having children, something had happened to her life. Truly. It had gone off somewhere. Underneath she was still the person who had read *Finnegan's Wake*. She hadn't always worn hair spray, or these shoes. This was just the way she looked. That other person had just got lost or something. Had Lovely ever felt confused or unwanted. Had she always felt perfectly at ease, even with Leonard Kestenbaum. Leonard Kestenbaum who had been so old, with some kind of hot coals burning in his eyes, and those hot lips, and hands like tree branches, and a heart that had suffered and understood the universe and many other mysteries whose secrets he had, presumably, whispered into Lovely's tiny ears.

March pulled herself up and got the conversation going again. Well, here I am again! Pregnant again. Again. Again. The fifth. But two died. Just like a cow. Like a sow. Like a garden. Like a melon!

A melon. Such a good word. Full, succulent. A warm Indian summer afternoon. In school in Connecticut when they went riding, and the air was so heavy with the smell of leaves burning, and apples rotting, and the light was a little hazy, as though someone had put cheesecloth across the sky; and they would ride for miles through the woods to a student's country house where the horses were tethered; and they would all go into the house and drink cider, and eat sausages, and creamed chipped beef, and ham and pickled peaches, corn muffins, powdered doughnuts, mugs of coffee in front of the fire. The warmth of the car made her groggy and happy, made her think of Stephen Vincent Benét's poem *John Brown's Body*, and Wingate riding in the fall in the south, and something in the air, something stirring in the land. Soon a shot would be fired and the war would begin. She jumped when Lovely said something.

Why are you always having children?

Don't ask me, March said. She laughed.

But I am asking. You seem so . . .

The car had stopped on Barry Avenue, and March who was huffing and puffing her way out of the car leaned back a little and rolled her eyes, and heard Lovely say something, but March was already slamming the door, and the door slammed on the edge of the words.

You seem so . . .

So what? She stood there for a moment on the curb, wondering, and she wanted to run down the block and open the door, and say, what did you mean. Exactly what did you mean. She wanted to say, I just joke. Underneath it all I am not always the way I seem. *I am somebody else.*

Too late. The car went on around the corner, but picking along over the grass and mud to the apartment March screwed up her face and frowned, and banged her fists on her black leather pocketbook. A word. A word like silly? Or frivolous? A word you would use to describe someone or something without ties, without seriousness or purpose? Without identity? She kicked at the door of the apartment with the toe of her black leather shoe, and leaned on the buzzer until she heard a child coming along on the other side, shouting.

Who is there? Who is there?

Mother.

Who?

MOTHER!

OPEN THE DOOR! THIS MINUTE!

The door opened, and March marched into the front hall and past the two children, and into the living room where the sitter was sitting in front of the television set. She waved her hand in front of the woman's face, and nothing happened. The room was nearly dark, and she turned on a light.

Wake up, she shouted. Wake up. There is a lot more to life than *The World Turns!* The old woman jumped and opened both eyes. She had no idea where she was. She blinked, and looked at her lap, and stuffed her tiny hands into a large brown paper bag, and brought out candy wrapped in orange paper.

Everyone loves Mrs. Sunshine, she said.

⟨≈⟩

In December March had a vision of herself running all furious, and naked, and crazy through the streets of Chicago. A Malay, she thought, running amuck. A lunatic speeding through town, through Chicago, home for the past six years.

I think there's something wrong with us, March told Warren. You, me, Littlemarch, and Alden and the big surprise. The big surprise would not be born until spring, but they already included this baby in their talks.

Warren said he didn't want to think about this, but March thought about little else.

I've seen the handwriting on the wall, she said. We're not going anywhere. Six years and what have we got. Five moves, four jobs, three children—almost. Broken dishes, blackened silver, dust, bills. Take a look.

I'm doing my best. Warren said. Life in a new city isn't easy.

New, Warren. Six years!

Flick of the wrist.

You're telling me. I am still writing thank you notes. Dear Mrs. Thunderhead. Warren and I are wild about the darling flowered butter plates. They match our wallpaper. What butter plates? What wallpaper. That was our first apartment. I still think about that wallpaper. I still think I'm in that apartment opening barrels of presents, still planning a future. What future? We're like refugees. That's what we are.

The world is full of refugees.

Yes, but we have never been to war. We have never had to flee. We ought not to be refugees.

War is hell, Warren said. I'm going to take a bath.

Whenever she brought up the future Warren disappeared for a while, and March was left to think of ways to shape him into their leader before it was definitely too late.

We stick out, she told him during three Christmas days in La Rue. All of us. We're falling apart. Flying around. A blind man could see this.

They were staying in the glorious country house that had replaced the old house on Rivers Avenue when March was still in college, this house March's mother had dreamed of, the house so surprising in its size and setting that a cigar-smoking man had arrived at the front door demanding a weekend stay. Told this was not a country inn, the man had flicked his ashes and departed in a huff.

Only March seemed to have any affection for the old neighborhood. Whenever they were in La Rue for a weekend she would insist on driving there and giving Warren and the children a tour.

The girls seemed to agree with their grandmother's assessment. That neighborhood had gone to the dogs.

Oh you poor person, Alden said. The girls, who were bouncing around in the back of the station wagon, their small faces pressed against the rear window for a better view, would express disbelief, sympathy. You lived here. Did you have a bad time? Poor Mumbles.

It was my life, March would say. Over there was the willow tree she had climbed, and there was the skating pond. There was the house where the man who had been a spy lived, and next to his house was the Christian Science reader who sat in his window and read all night. The next house belonged to the fat widow who hid candy under her mattress. Way up there at the top of her own old house, under the eaves, was March's room. And the pigeons cooing.

Poor thing.

It's touching all right, Warren said. A little bit like a war zone, though. A little bombed out now. Mmmmm? But where our sweet dear Mumbles began life.

March would finish with a tour of the old downtown where she had shopped and wandered. The Green Meadows Ice Cream Parlor, the Red Cross Drug Store with the soda fountain, the shop next to the Venetian Movie Theater owned by two of the players for the all girls baseball team March had cheered for during the war years. On the corner of Main and 7th was the library where she had spent so many afternoons, and back behind Woolworth's, over there off the square, was The Kewpee where the hamburgers were flat as pancakes, wrapped in wax paper with pictures of cupids.

All tiny and sticky and dear, Warren would say. Our sweet Mumbles ordering a cherry phosphate, spending her last nickel on a bottle of Horlick's Malted Milk tablets. Hot footing it over to the Venetian that now says, I'm sorry to say, WE ARE CLOSED. But, once upon a time, featuring? March? Once upon a time.

Esther Williams. June Allyson. Clark Gable. Margaret O'Brien. Cary Grant. Peter Lawford. Elizabeth Taylor. March would list her old favorites, half pleased, half embarrassed. Then they would pass the last crumbling warehouse, and head north over the bridge, out past the zoo, and newer houses until they were driving along the lake; going by the lighthouse and turning into the drive that curved down to the new house which nobody but Warren called the new house.

Warren said he was mad for the new house because of the bath towels. He would describe them at length. Ninety-six inch, fully absorbent, soft, fleecy, monogrammed, all that a bath towel should be. A bath towel you could not only dry yourself with, but wrap yourself in, walk around in, live in. You put this towel down on the floor and lie down at one end and roll and roll and roll and when you are almost out of breath, you come to the end, and you are so happy, and dry, and warm, and tired you never want to move again; and you know that if you don't, it will be all right. You will be safe there in your new cocoon.

The bath towels were wonderful, and the bathrooms were wonderful, and the kitchen was wonderful, especially during the holidays. A true celebration, Warren said as he circled the room, eating turkey dressing for breakfast, or caviar in the middle of the night. Anytime. He loved drinking expensive gin out of the heavy spotless glasses, drinking champagne, eating stacks of Christmas cookies that melted in his mouth. He put the cookies on his tongue, one at a time, to prove his melt-down theory. He ate caviar sandwiches on toast, munched sizzling cheese puffs; scooped up handfuls of pistachio nuts, spoonfuls of creamed oysters. The bounty, he would cry. The plum pudding, still moist, the orange and grapefruit segments which have, dearest March, been sprung from their troubled homes, from their bitter piths, a terrible time-consuming effort, and placed in great abundance in small containers. The kindness of others!

Sweet sweet segments, he called them, and popped them into his mouth at a steady rate until his arm wore out; and he just sat there beaming, and wiping his chin on his sleeve, at four-thirty one morning, in the still, polished kitchen where he had come with great excitement and a sense of adventure, dragging March with him, swathed in his great moth-eaten flannel bathrobe, dragging the puff from his bed to spread out and picnic on, to throw over himself should someone hear him, and interrupt the fun.

If your mother could see me now, Warren said. He chuckled, and March shuddered. I wonder if they ever come down for segments. Old Noonie and big Albert. It's a thought. He popped another bit of orange into his mouth. It's like a tropical country here. Like Bora Bora. Yes, I'm sure Bora is like this. Warm and breezy. He poured a glass of champagne.

Once, Noonie and Albert did find me down here, Warren said. Did I ever tell you?

I don't want to hear about it, March said.

No. No. It was a great story. It was. It is. I was here one night having a bottle of Squirt, and I heard sounds in the pantry. Who's there. Who is in our kitchen? Then Albert and Noonie burst in. Through the door. Like Rough Riders. Albert stood there without any loss of nerve at all, and your mother didn't look too bad either. I was the one who was terrified. I've always been terrified of Noonie and Albert except when I'm in Chicago, and they're in La Rue or in Europe, but this time I held my ground.

I said, Warren here. Just putting out the fire. And off they went! The loving couple: Albert looking solid, brave, Noonie especially fetching in her pink outfit. And it made me think. Do you suppose they ever? Hmmm? March? Do they? You know?

I wish you'd hurry up, Warren.

Do you ever think of Albert as a sort of Marlon Brando in disguise, March? I mean someone who, but for fate, might have been a motorcycle type. Someone on the road, aching for trouble. And then. One night he wanders into this little café and there is Noonie doing something behind the counter, and Albert ambles over and says, hey, you. And Noonie says, Hey man! Que pasa? And Albert closes his eyes until they're just slits, and runs his tongue over his lips, and then he does this half smile, and Noonie sort of gasps and says whatever Noonie would say. And then. Then old Noons puts down her spatula, and comes around from behind the counter. And right then. Guess what happens next!

I know what happens next. One part of March wants to hear. Part of her never tires of these stories, these outrageous family dramas Warren concocts with such ease, but the other part of her wants to get him out of here before her father comes down and sees them, or just starts shooting before he sees them.

Guess, March.

Someday we'll be shot, Warren. I think about that all the time. Albert shoots things you know. He shot a raccoon. We'll be next.

Nonsense. All taken care of. A little blood on the stairs; but Albert is up in his bed now; in his snuggies, dreaming about this movie. Guess what happens.

What always happens. They ride off. Into the sunset.

No! Fooled you! Now the camera switches to a meadow and a river. We see pebbles hitting the still water and ripples expanding, and we sense, March, but don't actually see. This is all very subtle. We hear music, but we don't know. Everything is suggested. Pause. Finally we hear the sound of motorcycles. We see dust rising, and from far away we hear Noonie singing. That's right, our Noonie singing a dreamy western number about a man who loves her, but has to get back to the open road. Then cut to a grill. Eggs frying and more motorcycle sounds, and the spatula lifting the eggs very slowly. Well? Will it fly in La Rue?

The part of March that knew Warren was going to lead them all down the road to disaster one day, might have already, made her begin to feel crazy.

You have to get up, Warren.

The clock hummed and Warren ate and frowned and ate again, and March hopped on one foot and listened for noise on the stairs. Warren could never be hurried. He was large to begin with, and growing larger all the time, and though this had once seemed a point in his favor, his impressive presence, it had begun to seem more of an impediment. The hulk that was Warren.

March, if I didn't know Noonie better, I'd be worried, Warren said. He held out a bowl of something white. What we have here is—I think—very possibly, a dip. A clam dip. I could be wrong. I don't see Noonie sinking to dips, but I wish you would taste this and vote. He held out a spoonful of white glop. March shook her head, and Warren chuckled and yawned and got up.

Dragging his robe behind him he headed for the door. March put the dishes in the dishwasher, and followed along through the pantry, and the long hallway, and up the stairs, and down to their room where Warren was already under piles of slippery satiny covers, the ends rolled under him cocoon-like, his face buried in the big feather pillow, dreaming and snoring and snoring until the whole room vibrated, and the wind and snow blowing in from Lake Michigan, and the storm windows rattling, and the tree branches and ivy scraping were hardly noticeable.

⚜

WE ARE not like other people. March would zero in on this fact. Working her way through the house, getting the children into clean clothes, getting their shoes to shine, wrapping packages, unwrapping packages, sorting the loot, trying to attach cards to objects; eating, drinking, talking to people from La Rue who dropped by; wiping up the children's spilled Coca-Cola, persuading them to take naps, taking them out in the snow, changing their clothes, getting them to sit up at the table, getting them ready for bed, bringing them down to say good night, finding a lost doll, putting them to bed, telling them a story to put them to sleep, coming downstairs, going back upstairs to put them to bed again, trying to fix her dress which was bursting at the seams, crawling around under beds and chairs trying to find the check her parents had given her, finding the check in her pocket, putting the children to bed again, March thought about talking to Warren.

On Christmas afternoon she found him reading magazines in the bathroom and told him he had to look more alert. Like you know what's going on. Take charge. Talk about your work. Your business. You sell time. Tell them about selling time. Stop pretending you don't know about the real world. Stay out of the bathroom. People think you have dysentery. We need to look normal.

Warren said being a guest here was no picnic. He said it made him dizzy. Don't get the impression I'm not working, March. Noonie has been on my tail since we got here. She's after me with coasters and ashtrays wherever I go, and she's into real paranoia about her blanket covers and the goddamned plumbing. Watch the rumples in the silk, Warren. Don't sit on the bed. Watch the wet towels. Stop putting too much toilet paper down the toilet. The last time you were here we had to dig up the lawn. We had to put in a new septic tank. We had to drain Lake Michigan. Install a toilet paper guard. A little net that deflects the paper you are trying to kill us with.

The C.I.A. would hire your mother, March. Proud to have her aboard, as they are always saying around here.

And let's talk about old Albert. I feel his eye on me, and I have trouble relaxing. I feel him seeing into my life when he's downstairs, and not even thinking about me up in his room checking out his wardrobe, seeing what he might want to share. He sees around corners, March. I feel him. I'm up in his bedroom looking for a new tie, and he is down there thinking about my goddamned life. He wants to know where it's going. He wants to have a chat. He wants to ask about my program. He wants to know if I have a program. Any minute now he's going to ask me to sit down in the library with him. He's going to bump into me in the hall and say, Warren. I'd like to have a few minutes with you. I'd like to hear about your program for the coming year. How would you say it's shaping up?

You hide upstairs. People think you're sick.

The only place I'm safe, Warren confided.

Nevertheless. March was going to get to the bottom of this. Busy as she was, she was going to consider how to reshape Warren and herself and the children, and make something of them. Something normal, even admirable. First she would pinpoint how they had got off the track, then find out how to get back on. Had they ever been on? Maybe not, but change was always possible. She knew. She had had years of practice. The Wisconsin state motto was Forward! She did not know about Illinois, but she knew that given time and the desire to change, lives could be altered.

Trudging through drifts, pulling the sled along over the golf course, and coming down off the hill and into the ravine, looking up over the children's hats and scarves to the hill beyond where Christmas lights shone on the pine trees, where bells rang, and torches lit up the drive, March felt less the joy of the season than the desire to be warm, but she gave the rope on the sled a yank and they all started back up, March tugging, and trying to bear in mind that it was Warren's face that shone in the sky, that shone brightly, that guided them home. Warren as savior. All the way back through the snow, late on that Christmas afternoon, March thought that odd as this idea might seem to Warren, he must be made to picture himself in this way. As savior.

Leading the children into the garage, hanging the sled on the hook, removing boots, snowsuits, scarves, mittens, taking them up for their baths, March thought only of getting to Warren. Warren wake up. Warren come out. Where was Warren? Hunting through the house, March found him upstairs in her father's study, wrapped in her father's Italian silk robe, paging through a history of World War II someone had given her father for Christmas. He was smiling, and puffing on a cigar, drinking a bourbon and soda he had made from the bar he had set up on her father's desk.

Nneoooooooowwwwwwwwwwrrrrrrr. Rrrrrrrrr. Chhhhhhhhhh! Watch it! The Coral Sea, March. Midway. Remember? Jesus. His head dropped and he blew smoke. We have B-17's coming over.

You had better come back to life right now, Warren. The children are down there running around, and nobody can find you, and we're having dinner in twenty minutes. My grandmother is here. My brother and his wife are here. All these people. Downstairs for God's sake. My sister-in-law's father. And what is all this mess! What about these cookbooks? Those are my books. I opened them this morning, and when I did there was a beach on my lap. Sand all over me. What was all that about?

Warren opened his eyes. I got the books last summer. I was looking them over at the beach. There's no law against browsing. He began to explain about a mystery story, a novel he was writing about a gourmet meal and a demented chef. Hence, March, Volumes I and II of *Gourmet* for you. And me! Something we can share. The whole plot turns on the deadly poisonous Charlotte Malakoff.

He puffed on his cigar, and March noticed a large burn in the leather top of her father's desk, but before she could rub at it or cover it, her mother came into the room and spied the same hole. Then all hell broke loose until her father came in and reminded everyone that this was Christmas, and Warren would certainly take care of any repair bill that might be entailed.

And so to dinner. Working her way through the pheasant, and wild rice, and three vegetables, and meringues and ice cream and Christmas cookies, March did her share of talking and nodding, and joining when they all sang, The more we are together, together, the more we are together the happier we'll be, for your friends are my friends and my friends are your friends. O the more we are together the happier we'll be.

Thus, another holiday season slid to an end.

The next morning Warren said he had pressing business at home, and they beat it down Highway 11 to the tollway. Just before the Lake Forest oasis Warren said he didn't want to hear anymore about this business of not looking normal because he had enough on his mind already. I'm having nightmares. Every night. My leg is bad. My hip hurts like hell. My cough could be TB or cancer. Take your pick. Maybe both. The plastic tooth is loose again. Things are up in the air at the office. I'll probably be fired tomorrow. They're probably going out of business. Radio is over. Any day could be the kiss of death.

At the Oasis he pulled over for coffee, and when he came back to the car he made March stick her hand inside his mouth. Here.

He took hold of her hand. Feel it. Feel it. Feel the wiggle. I'm living on borrowed time. That dentist appointment was for May, fifty-one. Two-thirty in the afternoon, March. May fifty-one. Thirteen years ago. He gunned the engine, and they spun sideways down the ramp. Don't tell me our life is up for grabs. I could lose my tooth and my job tomorrow.

Before the week was half over, before the new year, Warren went to work on his mystery novel. He lay in the tub for hours, or sat in an old wicker chair and smoked cigars and typed. He stuffed his cigars in the sink and clogged the drain, covered the floor with crumpled wads of white bond, and told March to keep her fingers crossed for good. I'm not a salesman, March. I'm a writer. Fuck them. All of them. I'm going for broke.

February of the new year. 1965. The sixth year of the marriage. Four months before the baby was due. March lay in bed and listened to Martha, or Dora or whatever her name was, the latest one to come to help with the girls.

So this woman in Detroit was laid up for three full years. Her hair fell out. Her eyes turned yellow. It was some new disease the doctors had never heard of. Later it was discovered a miniature was growing inside of her bloodstream.

Fantastic, March said. Go on.

This girl who knew Elvis before he was famous. She lost sixty pounds. She got so small they made her a bed in a dresser drawer with high sides all around because they never knew when she was going to rise up and shout at the faces she saw. She saw the Virgin Mary. She predicts Mrs. Kennedy is having a illegitimate baby.

Mrs. Kennedy is not having a baby of any kind, March said.

So this woman fell down in a supermarket? She slipped on wet lettuce and after that she had a loose breast. It wasn't completely attached. She sued the supermarket, but then she passed in her sleep. Or she was possibly murdered. March just shook her head.

A man in Memphis sent away for a bride from mail order. When she came she turned out to be only three feet six inches. She was so short he had to make a place for her to stand on behind the counter.

When the choir practiced in the church next door she sang right along. It was like the choir was behind the counter.

Winter was a long, lonely season, but after January when the doctor had ordered her to stay in bed most of the time, the women came, and it was less lonely. March would call the employment agency, and one would arrive and stay for a few weeks, and then one day a new woman would arrive. A succession of sleepy strangers who managed the days: made lunch for Littlemarch and Alden when they came home from play school and kindergarten, made cookies, brought tea, stole little things, told stories about friends or strangers who had died or had unfortunate lives. The stories were wonderful, all different, but with similar connecting threads. The people in the stories seemed very real to March. More real than the life she lived with Warren and the children.

Warren said the women gave him the creeps, and the girls did not like it when March stayed in bed.

How come you lie there all the time? Alden said. She came into the room with a blanket in her mouth, pulling at the end of a rope Littlemarch was holding. They ran around the room for a while. Then they climbed up on the bed. How come?

Where's Lucile? Tell Lucile it's time to go to the park. Get your shoes and boots. If you don't go soon it will be getting dark.

Luana. Her name's Luana. She's resting. She said she's gonna die pretty soon. She said we're all gonna die, but she'll come back and all the animals will be back and be gentle and the sun will always be out.

That's good news, March said.

That's what she said! Luana. The good news!

Good for her. Now get your shoes and boots. I'm reading.

March was not really reading. She was *trying* to read. Her father had sent her a collection of Joseph Conrad novels, and she was trying to get through them. Get through one. She had not read many real books for years. Now, when she opened this great heavy Conrad she would go along for a while, and then her mind would wander off and she would begin again.

I am reading, she told the girls, but they paid no attention. They crawled under the covers with her and started to play prison. They went down head first on either side of her, inching along on their stomachs toward the moat and the castle and the dungeon at her feet.

The dragon's waiting, Alden hissed.

They dug their fingers into March's leg and squealed.

Then March rattled the covers, and raised the sheet above her head, and saw them down there, and after a minute she went down there with them, and they all lay very still and waited in the dark with their breath coming in uneven puffs, until March *threw off the covers!* Then the girls rolled onto the floor at the foot of the bed. Out into the cool air, panting, *saved!*

Do it again. Again!!!!

No.

Yes.

OK. One more. They all went under the covers again.

Again.

No. Now I have to read. I have to read this book. Go away, away, away, away. She waved her arms and they ran away. They went off for a few minutes; then they came back to the door and crept up behind the dresser and around the back of the chair. March pretended she did not know they were in the room. She held up her copy of Conrad and covered her face until they sprung up on either side of the bed.

MUMBLES!

March lay perfectly still with her mouth open and her tongue out and her eyes crossed.

MUMBLES LA RUE! Is you dead? Is you DEAD?

March sat up and stuck her tongue up under her lower lip and closed her eyes.

Ahhhhhiii. Ahghhhh, she cried. She got up and lurched around the room. Then she got back in bed. Now out. To the park. Out! I am reading. *I am reading Joseph Conrad!*

WHEN THE children were out the apartment was quiet. And dusty. March wandered through the rooms and ran her finger over the tables and thought about what the children must be doing now. What about children? What about them? They were so strange. So unpredictable. What happened inside of their heads? Why did they do strange things? Howl, bite, write on the walls, jump around. Why did they throw themselves on the floor and cry. What were they crying *about?* Why did Alden cut off all her hair except for little clumps, like little bits of mouse fur left over? Why weren't they tired at night? Why did Littlemarch creep into the hall and spy on her and Warren? March often caught sight of her behind doors; edging up behind a chair, quivering with excitement, eyes gleaming.

Children. How were you the parent supposed to know what was right? How was a person supposed to work out a relationship between someone so old and someone so young. Someone her age and someone five or three? She had read books, but the advice, the demands, seemed extraordinary. Why would anyone want to be responsible for what an important child psychologist called, pouring the water of life into the empty sponges. How could she be responsible for every brain cell, every idea.

Sometimes she made up her mind that the authorities were wrong. Then, a day would come when she would be overwhelmed by the certainty that *she* had been wrong. She would see a child of three reading, a child of four playing the violin, a room full of children on television repeating the time of day or the phone number of some fire department. Things. Things she herself didn't know. She would buy puzzles, reading kits, send away for learning toys. For weeks she would be after the children to learn. Come on, guys. Clock time. Puzzle time. They would look at her like she was crazy. They hated the clocks and reading kits. They cried when she took out the puzzles. And so, after a few weeks, March would give up. OK. OK. Don't. Forget it.

When the children were around there was no peace. But when they were off somewhere March spent her time imagining what they were doing. She waited for them to come home. When they did come home, she wanted them to leave again. Children. How did you know what was right? At the zoo you saw a mother shaking a little boy in his old man's coat; and you saw the feather in his green old man's hat tremble; and you heard the mother shouting into his dumb, pale mouth. And you felt sick, and that was you, and you shuddered. At the Art Institute you looked at a painting. You saw a woman holding her child. You saw the fat pink legs, the dip in the child's neck, and your teeth ached. You saw the mother bent over her child, her eyes all drowsy with love, and that was you.

While she waited March worked on the stories she wrote for an educational publishing company that paid her poorly, and rejected anything that did not abide by certain healthy topics, certain word lists, word sequences. She wrote about ants, moles, whooping cranes, gorillas. One morning this poor poor gorilla named Vincent decided to do something about his ugly brown hair. (Please do not use the word decided, the editor wrote.) One morning this poor poor gorilla named Vincent made up his mind to do something about his ugly brown hair. Tell me, he said to his girlfriend. (Please do not use the word girlfriend. Wife would be better.) Tell me, Vincent said to his wife. Tell me if I am good in bed!

❧

WARREN CALLED to say he was bringing his friend from Montreal home for dinner. A man who came to Chicago once a year, the same man who had told March when Littlemarch was born that even if her own life ended tomorrow, she would live on in her child. March felt like telling him that she did not like that idea. What a crummy idea. She told Warren to keep this man out of her life, but Warren liked him.

Old Trucker, Warren would say. Poor old Trucker. You have to appreciate someone who seriously wants to wear a hair shirt. He owns one! He had it made in England, and he wears it when he wants to remind himself that he's fucked-up. He wants to be a saint, but he can't be one so he lives in Montreal to be saintly. Not only that, but he has a breathing problem. Warren's face would be scarlet and covered with tears, and he would be holding his ribs, and trying to get his breath to go on with his story.

So the thing is. The thing about Trucker is. He was in the air force and he was in England; up in some terrible town in England where he was supposed to be working on D-Day. He was very important. Very small, but important. He was in intelligence or something, he was practically running the war, and he was having trouble breathing. He had to go around almost all the time with this paper bag over his head so he could get the right amount of oxygen. Without the paper bag he got too much oxygen. He gulped oxygen and it made him dizzy and he fainted a lot, but with the bag over his head he managed to come out fairly even, most of the time.

So he was up there with his paper bag, and he was making all the guys he was working with nervous as hell because they were worried and nervous anyway without having him come around with his bag. He had cut holes in it for his eyes, and they couldn't stand looking at him, and they wanted to get rid of him and he knew it! He suspected they wanted to kill him, and the more he thought about this the worse his breathing problem got, and the more time he had to spend in his bag. But, then. Then! Just when the whole thing was getting out of hand. He! He told me this at lunch. He told me about this thing with his dick. He got something like a cold in it. Like a cold in your nose. And he had to go to the hospital. I swear to God, March. He described this whole problem. At lunch. I was having a Bloody Mary, and he was telling me this amazing story. But the thing is this situation spared him. He missed D-Day. He was in the hospital. People stopped wanting to kill him and he could breathe better. A happy ending.

When March said she didn't want to have Trucker for dinner, Warren said it was too late. He had already asked him. How could you cancel an invitation when someone had so much trouble with life?

That night they sat in the living room and drank gin. Trucker said he was fine with V-8 juice, but Warren and March drank, and Warren went in and out of the kitchen, and finally, around nine-thirty, Warren came in with a plate piled high with burnt spareribs, a bowl of lettuce with cucumbers, tomatoes, onions, avocados and Roquefort dressing, a loaf of French bread, a bottle of wine. He held up the plate of blackened meat.

I cook this on a small hibachi on the fire escape. The neighbors look down from their windows and see smoke rising and assume the worst. They call the fire department. Then the fire department comes and finds this little pot of coals and nothing to do! They come in with axes once or twice a month. Very nice guys.

Incroyable, Trucker said.

Warren smiled happily and proudly, and dropped the plate of spareribs.

Say there, Trucker said.

Warren picked up the spareribs and dusted them with napkins, and heaped their plates with the meat and salad. My best salad in years!

Here, here, Trucker said, while March noted that the barbecue sauce had left small red marks on the floor, so that it appeared that someone had been wounded during the evening. Trucker noticed this too, and said something, but Warren told him not to worry.

No problema, no problema.

They began to eat, but the girls were suddenly there, telling Warren he had forgotten about their act. Remember, remember, Alden cried.

Of course Warren remembered. He put the girls up on the windowsill, and drew the curtains on the enormous and dusty picture window. They disappeared behind the swaths of yellow material that had been left by the last tenant, and all that could be seen was a lump on the left side of the window and a lump on the right.

Then Warren seemed to forget about them. Avocados, he cried. You can't buy good avies in Chi. They have no taste here. You can't buy good tomatoes here. Or lettuce. Poor old Chi town. He poured red wine. You can't buy good wine. Or crabmeat. Or pickles. Or oysters.

Daddo! The girls were shrieking.

What? What's wrong. Why is everyone shouting? Warren winked at Trucker.

The act. We're back here!

Act? What act? Warren got up and went over to the window. I forgot.

I forgot about the bunnies. He waited again; then drawing himself up, waving his arms, throwing his head back, he became the carnival barker. Now. Now. Attention please. LADIES AND GENTLEMEN. Announcing. We are now announcing, the one and only, the most amazing act of all time, the one and only, fearless, flying Zucchini sisters! Three cheers for the little Zucchinis!

Warren clapped and cheered and pulled the curtains; and there Littlemarch and Alden stood, in the black window, trembling with excitement, flapping the arms of their long white nightgowns.

Three cheers, Warren shouted. Three cheers, Trucker.

Trucker said nothing for a moment. Then, that's a little offbeat. To do that?

Later that night March said maybe Trucker was right. Maybe that was a strange thing to do. It was funny, in some ways. But strange? Yes?

Let's not get started on that, Warren said.

⟨≈⟩

Bunnies, Warren called when he came home from work at night. Bunnies! *DA BUM!. DA BUM!*

In their room the girls shrieked, and were still; Warren started down the long hallway. *DA BUM!*

At the end of the hall he turned into the room, and the children squeaked to let him know where they were hiding. He moved slowly toward the armchair. March could see the girls' feet. She could hear them breathing, panting really. In a moment Warren would be past the bookcases and directly over the chair, and then!

But it was only a game. Warren was a circus bear, not a grizzly. He did not lunge. He did not capture them. He laughed. Funtings! Rabbits! They came out and jumped up and down around him, and jumped on the beds, and took turns being thrown high in the air and landing on their backs. After a while Warren lay down on one of the beds and closed his eyes. Ol' Daddo tise now. So tise. Daddo wie down do feepy. Ni-ni. Ni-ni.

He slept.

The children leaned over him, to see.

He was sound asleep.

Then. BABY TRAP! BABY TRAP! Warrren was not asleep after all. He was wide awake, and the rabbits were his prisoners. They were trapped in his arms. They could not move. They squealed and giggled. They struggled but it was no use.

All go ni-ni now.

<hr/>

THE CHILDREN wanted pictures of their lives, but there were no pictures of their lives. How come, Littlemarch said. How come we don't got pictures of our lives? Other people have got albums. They have hair, and teeth, and shoes, and everything from their lives. In little boxes.

We have pictures, March said. All over the place. Everywhere. But she could not find many. Looking, she found no more than a dozen snapshots. In drawers and in closets, on bookshelves, she found five Instamatic cameras and tangled rolls of film, but she could not find the pictures. There were some from their wedding in a white leather book, and there was Littlemarch's christening picture, a Christmas card that said Seasons Greetings from March, Warren and Littlemarch. People with empty open faces sitting on a red Naugahyde couch (Warren's mother) leaning toward a butler's coffee table (March's mother). On the table were objects displayed as casually as possible. A Steuben glass ashtray, a silver bowl, a copy of *Art in the Eighteenth Century*, an Oriental bowl with blue and yellow paper flowers, and caught in the window, a fine December moon, or what was thought to be, until Warren decided it was not the moon at all, but the flashbulb reflected there.

There was another, a Polaroid shot of Littlemarch and Alden and a young woman standing on the cobblestone platform, beneath the arch at the train station in La Rue. The train no longer stopped there, and March herself no longer wore her hair that way but the resemblance was clear. The little girls were wearing sundresses and white shoes and straw hats, and they looked so happy and excited; and she too looked young, in a dress she remembered wearing just after the birth and brief life of the son whose early birth she might possibly have prevented, if they had stayed in Chicago instead of traveling to La Rue for the Fourth of July weekend. If she had not given in to the children's pleas, if she had convinced the doctor in La Rue to keep her in the hospital when the early labor began instead of sending her home, telling her only to be careful, to take it easy, when she knew, she knew. When she damn well knew there could be trouble coming.

Warren had come into the hospital room after the baby was born. Christ, March. Even his balls are blue. You have to see him. He's not as big as my hand. March knew he would die and when he did, that night, she told Warren they would have another, and they would.

As for the baby she had named Blue, they released his body to the hospital. The weeks passed. It was as though nothing terrible had happened. They did not talk about it. March left the hospital, Warren went back to Chicago, and after a week in La Rue March and the children followed. She looked at the picture taken on the day they had gone home and wondered what it was they were gazing at. The train? Someone? She was holding an armful of flowers from her mother's garden. Alden was standing on one foot; her small round body looked as though it was about to pop the buttons on her dress, as though she was about to pop with joy. Now two years later Alden was so thin and she hardly ever smiled.

Alden wanted to know why there were more pictures of Littlemarch, why there was no picture of her in the long white dress— the much fussed-over christening dress—and March knew the answer. When Littlemarch was born her mother insisted they have pictures taken. A photographer had arrived at the apartment; the result was a formal photograph of Littlemarch on March's lap, paid for by her parents. When Alden was born her parents did not offer to pay for a photographer, and March and Warren did not have two hundred dollars. Nothing was done. Then, one fall afternoon when the apartment was a wreck and March had a cold, a man came to the door with a rose for March, and his camera ready for Alden. He said March's name had come from the diaper service. He knew all about this new baby.

Come on, cookie, the man kept saying to Alden. Pucker up for the birdie. Give Daddy a smile.

When Alden finally smiled he said, Three cheers for the cookie in the little blue robe. March would have taken her out of the bathrobe with the cereal on the collar, but the man said he had no time for costumes. He had to make a living. He returned a week later with the pictures and the bill.

Forty dollars, March cried. I thought this was free.

Some mother you are, the man shouted. Bitch! He took up the pictures and she heard him slam the front door.

Now, going through drawers and boxes, opening book pages and envelopes, March felt a certain dread. There was no record, and now it was too late. For those years. So where have you been, she asked. Out of cameras? Out of film? Just out?

⬥⬥⬥

Early June. There are cramps in her toes now. Look at them sticking straight up. Cramps in her legs too, and when she bends down on all fours and sees that gigantic belly hanging there she imagines herself zooming through the skies, dropping fruits onto crooked back stoops and into the canning factory, a bundle for the back of that pickup truck going down Route 13, a heap for that burned-out, flat, black patch of ground alongside that barbed wire fence with the broken gate; oranges, pineapples, plums. Bang. Squash. They hit the land and spatter. Sweet pulp. Fruit and fruit juice everywhere. Blessings.

Down there on the floor beside the bed in the light of the street and a full moon; working out another cramp; celebrating another year—thirty-one candles on the cake from the kitchen in La Rue—listening to Warren up there on the rumpled bed. Warren sweating away another night, dreaming, snoring, nose pointed toward heaven, mouth open for rainwater; and on the bare floor March lies pinned by her own body and a heavy June night. The final settling inside of her. Nice, she thinks.

The cramp eases and she stretches a little. Better.

Soon. Tonight, this morning, after the birth; after she's up and around again, she'll set things straight.

There is a downward pressure that lets her know it won't be long. She gets up to lie on the bed beside Warren. We'll begin again, she thinks. The years go by and you have to mark them, take note and direct them.

She thought then of November 21, 1963. She and Warren's mother had been having lunch at a restaurant before going to look again at a house March had thought of as a way of giving some kind of stability to their lives, some order. Then the news came over the radio. President Kennedy is dead. The appointment with the realtor was cancelled and they went home to watch the news. That night Warren's parents insisted on dinner at the Cape Cod Room to mark hers and Warren's anniversary. Two days later March watched as Jack Ruby shot Oswald. They never went back to look at the house. The plan was put aside, then abandoned.

At last you begin to see what life is not. It is not collecting chestnuts, or stuffing little potatoes into piles of burning leaves in the fall, riding over trails, through some farmer's dry creek bed, and it is not writing stories or poems, or dreaming of fame or dreaming of an old love, not fancying you were in love, when you were not. It may be this great web in which you are now caught, with someone who has helped to weave the web; this web from which there seems to be no escape, no way to untangle yourselves. Finally, love is not a ter-rible aching to be in someone's arms; the need, the desire—so over-whelming—so fierce to make love until your mind goes; until you are just a body there, with no brain clicking, no thoughts, nothing; no that is only a moment, that desire, that madness, that is no more than a bolt of lightning before the long roll of the thunder.

Warren, March says. *Warren*, she says, as the sky begins to lighten and the birds begin to stir. Time.

FEET FIRST, March reported to her parents, listening to the echo, because they were using two phones.

I'm in the library, her father said. Your mother is in the pantry. It's Lenora's day off.

I looked up at the mirror and saw blood and feet like little pig's knuckles, March said. The room was still and full of light.

Is the baby *all right?* Her mother sounded alarmed.

Of course she's all right.

It's hotter than H-E double toothpicks here. I hope you have air-conditioning. Something's burning in the kitchen!

We're all delighted with the news, March. Three lovely girls. But time to call it a day, don't you think?

It's the rice. The rice is burning.

Daddy?

I'm here. Your mother is having some trouble out there. Something's burning.

It was so amazing. I felt this power. Like I could do anything. That I had this power and control. You know?

You can. You can, March.

I used to feel that way. A long time ago. I'm afraid it might fade?

It was the rice. I've forgotten how. The double boiler melted right into the burner. The house could have burned down.

Do you want me to come out there?

Don't be silly. The burner's off.

We'll call in a day or two.

I stretched my arms over my head and made a long low noise. Like a bellow that went as far as the windows and back again, and faded. Then the only sounds were the sounds of people breathing over their work, and small hot squawks.

Love from both of us, darling. Congratulations to Warren.

I've got to get out of here, March told Warren when he came to the hospital that night. Warren busy handing out dyed pink and blue daisies; almost touching in their ugliness, clutching newspapers and brown bags, gin and tonic, bourbon and soda, ice and plastic cups, cigarettes and matches, one paper bag already soggy, the bottom of a bottle poking through, his chin glistening, his shirt damp, the sleeves rolled, and sticking out from the last of the bags a bundle of shrimp-colored gladiolas.

It's hot out there, rabbit. Ninety-six. I'm dripping. You're lucky to be here. The bunnies miss you. 'Tell feet ol' Mumbles we miss her.' He unpacked his treasures and began to settle the empty spaces the way you might settle a home, ripping papers, arranging, distributing his wares, lighting a cigarette, blowing smoke, sighing. Suddenly he put both hands over his face.

What?

No opener.

Somewhere.

No. Oh Christ.

I'll ring for the nurse.

She won't have an opener. She'll throw us out.

There's a place near here.

There is nothing out there. Vacant lots. Muggers. Vermin. A ghetto.

But look! Nail clippers. He beamed. Never say die.

He drove the top of the soda bottle against the edge of the radiator and pried at the same time with the nail clippers. Success. Then the tonic bottle. The cap flew. He held the bottle at arm's length, but the tonic was already spraying his face and suit and the tabletop. He turned up his palms, snatched a towel from a chair, grabbed a pink blanket from a wad of tissue paper, swabbed, extracted cigarettes from the edge of the ruins, tossed his suit jacket on the bed and poured the drinks. He handed March a gin and tonic, tasted his own bourbon and soda, grimaced as he always did and drank again, sighed, smiled, settled into a chair.

Cheers. He raised his eyebrows and his glass. The bunnies sent the daisies. The gladiolas are from me.

It's very dead around here, March said to a nurse. Very dead.

She had too much energy. The baby, Mia, was brought in for feedings, but mostly March was left to herself. She sat on the edge of the bed, swung her feet, called people, read, paced the corridor. Nobody about. WHY DON'T THOSE WOMEN OPEN THEIR

DOORS? She climbed up on the windowsill and forced the lock on the window; opened the window, let the air in. Out there along the expressway and in the parks it was summer. Flattened against the window screen she took deep breaths. She could not get enough. She could taste the heat. She imagined a reckless, nervous surge taking place out there, and the racket! She listened and watched and felt uneasy. Later, she noticed the smudgy screen marks across her forehead. They seemed to fit.

I'm a guest in my own house, Warren complained after March and Mia had been home for a week. That field marshal runs everything. We eat at six. The place closes down at eight. Fire her. Fire the goddamned German.

Her name is Caroline. She's a gift from my parents. I can't fire her. I don't want to fire her.

Well you can count me out, Warren said. March saw how the entrance of an outsider had unsettled him, diminished him, and she was embarrassed by his behavior. The peace and order in the apartment were new to her. She was not alone. She had support. She was grateful. She wanted this to last.

This is how it should be, Caroline said. At night March and the girls sat with her at the dining room table. They ate noodles and wiener schnitzel, and shredded carrots arranged around hard-boiled eggs with raisin eyes. The windows were open and they listened to the street sounds and watched the candles flicker. In the back of the building their neighbor waited for the night, and then his old films would flash on his garage wall, bringing Louise Brooks and Colleen Moore with her amazing eyes rolling on the white stucco background, into their odd, sticky world, bringing music and the sound of voices and people clapping from their windows.

Warren sat in the living room. He listened to his radio and walked through the dining room to the kitchen, to the living room again. He read his paper and watched them through a hole he poked in the paper's sides.

They ate Jell-O with whipped cream, and looked up as Warren came through the room with something white. For a moment it looked like a dish towel draped against his chest and caught under his armpit. Sweet Peaches, he crooned.

Caroline got up to clear the plates. Littlemarch and Alden held bits of paper napkin near the candles. March blew the candles out. Warren sat in his chair and smiled and sent smoke rings out over the baby's head.

Long after those weeks March would look back, realizing then that in those summer days and nights it had been just weeks before she would actually hear, she would claim, and actually see, she would claim, the framework topple. When she would look up to watch what seemed to be an immense balsa wood dome go, piece by piece, plinking slowly down, down, until nothing was left but sticks on a scrap heap.

WARREN WAS thinking of changing jobs. A golden opportunity, he announced. Northern could fold any day. With Erelemeyer he would have the chance to take over the whole operation. A two-man office. He couldn't lose. Erelemeyer is dying, March. You take one look and you can see it.

What kind of job was he talking about, March wanted to know.

The same as Northern. Only I'll be selling space instead of time. TV instead of radio.

Not exactly the same. March thought it was a joke. First selling time, now selling space? She laughed, but Warren ignored this. It was complicated, he admitted. There were certain things he didn't know, but Erelemeyer was excited.

Erelemeyer is willing to invest his future in me, and personally, March, I'm flattered.

What if he dies?

He will.

Before you have the future invested in you?

He won't.

I thought you were going to talk to my father.

What about?

Business. The business world.

Right. But this is definite. The way I see it, things are looking up. Or, they're going to. I'll finish my novel, and take this space job as soon as the heat wave's over. I'll buy a new suit, a stack of pens, new socks. Thirteen socks to the bag. Remember the old days. Thirteen instead of twelve and then if you lost one? He snapped his fingers. As soon as I'm settled, we're going back to California, and say hello to the boys.

I've been thinking we should go back now. Live there.

Not yet. Not until I've made it here. When I go West I'll be someone. I'll have money and copies of my mystery. I'll show the boys. The boys have never done anything.

True. March remembered the one who had come when Littlemarch was born. He had stayed for a month; sleeping on a cot Warren had rented, going to a health club during the day, keeping Warren up at night. A long time after March had more or less thrown him out he sent them a French corkscrew from North Africa. Thinking of getting into imports, he wrote.

We'll go back, March said. We'll live in a small town. We'll open a business. A small farm or a store. You'll write your mysteries. I'll have time to write too.

I'm not going back and live in some dump and raise artichokes.

You love the land. You love the West.

I'm not cut out for farming.

I'll help you. We could open a hardware store, a general store. Something for everyone.

Sell fucking screws!

So? You sell other things. Films, ads, space, time. Anyway, you wouldn't have to have wet feet and cold hands. You wouldn't have to go calling on people who didn't want what you had. You could just be whoever you were meant to be.

You've finally flipped the sweet lid, March. He came up behind her and put his arms around her. Flipped the sweet lid.

March said she was writing the rich aunt. Warren said fine.

She might ask for a loan, and while she was at her letter writing she might ask Albert for help.

Your father would love to set us up on a farm, think about you running the rich earth through your tiny fingers, March.

In fact, her father did not seem anxious to offer more than advice. He said the money seemed to go as fast as he gave it to them.

It makes Albert nervous to hear about our money problems.

It makes me nervous, Warren said. If I had money I'd have time to plan my life. As things are now, I'm always in a hurry. I don't have time to sit back and think of how to handle the world.

You see Albert and I'll write your aunt.

At the end of the week Warren reported on the lunch with her father. Albert was in perfect form. We went right to the Empire Room, and before we looked at the menu Albert was drawing graphs in blue ink on the tablecloth. I mean it, March. A goddamned fountain pen. I knew he was concerned, but he was on a tear. He drew and outlined how income ought to ascend in direct proportion to a man's age. One graph for me. One for some other guy, Mr. Theoretical.

Warren was sprawled on their bed, drawing with a magic marker on the sheet. At twenty-five a man should be earning x, at thirty xx, at thirty-five xxx. Always more. Anyway, March. *My* graph is here. As you can see it goes sideways more than up. All the way over here to this circle. This is the butter plate. But then! We take the graph of your man on the rise, old Mr. T., and the line just takes off. Keeps going over and up. Way up. So I have to move my glass which is here, and now my silverware and finally, I swear, finally my goddamned chair. I am over here.

In fact, Warren was at the foot of the bed.

You would have to see the tablecloth to appreciate Albert's talents. The waiters were spellbound, March. We were all spellbound. I kept thinking Albert could get into a whole new career himself if he wanted to. Just because he's stuck making those machines, there's no reason why he couldn't try to think of himself in terms of art history or cartography. With his skills. I tell you if I were A. I would seriously think of getting out of manufacturing and into something more exciting. I'm going to take him to lunch someday.

Did you ask about the money?

No time. We hardly had time to eat.

So nothing happened?

A. was busy with his drawing. And it was noisy. You can't talk about the future when there's a hum in the room. Violins. I mean it. Guys playing violins. Not good.

I wish you'd stop wearing his clothes. I'd think he'd notice.

Nonsense. A. has good taste and that taste should be shared. If he lacks imagination, we excuse him. He's high on quality. Quality counts. The next time he calls, I want you to say, Warren is enjoying the socks and ties. And the handkerchiefs. Let's not forget the handkerchiefs. You can't beat good cotton.

Warren rolled over again and picked up the phone and held the receiver over his head.

Calling La Rue. La Rue, La Rue, Lilly Bolero. Where? Wisconsin. Collect? Of course. Straight up the road, collect all the way. Right. Hello? Albert? Warren here. How are we doing with the program I outlined for you? You do remember our lunch? I'm just checking on your progress, Albert. You haven't made any? I'm disappointed, but I want you to stay with it. I think we have a good crew. I'd hate to see one poor sailor make the ship hit the rocks. The ship. Yes. You know the story. With a little more effort and tenacity we could look at ourselves and say, damn it all we are running a tight ship. And we're proud of every man on it. Right. We want you on board, Albert. Give 'em hell!

Warren dropped the phone and rolled off the bed. Oh Al. Al says he wants to make the team. He does care. He wants. He wants so much. He says he. He dreams of. Of. Oh Albert. Sweet Albert. Al. Al!

Warren lay on his back, clutching a pair of her father's good black socks. Albert says he's depressed because the Empire Room is suing him for ruining their tablecloth.

March wrote to the rich aunt. The aunt sent the letter back. What is all this about money? I have no money. I wish you well.

WARREN SAID, This time next year we'll be eating avocados in Malibu, sunbathing with Marlon Brando. I'll have my tooth fixed. I'll do something about my hip, get something for the pain. I'll get the army to pay for it. The army was responsible. He would tell his story about being wheeled out of the operating theater just as the question about his ever walking again came up. He would laugh. It was a good story, wasn't it. And he deserved a new hip. He was always in pain. There were half-empty bottles of aspirin in every room.

But next year. Next year, just off the Pacific Coast Highway, there would be a Cadillac, a Cadillac that would blow the sweet March mind, out there glistening in the dazzling sun; facing the dazzling surface of the Pacific, prepared in its heart of hearts for a brodie spin over the ocean, kites flying from the windows, beautiful green bills flying from the kite tails.

They had just finished dinner. It was after ten o'clock. We won't be in Malibu, March said. Or anywhere off the Pacific Coast Highway. We'll be in Chicago. In another apartment. And you'll have another job. It will be late. The children will be running around. You'll be dreaming about going somewhere, but we won't be going anywhere. There will be tails on the kite, but the kite will not be up in the air. It will be stuck in a tree.

Warren was on his feet. You have an evil tongue, March. You know that?

March did not answer. She knew what was coming. She was afraid. She was always afraid when things went this far.

You have an evil tongue. And dirty feet, and you are a crappy mother. And a lousy lay. You are getting lazier and messier every day, and pretty soon no one will want you. I personally had no choice. I had to take you on. And you are right about being stuck here. But you will be here alone. I will be in Hollywood. With the rabbits.

I don't think you will ever go to Hollywood, Warren. I don't see that in your future. I don't think you will finish your novel. But should you finish it; what makes you so sure it will be a success? You have never written a book before. You have never written a letter. Now you find yourself writing about a mythical war on a mythical island off the coast of California and on top of that you have another myth. Warren in Hollywood. Warren's wet hands in the wet cement outside that movie theater. Warren and Elizabeth Taylor splashing in pools filled with gardenias, and rum, and orange sections, and cherries and lemon twists. What I think, Warren, I think you should stop drinking. You are drunk every night. You are going down, and we are going with you.

Evil tongue, March. Full of very very sour, soggy, rampant grapes. Rampant. Very rampant. Extremely rampant, I'd say, thinking it over. I'd say that, March. Fucking rampant. He sat down and drank and got to his feet again.

What we have here, March, is a worn-out, middle-aged woman who is getting flatter on the top and larger on the bottom. A pear-shaped woman who keeps talking about how much she has to do but actually does nothing. Nothing at all. We know she talks a lot about going back and recapturing that old college energy. Becoming a writer. But we watch and what do we see? We see this pear at the typewriter all right, but we do not see the keys moving. No. The little typewriter is dusted every morning; the pear hovers over it, examines it, breathes on it. The pear frowns at the typewriter—growls in a soft anxious way—makes noises that indicate something clicking. A thought! This could be called the agonizing moment of March on the verge of putting down a word. Will she or won't she. We hold. We hold. We hold our collective breath.

The real truth, Warren. The real truth is I don't have time to write. You don't either, but you take the time. You live in the bathroom. You live in bathrooms everywhere. Even at Northern. When I call, the secretary says, I believe he has stepped down the hall. She may not know what that means, but I know. I know you are in the bathroom. At Northern or Walgreens or Charmet's. At the Drake or the Ambassador. At Woolworth's. Somewhere, in a bathroom or a coffee shop; writing when you should be out working and earning money; and getting somewhere in the real world, like real people, like other thirty-six-year-old men. Pretty soon you'll be forty, and you'll be talking about these big plans, but time is running out. Time is flying, and even when you're home you are in the bathroom with *my* typewriter.

That's enough. March.

It's true.

You asked for this, March. Zoom. Zoom. A dinner plate took off. Bye bye, wedding presents. Dinner plates. Butter plates. The old Singapore Bird. Ta ta, birdie. Poor birdie. The sweet ugly fancy vase your parents lie awake worrying about. The special vase. The wineglasses. Made in China. Made in Venice. Underwater by frogs. Oh the china, what has become of all the bloody china. Where has it gone? Who knows? The Shadow knows. I know.

Zoom.

Yeoowwwww. Cachung! March, call Washington. Tell them we have news about the UFOs. The great mystery has been solved. They are not UFOs. No, something else is lighting up the Chicago night. All this time people were out there wondering. What can it be? Lights in the night? When all the time there were our hundred dollar a shot wedding plates from Spaulding's on Michigan Avenue lighting up the night. March, get on the phone, call Washington. Say, this is March the Pear. My darling flowered dinner plates. Observez. Observez!

There is a rhythm to the violence. It builds slowly over an evening, pauses, builds again, pauses, stops. It is that full stop that marks the probable shift to a much faster pace, a time to take care, a time to smooth things over, to say something calming, to say nothing, to consider—assuming you are able to consider anything sensible, anything reasonable—whether now might be the last chance, to restore sanity, civility, peace. March is aware. This is nothing new, this behavior, the accusations, the drinking, the violence. All is familiar and reckless. She lets it slip by, though—the chance to draw back. She is too slow, too frightened.

When it is over and Warren has gone to bed, she sweeps up the pieces and turns out the lights. She has a bloody lip, a swollen knee. She checks on the children who are sleeping (though once or twice she has found Littlemarch in the hall). She can hear Alden stirring now, having what sounds like a nightmare, so she sits beside her for a while. Later, in a chair at the window in Mia's room, she rubs her bruises, puts an ice pack on her knee, listens to the baby breathing, the pictures rattling in the breeze. The summer helper who had come for a week in August had left photographs, magazine pictures of movie stars clipped to strings strung across the room. Handsome men and pretty women. Above March's head they flutter in the night breeze.

Just one break, March. Just one. Right?
Right.
It will come.
Yes.

It was not quite morning. They sat at the kitchen table, making promises. Many years later she would remember Warren like that: in the green plaid bathrobe, with the burn holes; sitting at the kitchen table; a man—no longer young—troubled, bewildered, hopeful, desperate; steam rising from his cup, the creamy pink of the shrimp soup on the spoon.

⁓✦⁓

THURSDAY IN September, the first day of the school year. Once in March's own life it had been a time of intense excitement, as she believed it ought to be for her children: a time for new sweaters, new shoes, the delicious smell of new pencils, a pocket sharpener to capture the pink shavings, one art gum for whatever, for chewing, for picking at, and throwing at someone. A time for a jump rope, and marbles in a pouch, a book not yet smudged—one of those happy family books—a book with green lawns and small dogs, the father doing something in the backyard and the mother smiling in the kitchen; flowers in bloom and children on swings; nice Aunt Jane coming around the corner with a pitcher of lemonade. She couldn't read those books anymore. Couldn't stand the sight of them. How come those people all look the same, Littlemarch had asked. All pink and everything?

On this morning she left Mia with Annabelle who was babysitting and supposedly cleaning, and took the girls to the doors of their classrooms, Alden to junior kindergarten, Littlemarch to first grade. It was eight-thirty. She went out to sit in the courtyard until the ten o'clock bell. This was no ordinary school. It cost a fortune—two thousand dollars per child per year—paid for by her parents—so that the children could be introduced to sunlight and brick courtyards, to fish ponds and birdcages, and charming white mice and guinea pigs; so that the children could smell flowers, lounge on rugs and floor pillows, thrive in sunlight and pretty breezes, play on seesaws and jungle gyms, frolic at school assemblies when Christmas came, and the upper school performed The Twelve Days of Christmas, and the small children clapped and parents wept; or, so that on a perfect day in the fall, when the warm breezes caused red leaves to fall, bagpipes would pipe the entire school on a walk to the park. March was grateful that her children could be here, but she felt like having a drink whenever she had to be at the school.

On this particular morning she did not feel too well. She thought she did not look too well, either. Most of the other mothers looked better than she remembered. It was not only their clothes, their huge, soft sweaters and colored shirts and their shoes, it was their hair, and well cared for faces, their smooth skin. Yes, and their hands: their almondy nails, and the tan fingers, the way they talked with sweeps and curves, spreading their fingers and flicking their wrists, their rings and bracelets flashing in the expensive sunlight. March's hands were red on the palms, bright red. And she had no life line. Nada, a woman in a tearoom, had told her. Also, her nails were cut short; and aware of them now, she sat on them.

Hey, March. Where've you been?

March, how was the summer. Haven't seen you around. How's the babe?

Gorgeous day!

Who's got my lighter?

Margo, Sally, Betsy, Lizzy, Daisy, Lynn. Her friends. The people she saw in the park, at parties, at dinner sometimes, at meetings. Their children went to the same school. This school, not the Latin School, which was considered too conventional, too conservative. Here they were. Her friends.

There were many groups of mothers in the school. There were some with new cars, and clothes and frozen hair. Then there were the ones who drove old cars, and never got dressed up, and had long straight hair. They were younger looking than the first group. They did not seem to care how they looked, but they always looked beautiful to March. She was more or less on the outer edge of this second group, and she was crazy about them—the mothers. She would notice them at the beach in the summer and her mouth would water. They had fat, brown children with white, white hair. They played games in the sand, and on weekends the husbands came along. Then they drank white wine, and brought out bowls with strawberries as big as the moon; and once, sitting with Warren and her own children, she saw her favorite—Lovely Blades who had four boys—put on a funny hat, and put hats on the children and take their pictures, and when the small boys had run off to the water, Lovely lay down beside her husband and put all of the fingers of one hand into his gorgeous, big pink mouth.

March said these people lived in a magic circle. Warren said, oh balls. They were just people. As far as he was concerned they all looked alike. Inbred, he said. If March ever looked closely she would discover all kinds of hanky-panky. Six fingers on some of those hands.

A third group of mothers at the school, whether rich or not, were Japanese or Chinese or best of all, black, a group everybody in the other two groups, and people in no group at all, adored. The school was especially proud of black families. Parents in the first two groups fought over them. They asked them to dinner all the time, over and over, and despaired of the fact that there were not enough of them to go around. March said it was disgusting the way people she knew stole these couples from one another, and passed them along like hors d'oeuvres. Have you had so and so. We're having them tonight and tomorrow we're playing tennis with them. We had them last week! Still, March also imagined it must be terrific to be in such demand, to be asked out for dinner all the time.

March! Someone touched her shoulder. Leslie Chum. Leslie, from her old building. They sometimes met in the park, though they no longer had the same park.

Boy, Leslie said. This place hasn't changed. Everyone in Charlie's class is already fighting over the new little Chinese kid. What are you doing this fall? I can tell you one thing I'm not doing. I came back from Maine and I resigned from all those stupid boards. I thought about my life this summer and I decided to go back to school. And Peter is thinking we might go out West for a few years. I don't know. But we're not sitting around anymore.

March nodded. Her chest hurt, and she wanted to run. There was so much noise. Then there was a kind of sonic boom, and she thought she heard all the glass in the school windows breaking and sprinkling down. Then it was quiet. She could see all the mothers around her talking, but she could not hear. She waited. Then she heard Leslie talking again.

You have to read it! This book has changed my life. Everyone in Maine was reading it. All about housewives and their dumb world, and how we're wasting our time. When we could be doing something with our lives. And she's right. The writer. She knows. Betty Friedan. Betty Friedan. You have to get this book.

March knew about the book. It made her crazy. She suspected this woman was right. That her own life was a stupid waste. The book was about everything she hung onto and wanted to let go of, everything she could not let go of, and did not understand, and could not figure out, everything she had given up so much for, and had been wrong about and did not want to think about. The whole world had heard about this book.

I know about it, March said. I don't want to hear anymore. It has nothing to do with my life. It makes me sick.

She got up to run, around the courtyard, and into the building, and up and down the hallways, and back outside. She tried to remember where the classrooms for her children were, but when she looked into a window she saw two bat eyes, a little jaw, a face, part of a steering wheel, a car. She ran back into the building.

When she found the girls at their classroom doors, she took their hands. We have to run, she told them, and they ran, racing down the street, and racing across the park, and up to their building, into the hall and up the steps where Annabelle stood at the door, in her purple slip, with a dish towel around her head, and a broom and the baby in her arms.

I need things, Mrs. Wright. Endust. Mr. Clean. Easy-Off. Comet. I try to do my best. I tries. I tries. I works hard. But. I am not Lady Miracle.

She followed March into the bedroom. March said she was sorry about things, but she needed some help, and maybe Annabelle could just take the children and give them cookies, because personally she was very sick, and it might be a good idea not to stand there in the doorway and watch her die.

How are you sick? Annabelle wanted to know.

March shook her head. I have to keep walking right now, Annabelle. I have to keep moving. She walked into the bathroom and back into the bedroom, back to the bathroom, into the bedroom. She lay down on the bed. How did people know when they were dying. If a person was all alone did that person just wait and hope? In the middle of the night, in a hotel in Mexico, did a man lying on the bed call for help, or did he wait and wait too long. Did he lie there, sweating, watching the neon lights go on and off on the sign across the alley, hating the loneliness and the fear, but waiting, still ashamed to call, even the night clerk, because maybe he wasn't dying?

She could hear the vacuum cleaner, and the scavengers who picked up trash in the alley behind the building were shouting. A dog barked. Then something kicked her hard. She felt the blow. Slowly, carefully, because her hands were numb, she dialed Warren's number with her fat, stiff finger. Strangely enough, Warren answered. She thought that if she were dying she would like to have him with her. He was like an old pillow, a blanket. He was the only person she knew. He was the only person who knew her.

Warren, listen, I'm sick. Something's wrong.

What?

Warren. You need to help me. I'm paralyzed.

Jesus, March. What do you want me to do?

Do something.

Jesus. OK. Just stay where you are. I'm calling a doctor. I'm putting you on hold. I'll be right back.

Warren?

Nothing.

Warren?

March hung up and dialed the fire department.

Littlemarch came to the bed then. You talk now, she said. Talk, Mumbles. Say something nice.

Annabelle had planted herself in the doorway. Mia was in her arms, and Alden was hanging onto her slip.

We must all pray to the Lord. Everybody. Down on your knees, Annabelle cried, sinking to her knees, dragging the girls with her, holding Mia up, like an offering, toward the ceiling. Oh Lord, she cried. Oh Lord! Take this evil spirit out of here and spare this family. Do your work for this poor dying woman and her children. Show us that You do care because we know that You do care and we are needy people and this lady needs You now and we ask You to show us the way.

March heard a siren, then pounding on the door, the door breaking open, firemen in blue crashing past Annabelle and opening a small wooden box that looked like a child's coffin. From the box they brought out an oxygen mask, and fit it over March's nose and mouth.

It's no good. It doesn't work, March cried. You have to help me! You're all right. You've had a shock.

I have not had a shock.

This happens a lot. Anxiety. This happens to women, the biggest fireman said. The smaller one, no shrimp, smiled and nodded. Neither of them seemed worried. They stood there in front of her, shuffling their feet, and she saw that they were too large for the room. The ceiling was too low. The furniture was too small. The scale was all wrong. It seemed to her that they should not be in here together. In this small pink room. She wished they would sit down.

There was a crash in the hall, and Warren rushed in. March. You hung up. The rescue squad. I saw the squad. I saw the squad.

You put me on hold.

She's not in any danger, the men said.

I'm sorry, Warren said. You're awfully nice to come by. I'd like to give you a little. I'd like to. He took his billfold out of his pocket. March saw he was going to tip them. A little something for all your trouble.

Not at all. It's a service.

No kidding. Free? His face brightened.

Taxes.

I'm sorry. Very. It's embarrassing. All this. My wife. Warren waved a hand.

Not at all. Glad to help. Sorry about the door though. We didn't want to wait.

You did the right thing. Just a door. How could you know this was a false alarm?

They trooped back down the hall and March sat on the bed. She had made a terrible scene, but how was she supposed to know. Still, she had terrified the children. Would they remember forever? Would they think they had seen death? And there was the door. Was it all in pieces? And still she could not breathe. And could not feel her fingers.

You won't do that again, March. Will you? They had stopped at March's doctor's office and picked up a prescription for Valium. Now they sat at a wooden table in a beer garden Warren claimed was famous. The guys from the brewery come over here for lunch. You can get a salami sandwich, a beer and a hard-boiled egg for nothing. He ate with enthusiasm.

I wanted you to come because I thought if I was dying I wanted you to be there, March said. Isn't that strange? I thought I wouldn't mind so much, if you were there.

But you won't do it again. Because you scared the hell out of all of us.

She was too tired to say more, and though she felt foolish, she did not feel certain about staying away from the rescue squad. She might need them.

WITHIN THE month March had seen three new doctors. She had started lying about her name; saying she was just in town for the weekend; saying she was someone with a theater troop, a model at the housewares show, in for a few days; having a little trouble. Doctors seemed to believe her. They checked her blood pressure; wired her for electrocardiograms, gave her more prescriptions for Valium. One took an x-ray of her heart! She had not thought that possible. One who gave her a shot of something seemed nervous. Afterward, she sat in a dump of a coffee shop on South Wabash, and waited for the air bubbles to reach her brain or whatever was left of her goddamned heart.

"No LONGER will man be able to see himself entirely unrelated to mankind, neither will he be able to see mankind unrelated to life, nor life unrelated to the universe." At the swimming club, on the far north side of the city, March read from her water-soaked copy of *The Phenomenon of Man*, and hung onto her belief that the book would keep her alive. She read a line here, a passage there, listening now and then to the other mothers and children. It was the third Saturday in September, an Indian summer day, the sky a deep blue. There was a light breeze, and now and then a leaf floated onto the surface of the pool. Children swam and mothers gossiped. In their carriages the babies slept. A peaceful day when the framework of her life seemed exceptionally precarious. She kept a hand on her throat to keep track of her heart. Still beating away.

The calm was broken when Leslie, one of the few mothers March felt comfortable with, suddenly got up from her chair, and pointed to a distant roof. Up there. On the edge. Other mothers sat up. A chair tipped over. Pages from *Vogue* and *The New Yorker* rattled.

Where?

There.

What? The children wanted to see too, and it was hard to see. Where should they look? They pulled themselves up over the edge of the pool and wiggled onto their stomachs, pushed up onto their knees.

It's a post.

No, definitely a man.

I'm calling the police, Leslie said. She picked up a phone that hung on a tree.

March so loved that phone on the tree. The pool and the land, the running and swimming were good for the children. The phone on the tree was good for her.

They're sending someone, Leslie reported. But of course, March thought. In a flash. No charge. All around there was the hum of mothers and children, mothers and children. Don't look, darling. Over there. That high building. No, he won't jump.

Where were her own children? March saw them over on the terrace, wiggling around under the tables where elderly ladies sat with their drinks. Mia was asleep in her carriage.

She watched the roof. Warren's face floated up. She knew it was not Warren up there, but she saw his face. She hung onto the sides of her chair.

A man was running now, along the edge of the rooftop. Oh, boy, watch it, March whispered, but he was trapped. Or saved? Two policemen had come up behind him, and that was all there was to it. The threesome retreated from the roof's edge, vanished from sight. Far away the noon whistle sounded. The women returned to their chairs around the pool.

I think we all need a drink, someone said.

March? Leslie stood in front of her. What did you think?

About what?

The man. You just sat there. Did you even notice?

I was thinking that maybe he was watching the water, or the city. Or us. Or maybe he was bent on self-destruction. A man itching to end it all, and maybe for good reason. Now you've saved him, and he has to start over. He has to put his life back together. That may be a good thing, or not.

I worry about you, March. I really do.

They moved along to the tables set out on the grass, beside the screened-in kitchen where the door slammed incessantly as lunch trays were picked up. Paper napkins blew, cups of juice spilled. Bees hovered. Talk of suicide continued.

I can't imagine killing myself.

I wouldn't jump.

I'd never use a gun.

I'd take pills.

The ultimate egotistical act. A well-known fact.

March played with her hamburger. She was having trouble keeping her eyes open. Finally, when they were the only two left at the table, Leslie started in again.

What are you going to do, March? If you go on like this your children are going to be hurt. People have started talking about you.

I'm fine. My children are fine.

They're hysterical. Jumpy. Out of control.

March said all children were jumpy. All children made *her* jumpy.

Peter and I think you and Warren need help.

Mmm. Maybe. March picked at the ice cubes in her ice tea. Have you noticed? The ice here is cheap. Cloudy. The kind they should have is the kind we have at the lake. You chip it off with an ice pick. You put it in your glass and you have diamonds!

Peter said he saw you on Wabash. You didn't recognize him.

March threw up her hands and laughed. This whole place needs to be redone. Bigger ice cubes. More mayonnaise in the chicken salad. Better towels. The ones they give us don't absorb. They just don't absorb. Have you noticed that. The negative absorbance situation.

The world is changing, March. You have to get involved.

Leslie was right. She was out there making the world a better place. March knew that. She wanted to say that she wanted to worry about changing the world too, but she couldn't do that right now. She wanted to say that she would change the world as soon as she felt better. As soon as Warren stopped drinking and she stopped being crazy they would definitely do that. Do something about the world.

You should get involved, March. Things are changing. Peter and I are both up to our necks in committees. Changing the world or at least this world here, if we can.

I know. I want to do something, but I can't right now. Last year I taught, after-school reading in a terrible neighborhood, at a terrible school. Sometimes this huge nice kid would walk me to my car so nobody would rob me. One time a kid did put a knife at my throat and I gave him my money. He said that wasn't enough and I said that's twenty dollars, that's a lot to me, and he left. But I can't do that right now.

Littlemarch and Alden came to sit on her lap then, and March wrapped towels around them. Don't look now, she said. But I think the locker room maid is watching us. We brought our own, but she charges for towels anyway.

Someone in your neighborhood said you sit in the park and just look at a tree.

I don't know anybody in my neighborhood. Besides, we don't have trees in our park.

You and Warren should get help.

Warren's not too interested in help. But he's scared. I'm scared. We need a fresh start. We're thinking of moving.

Leslie was saying something, and now Mia was crying. March lifted her from the carriage and pressed her against her shoulder. Shhhh. Littlemarch and Alden huddled against her, shivering a little.

Listen, March whispered. She leaned forward, and put her finger on her lips. Shhh. And right then, before her eyes, in front of everyone, the earth tilted. She looked up and saw things falling: splinters, small, almost weightless bits coming down. Leslie did not seem to notice. She went on talking. Talking. Yet, the immense geodesic dome made of what seemed to be matchsticks, pale balsa wood pieces, was coming apart. Drifting, tumbling. Her life. Look at it. All coming down. All that she had been building for years, counting on, clinging to. She dug her bare feet into the grass.

March! Are you all right?

She shook her head. No. Yes. Yes. Fine. Fine.

Picking up the children's things, stuffing them into the straw bag, wheeling the buggy across the grass to the parking place, folding the buggy into the back of the trunk, opening the car bed, dropping Mia in, digging for her keys, calling to Littlemarch and Alden to come along, to hurry, to get in, get in, sit down, she started the car and shot onto Lake Shore Drive.

Later she often thought about that day, telling herself that watching any structure come apart and disintegrate could be mesmerizing, and that a silence at the end, nothing but a small wfff made sense. She was reminded of the time the man fell off the tightrope at the circus. The man was wobbling along up there, and he was almost all the way across, and then he was gone; but as he fell the gasps of the people watching accompanied him, rose as though to buoy him up as he descended, but just at that moment he hit sawdust in the far ring. Then there was dead silence. When he hit the ground there was just a whump, and then a little wffff.

AFTER THANKSGIVING Warren moved to a hotel. Not a hotel, a cat house, he complained. Listen to this. He would hold the phone to the door of his room so that March could hear people laughing and shouting. Also, the bed was killing his back. He came daily to the apartment on search and destroy missions; looking for things he could not live without, searching for the ice bucket, for cookbooks, for the electric can opener, seizing ashtrays, bath towels, coat hangers, glasses, two corkscrews, another pillow.

All thanks to you, March, our new Elizabeth Taylor! Liz would try something like this. But March was no Liz. He was no Eddie Fisher. Other people, rich people, movie stars did things like this. Tried a separation. Took up hotel living. Invented a new lifestyle.

Call up Eddy, Warren shouted one night. Call up Richard. Call up Sibyl. Call up Debbie. Call up Harry.

Harry who?

Jesus, March. Harry Karl. You know perfectly well who. Harry Karl. Married to Debbie. After Eddy. Who was married to Elizabeth before she married Richard. Harry fucking Karl.

MARCH WAS busy looking for that book, looking everywhere for *The Naked and The Dead*.

At one of those awful moments you read about and did not forget, soldiers had been scared shitless. She had read that and at the time wondered if it was just a figure of speech, or was it an accurate physical description. Then, she had not been able to imagine such fear, but now, now she understood that the description sprang from the truth: sudden fear of sudden death, the kind of fear that could squeeze miles and miles of intestines with pressure so great and a speed so incredible that one had, at best, a few seconds to find a bathroom. And she was lucky in that respect. There were bathrooms all over Chicago because Chicago, it turned out, was practically made of white porcelain. March had found bathrooms in supermarkets, in Laundromats, in liquor stores and drugstores that might never have been seen by anyone but employees or small children. Small rooms down hallways made glamorous and historical by the graffiti she had discovered, in blue ink and red pencil, in lipstick, and black marker: We like Ike, Donald Duck is a Jew, Kilroy was here, God is dead, Shakespeare is a fairy. A person could tell the dates from the messages scrawled.

And there were messages for her as well.

You should get out more, March.

Get a job.

Pull yourself together.

Think of your children.

She heard. She might not answer, but she heard all right. In fact, some of the messages seemed to come from space. Her knowledge of physics was vague, too fanciful to mention; but she was on the receiving end of matter, of energy, of light waves, of jolts. Messages arriving from great distances in space, entering through the millions of hair follicles on her small frame, or in some other fashion, but entering. Sparks, jolts, shot through her, treated her as a receiving station, as part of a space center, not exactly as a person.

There were, strangely, some good days; when she was fooled into thinking she had come through, times when she looked at the world and felt like she was falling in love with it, with all the people out there, all the men, and women and children who had the courage to get up, go out, fry an egg, stay out of jail, get out of jail, survive. What courage, what talent, what guts.

She thought at those times that she might indeed be looking for a job. She might be working on her novel again. Why not. It was a good novel. An important novel. To her. Why not to others. And she might have people for dinner. A soufflé. She would beat eggs, make something that would rise. She would clean the apartment and buy flowers. She would bring the children into the living room and wrap blankets around them and read to them, and they would smile. Then she would be reminded of the joke a friend had told years ago, the joke about the tipperary: the poor animal that had been dragged everywhere in the back of a truck, and then one day he was dumped out the back end and over a cliff and as he went he cried, It's a long way to tip a rary. A twenty-minute joke when done right, but maybe not so funny after all, because by then you cared about the rary, really a very warm, odd, frightened animal.

SHINEHOLTZ. Dr. Shineholtz did not believe in good days. A woman March barely knew had found her sitting on a pile of coats in the bedroom where she had retreated one night after ten nervous minutes at a cocktail party. I hear you're having a bad time, the woman, Joan somebody, said. Call my therapist. Ed Shineholtz. Fantastic guy.

But Fantastic Shineholtz had not taken to March.

What I would recommend, he said. What I would seriously recommend, Mrs. Wright. Is this. Commit yourself. Put yourself in a hospital for a time.

March shook her head. She would not do that. She would never do that.

Shineholtz pressed on.

I look at you and who do I see? Somebody who came in here because she got my name at a cocktail party. She got my name at a party, and she picked up the telephone the very next day and called, *from a pay phone.* In the lobby of some Loop hotel. And begged. Begged to put her life in my hands.

I got your name at a cocktail party, March agreed. So what's so bad about that? How are people supposed to get news of you?

Shineholtz rapped his knuckles on his desk. The point I am making is that you went to a cocktail party, latched onto my name the way you would pluck an hors d'oeuvre off a plate.

All right. I'm sorry. I picked up your name at a cocktail party. I was trying to have a decent time for a change. Trying to make an effort. Talk. Eat a couple of olives. Laugh. It wasn't working so I went into the bedroom and sat down on a pile of coats, and Joan Perz, your patient, came in, and asked if I was OK, and I said, not so hot, and she said, call Shineholtz. She gave me your name and number. Why is that so terrible?

It's a question of doing things properly. You don't pick a doctor with whom you want to have an important relationship, with whom you may well be spending five, six, seven years of your life, by asking someone you hardly know, at a cocktail party, for a name, in a bedroom full of coats.

March sighed. You take everything so personally. But look. I'm here. You tell me what time to be here. I do what you tell me to do. You make a big deal about time and money. I am two minutes late and one payment behind, and you start complaining about the party and the bedroom full of coats again.

That isn't my point, Mrs. Wright. I am not interested in the party. I am asking you to commit yourself. I do not think you will hold up as a patient. I personally don't.

I am not promising anything, March said. I'm just scared. I'm afraid my heart will stop, or my brain will split open. I think I might die, and I want to live. It's a bad circle.

Do you know who I see, Mrs. Wright? I see a person who wants to be saved. I see someone who is crying, make it all better. Right now. Not tomorrow. I see someone crying, help, fix me.

What is wrong with that? Someone saying I'll be all right?

However. I cannot say that. No, I cannot say that. Maybe you will be all right. Maybe you won't. I see a lot of people like you, Mrs. Wright. A lot of women whose lives have fallen apart, whose marriages have collapsed, who want Daddy to make it all better, but I am not Daddy. No, I cannot promise you I will make it all better.

March sat in her corner, and wondered why he didn't say it anyway. What did he have to lose. A small, mean-tempered man with thin lips, in his dreary brown suit and gray shirt; sitting here in his room with the brown carpet, the ugly green plaid furniture; a Jewish man she would therefore have expected to be attracted to, to have loved, but instead, she had taken an instant dislike to him, this emotional tightwad with his creepy thread of hair wound around his skull, this man whose help she needed, whose help was not available to her. She started to cry. Shineholtz was not moved. He handed out a giant Kleenex, checked his watch, moved his fingers as though he had a piano on his desk.

March thought about what he had said, about committing herself, but she could not do that. Once you went to a place like that, once you gave up and went away, you might never recover, or you might go again, and again. You would have to go through your days knowing you had given up once, and you might need to give up again.

Time, Shineholtz announced, and March was reminded of the day of her oral exam at Vassar, her craziness then. She went out into the hall, and opened a fire door and sat in the stairwell until she had stopped crying. Then she went to wait for the elevator. Shineholtz came out of his office and waited too. When the elevator came they rode down in silence. He headed north, and March followed him along Michigan Avenue and over the bridge which shook and seemed about to give. And people did jump. Right, Shineholtz! From bridges. Into the bloody Chicago River.

❧

OF COURSE the dress looked terrible. The sleeve was just plain disintegrating. After four months of being cleaned at the coin-op, it smelled of chemicals, and sweat, and dust, and smoke, but it was comforting. This black and white sack. She should probably take a bath, but she was worried about getting in and slipping all the way down and not getting back up. The shower curtain was all ripped to shreds so a shower was out. Warren said she made excuses for everything.

Warren, on the other hand, had never looked better. Stronger. Healthier. In spite of March forcing him to leave at the worst possible time, in case she was interested, when he was just getting going. And yet! After all. He was starting a new life! Making new friends. Seeing old ones, couples she had dropped. And he was thinking of taking up flying again. Take the bunnies up for a spin! Spending a Sunday in the sky. And he was writing well. Oh, yes. Writing and writing. Another story, just last week. The mystery almost finished. If only he could type faster. She imagined him lighting a cigar and rubbing his fingers for a bit of luck.

He would rummage in the refrigerator, look for books he needed, stuff the girls into coats for a trip to the park, wander through the bedroom where she had her desk.

What I would suggest, March, if I may, he began on that Saturday. What I would suggest. Is this. Stop the brooding. Stop the business with the rescue squad, and taxpayers' money. Get dressed, get out, date.

DATE?

Date.

I should date. Someone. Why?

That's what people do.

They date.

Yes.

That's what you do, Warren. Good for you. You hit a wall, but you bounce off it. I'm impressed.

You might be interested in knowing that I am good in bed again. After years of your exhaustion, your many pregnancies. I'm just beginning there. These may be my best years. He raised his eyebrows. A new era. March wanted to laugh. He looked so pleased. And because he seemed to have gained weight, swelled up with all his good times and good sex and dating, he looked like a gigantic mattress, wrapped up in plaid. Or a carnival barker. The sight of him made her want to throw a rubber ball at him, and win a stuffed bear.

He went over to her typewriter, and looked at the paper sticking up. What's this? *Summer is going and so am I*. Oh, wonderful, March. My nervous breakdown. A guaranteed best seller. Guaranteed to scare the hell out of any editor. Even a brave publisher. Have you ever thought of something that would not scare readers, something that would not be guaranteed to depress any future audience. A cookbook? A romance? A tiny mystery?

I don't know about anything else, March said. My life. That's all I know about.

I am merely suggesting something that might sell. In the time that I have been writing I have considered the marketplace. Sales. Economics. Marketing strategies. The odds. What are people looking for. And this investigation has paid off. I have, as you may know, or may not know, sold two to *Ellery Queen*. I have almost finished my novel.

He rattled the table, picked up her copy of *The Phenomenon of Man*. Whereas you, the artist, the wounded philosopher, the world's smallest existentialist, have now begun a story of your life that is almost guaranteed to bomb.

I wish you would stop saying guarantee, Warren. You sound like an insurance salesman. So it bombs. Or it doesn't bomb. Not your problem.

Warren went into the kitchen. She heard him opening the refrigerator. She heard the girls talking, and after a while, the front door closing. The buggy banged on the steps.

She wandered through the empty apartment and went back into the bedroom and looked out at the alley. The snow was melting. Still, the street was empty. In a warm place people would be out, would be talking and leaning on porch rails. Her head and heart had started up again, but she knew what to do. She got a towel from the bathroom and twisted it around her head. Warren had seen that one day, and said it just proved, just proved. But she used this turban to protect herself, to keep things in place. It seemed absurd, but she was afraid that her head might split open, and the pieces would scatter, like the many pieces of a shattered alarm clock.

After a while it was better. This clock in her head. She got up and looked in the mirror. The blue towel, like part of a Halloween costume, her blank pale face, her skin that looked as though it had been folded over and over and saved, a piece of tissue paper or parchment that had been pressed between the pages of a heavy book. Never mind, she thought. I'm not through yet. Not by a long shot.

The door opened down the hall. The girls were calling. We're back! We're back!

March, Warren shouted. MARCH!

Mɪᴀ ɪs crying. She is crying her head off. Alden was shouting. Littlemarch said I should come in here and get you up. Right now.

Alden was on the floor, a few inches away from where March had spent the night, where she often spent it now, under her bed.

She is crying her head off, Alden said.

I guess she must not like it here, March said. Maybe she wants to pack her bags and be off somewhere. I wouldn't blame her. Some morning she'll probably tell us she's on her way to Florida. Adios, you birds, I'm off! We'll see her down there, splashing around near the fat man who is buried in the sand. We'll only see his face. Bright red. And we'll yell, Fly away home, Fat Man. Your face is on fire. Your ears are burning. Go to your room. Call room service for goop for your burns. Call your wife and children! But wait. Look! Mia is turning Fat Man into a castle! She is making turrets and rivulets. She is pouring water for the moat. Oh, Fat Man, you is going to drown in Florida.

Mia can't go to Florta, Alden said. She can't. She's in her crib. She can't go anywhere.

No. She's stuck. No Florta for Mia.

You come out.

Alden's face was right up next to March's now. She was breathing hard, and her dark eyes were furious. She stuck her hands under the bed and March could feel they were icy cold. Once she had been so fat and squashy, solemn like a Buddha. They had called her by that name. Now it seemed if you really looked, you might see right through her. She was all dressed up in one of her costumes, wearing bracelets, and pieces of ribbon, leather necklaces with terrible-looking pieces of cloth, and she had strung old chestnuts and seashells together, and pieces of fur were hanging there, and her brown fur pocketbook was around her neck. Why did she dress like that? Going off every morning looking like a gypsy, slamming doors behind her, shouting, telling the rest of them to clean up, pick up, telling them to lock the doors, pull out the toaster cord, pull out the blender cord. Keeping them, March understood, from being burned up, from being murdered in the night.

We is going to be late, Alden hissed.

Are. Are going.

Are going. Littlemarch can't find her boots. We have to be on time. You have to find her boots. We have to wear boots in school. For the playground.

March slid out, stiff from her night on the bare floor. She had thrown the bedroom carpet out the window, and the scavengers had laughed and taken it off in their truck. It was an old ugly thing with cigarette burns and worn spots, but now it was cold under the bed.

OK, she said. We're on. Where is Littlemarch? Where are the boots? Let's find the boots. Pretty soon Mrs.Whoseybomb will honk her horn and we'll be up here, and she'll send that little freak of hers up here to tell us to get down there or mothaaaa will have to go on without us. Talk about people with problems. Talk about ment-uls, as you would say, Alden. Come on. Sweaters, coats, mittens, scarves, fifty below, and we'll all be hanging from the ceiling by spring.

They were running now. A horn sounded. The boots were nowhere. Never mind. Don't go out for recess. March threw a coat over her pajamas, hustled them out the door and down the stairs, out the front door to the street, just as the little kid was getting out of the car.

She ran in her bare feet, and opened the rear door, thrust the children in and stuck her head in after them. Sorry. We're so.

The car was dark and warm. Music was playing on the radio, and coming out of the backseat through a hole, a speaker? Mrs.———? Sue? was sitting at the wheel in a coat made of white and honey-colored fur. What animal would that be?

You'll freeze, March.

I know.

Minus six! Winter wonderland!

Right. Sorry we were so.

March slammed the door, and went back up to the apartment, and took Mia out of the crib. Don't cry. Please don't. We're going to be all right. She pressed the baby's tiny head against her chest, and felt her small hot hands dig into her shoulders, and smelled her damp cheek. The last one. She could still carry her, kiss her, take chunks out of those fat legs and knead them. She buried her head in the soft fuzz above the hollow at the back of her neck. She listened to the hiccups, felt the stiff little jerks as the crying stopped.

There there. Remember when what's his name said that in *Catch-22*? You don't. Well I remember. He did say that, and it seemed so comforting. Henry James thought a summer afternoon was lovely, but I think 'there there' is what you want to remember.

In the kitchen, she sat next to Mia's highchair while she fed her pieces of banana and toast. That's right. Just mush it around. She fed her milk from a tiny silver cup. There. See? That's right. No more? No more. She washed the baby's face and hands, and picked her up, and pressed her own face against the small pink ear.

Now what we're going to do is wait a little while, and see if somebody calls us. See if someone might come to see us. If nothing happens, and probably nothing will, we'll bundle up, and go out, and go up to the corner to the Laundromat. OK? Then we can sit around the gas fire and see people. We won't be alone, and there will be people, in case something happens. Nothing is going to happen, but just in case. We'll sit there and then we'll come back here when we feel like it. OK?

Now we are going into the living room and getting into the playpen. She lowered Mia into the playpen, and climbed in with her. March curled up on her side, and Mia settled herself on top of her, huffing and puffing, drooling, stuffing wooden beads down the neck of March's sweater.

You want bangs? The hairdresser patted her head.

No.

No bangs! That's a joke! *Get it?* Bangs!

March got up and went out into the hallway. She leaned against the wall with her hair still piled high with red plastic rollers. A woman waiting for the building elevator asked if there was a problem. March said she had a little something.

You can come up to my apartment, the woman said. You come right up with me. I'll give you some ginger ale.

March sat in the woman's apartment and drank the ginger ale. The woman sat on the couch and smiled at her. Four years ago my mother died, the woman said. After that day I couldn't ride in the elevator alone. I had to have someone with me.

That must have been awful, March said.

Yes. It was. Now I can go alone, but every once in a while I still get that feeling. Then I have to wait for someone to come along.

But now it's better? Most of the time?

Yes.

I'm glad, March said. That's encouraging. She went back down to the beauty shop and had her hair combed out. One of the things she was not going to be able to do again was have her hair cut. There were certain places that were bound to be a problem for her. But wasn't it strange that a person, a woman she had never known before, would probably never see again, could make her feel better.

The children stayed with a sitter for the night, and March went to La Rue. Her father said he knew what she was going through. Once, a long time ago, when he was her age, something like this had happened to him. That night she sat in her room with the light on, and

129

when it was morning her father drove her to the station. You don't sleep here, do you? he said. He was helpless, furious. He slapped her across the face. You don't feel better here. You feel worse.

On the train she took a window seat, and looked out at her father standing on the platform. He looked old and tired. She wondered what had happened to him so long ago? The train pulled out, and she could see him standing there, looking after her. All the way to Chicago she talked to a sailor, and thought of her father back there. It seemed to her that if she kept the sailor locked into a conversation until they were in the city, her father would be safe.

❦

A SATURDAY in spring. March took the children to the zoo. They bought balloons, and went to the shoe store for new sandals and to the bookstore. Mia who was wearing shoes now, chewed on her book, and said, book book. At noon the babysitter who lived upstairs came to take them to the park. March listened to the stroller and the bikes bang on the landing. Good-bye! Good-bye! And don't come back 'til midnight, she whispered. She lay down on the floor in the living room. She wanted to sleep forever.

March.

Listen.

March Rivers!

She jumped. Who was calling her. What day was this? What time was it? Where were the girls. The children. She opened the front door.

I thought you were out, her mother said. I've been ringing for hours.

What in God's name was her mother doing here?

Were you asleep?

Me?

Where are the children? Are they out? I thought we could have lunch before I took Littlemarch back.

Oh my God, she was taking Littlemarch to La Rue. For the weekend.

Her mother followed her into the living room.

What happened to the curtains?

What curtains was she talking about?

The children are at the park. I'll run and get them. It won't take a minute. I'll be right back.

Did you order the curtains?

March stared at her mother. Was her mother crazy?

What?

At Field's. The ones we discussed. The drip dry. Two pairs for each window. To give fullness. A sense of finish. One pair would look skimpy.

Yes. I'm going to get the children. I'll be right back.

I don't see how you can live without curtains.

March ran down the stairs, out through the door and down the street, panting, frantic. She would find them. She could do that. How could she have forgotten? She ran and ran, her hair flew and her fists were up; her eyes were popping and she felt like a child, little and late again. Where were they? She could not spot them, but she knew they were there, somewhere, sleeping under a tree, stuffing popsicle wrappers in their ears; chasing pigeons and getting impetigo, throwing sand and peeing in the bushes, tossing twigs in the fountain. And Mrs. Smith—glued to the park bench—would be gossiping with the other sitters, gazing at the sky.

There they were! Noonie's here, she shouted through a hole in the fence.

COME ON!

At Jacques March and her mother ordered martinis on the rocks with a lemon twist, and studied the menu. They sat in the garden and March listened to the fountain bubbling, the clink of forks and glasses, the crunch of breadsticks. The sounds merged with the warm air, the drooping artificial trees under the bright light of the Plexiglas bubble set in the roof.

What is that on your face? her mother said.

March's hand shot up and touched the spot where her skin had begun to break out in a perfect semi-circle at the side of her mouth.

Skin cancer.

No.

No. Age. Stress. Distress.

Now when the rest of her seemed to be on a crash course toward old age and senility, her skin was retreating into adolescence. As we grow up we grow out, the shoe clerk had said. I'm only thirty-two, March said. He shook his head. Think of yourself as sand settling. And teeth falling, March thought. The back one's a cooked goose, the dentist had said, but we'll try to hang onto his neighbor. And her hair. She felt it becoming lighter and trembling a little, like delicate beach grass growing on top of her soggy body. Now the heat and the gin and the weariness that seemed to have settled over her made it difficult for her to keep her eyes open.

Her mother lit a cigarette. I wonder if you'll marry again?

I don't think I'll be married to anyone again.

Don't say that. You have to look ahead. Have faith in a future. Her mother ordered another drink and the sole. March ordered a salad.

Life is not a bed of roses, her mother said. You have to think of your children.

I take care of them. They keep me alive. Otherwise. Without them. Well, I'm grateful.

Her mother picked at her fish, and March wondered if she would have the nerve to do a tracheotomy if her mother swallowed a bone; if she swallowed a lemon peel or ran into a soggy biscuit. Where did you make the incision, the little hole?

Did you call the cleaning woman?

What cleaning woman?

Oh, March. I sent you her name a week ago. She's expecting a call. If you go to the lake you'll need her. You can't be up there without help. Now she's probably taken another job. Of course it's your life. I can't live it for you. But I have to know about cleaning. About your plans. I have to arrange for cleaning and I have to know exactly when you'll be there.

Right.

There was a long silence, and her mother said, The fish is dry. I think they're going downhill here.

March tried to think of a subject for discussion. Did you go to Michigan? See your mother. See Nana?

Her mother pointed her finger at her head. When I get that way, shoot me. She knows you for a minute and then she's off again. I wore my new hat and she said, Where did you get that awful old thing? Take it off! My brand new hat. They both laughed.

After lunch they went into the ladies room and March watched as her mother combed her hair, washed her hands and put on deep red lipstick and powder, and chatted with the attendant as though she had known her all her life. Now there was a workable relationship. They both knew how to handle themselves and what to expect. Quarters fell into the saucer, and the woman said, Now you have a nice day!

Thank you, her mother said. I'm sure we will!

Is that your daughter? She nodded in March's direction.

Yes. This is my daughter. She lives in Chicago, and I've come down for the day to see her and my grandchildren.

Isn't that nice.

Before lunch March had come in to take a Kleenex, and as she was leaving the woman had said to no one, Did you see that. Imagine just coming in here, and taking a piece of Kleenex. Just like that!

They waited for a taxi. Her mother said, Sometimes. She paused and pulled on new gloves, and snapped the clasp on her pocketbook with authority. Sometimes, I think you would be better off to go back to Warren. There's just no point in being so miserable.

At the apartment March paid the sitter and made coffee while her mother took the children into the bathroom. She could hear her mother chanting, Where's the soap, where's the washcloth, where's the towel? Then she heard her in the living room giving Mia a ride on her knee. Ride a cock horse to Banbury Cross, and see a fine lady upon a white horse!

All three of them were busy digging in her mother's alligator bag. Pennies, a white handkerchief, a gold lighter, another white handkerchief, a clean comb. March wished they could all descend into that bag and stay there.

I think we should leave now, her mother announced. I want to miss the rush hour traffic. But Littlemarch could not go without her white gloves and her blanket. She would not go without these things, she whispered to March. They stood in the bedroom, facing each other, hopeful.

You can go. I'll find them, March promised. Just go. Please. Noonie gets so impatient. You'll be fine.

I can't. Littlemarch was sobbing. March looked around the room again and looked at her small body, the sweet grubby face, her wrinkled dress. She knelt down and put her arms around her. I'll find them and bring them up, she said, to La Rue.

What seems to be the problem. Her mother came into the bedroom and March explained, and then for no reason March could think of, her mother headed for the hall closet. March and Littlemarch were right behind her.

Don't go in there. They wouldn't be in there, March warned, but her mother opened the door, and as they all stood behind her in a half circle, the Christmas tree tipped toward them, moving slowly, stiffly, armed with ornaments, balls and little birds, fish, boats, glass angels, all of these obliging the expectation of a good show by bouncing and shattering at their feet.

My God, her mother said. My God.

MARCH DID think of her children. She tried to remember them from the beginning, but it was hard to remember. Remember, she said. Remember? But who remembers? Who keeps track. Everything happens so quickly.

She thought of it in this way. I feel the years, but I have trouble seeing them; I was born, I am middle-aged. I was a warm wet creature, born early at dawn, a three-pound miracle, now a sort of mother, a worn-down clown.

Remembering the years she thought of the wind blowing, clocks ticking and pipes banging, cars backfiring, the smell of mothballs and the walls all slippery from the steam pouring out of vaporizers. Doors and windows closing. Morning sickness. Old butter.

Just for the summer she said in June. We'll have our own place, and a garden. We'll hear crickets at night. Mourning doves. Lawn mowers. We'll buy corn and raspberries at the roadside stand. We'll go to the parade, early in the morning on the Fourth, to see the parade before it really begins. We'll watch it from the curb on Main and Ninth which is the best spot. We'll buy flags, and ice cream bars and fur monkeys on sticks. At night we'll go to bed while it's still light. We'll listen to the crickets and someone down the block calling olly olly oxen free. We'll sit on our front porch and nod at the world. We'll make applesauce and jam. We'll get bicycles and ride around. She realized she was describing her own lost childhood, but as she described it, embellished it, she believed in the possibility.

The first of June. March's thirty-second birthday; moving day. At noon she put the last silver tray into the last packing box; sealed the lid on the last carton marked for storage; stuffed the last stuffed animal into the last suitcase; took the girls by their hands and followed Warren down the steps of the apartment for the last time.

Going home.

You can't go home again, Warren said.

For the summer. To catch my breath. We can't stay here. The lease is up. We'll have an apartment. It will be clean. Quiet.

What will you do there? Think about it, March. La Rue? Seriously. We'll find things to do. We'll have neighbors. It won't be so lonely.

They drove to La Rue in the car which Warren would keep because March said she couldn't drive anymore. They stopped at the edge of town, at a roadhouse where the waitress was setting tables for dinner. They were the only customers. The place reminded her of the morning she had waited at this crossroads for Warren and the boys to arrive from California. Eight years. It seemed like a lifetime, or yesterday. Warren ordered a drink, and Littlemarch and Alden had brilliant-colored kiddy cocktails. They spun a lazy Susan loaded with limp raw vegetables, and dishes filled with pale, lumpy concoctions around and around, ever faster, until March made them stop.

After lunch Warren drove them to the apartment and helped unload the car.

Not exactly Rivers Avenue, Warren said. It's a development, March. You're not going to like this. Believe me. Out here in the sticks. If you ask me now is the time to ask your parents to start dipping into the sweet trust fund.

It's clean, March said. Simple. In the kitchen she found a loaf of homemade bread on the table. In the refrigerator there were oranges, milk, apples, cookies. See. From my brother and his wife. From the woman next door.

Soon you'll be going to sewing bees. Church picnics.

Look at this. She showed Warren an invitation to a party. From someone I used to know. She has two extra men. Bachelors. A heart surgeon and a psychiatrist. Just what I need. She shook her head.

They sat on the grass for a while, Mia and Alden on her lap, Littlemarch jabbing at herself with a stick. March took the stick and rubbed at the scratches on her little legs. Last week her teacher had said Littlemarch made her ache. A waif, she had said. So small and fierce. So hard on herself.

You think there is thiefs here? Alden wanted to know. March said no, there were no thiefs. Warren said he had better be going. No telling when the movers would come. Moonlighters like that. And he had to get ready for his own move on Tuesday.

I guess you'll be busy, March said.

I'll try to get up soon.

Call or something.

I will. I'll call.

They all walked to the curb to wave and wave, to watch as Warren drove down the street, to see him turn onto the main road, pass the shopping center, and the gas station and the empty field, to watch carefully as he finally disappeared from sight while they were still waving and waving. March thought she had finally done something practical, something for the children and for herself, but she could not remember ever before feeling so terribly sad.

Two steps forward. One back. The gains were not remarkable. But there were gains. In the fall Littlemarch and Alden went to the school down the road. Mia played with the little boy in the next apartment. March had coffee with his mother. She did not expect to be suddenly, miraculously delivered from the feeling of despair she had grown accustomed to, but she believed that some part of her, some inner resilience she had hung onto, would enable her to go on. There came a night when she could not sleep, when she found herself separated from herself; when a part of her settled on the bedroom ceiling, unable or unwilling to return, until sometime before morning the episode ended, and she was all in one piece again. The memory of the separation stayed, but after that she noticed a change. She was aware of a turning point. Something had been settled.

She took too much Valium, and slept too much, a sort of awful drugged sleep, but she took care of the girls who began to seem calmer, enfolded by cousins and grandparents, her brother and his wife who had gathered the girls into the warmth and comfort of their Sunday suppers, who included them all in festivities March had trouble remembering she was meant to celebrate. She worked on her novel. When September came around again she began to correct papers for one of the high school English teachers. He suggested an affair. She declined. She began to think about graduate school at the university in Madison.

Out of the blue, and March had trouble taking this seriously, an editor at Doubleday in New York expressed interest in her novel which even now amounted to less than fifty pages, the typed and retyped pages she had sent to a friend in Chicago. The friend's mother was Colleen Moore, the silent film star whose films March was passionate about. It was Colleen who had once invited March to spend several hilarious hours with her and her dear friend King Vidor at a splendid golf club in a Chicago suburb where King was amusing himself by working on his putting, and intermittently on the screenplay which had after all come to naught. But now Colleen had sent March's pages on to a writer friend in Hollywood who had sent them to her editor in New York. Months had gone by. March had not expected to hear from anyone. She had not been waiting for an answer, but now the New York editor wrote to say, send the rest. Let us hear from you. An outline. We would give you a contract, but we need to see more. We love this woman you are writing about. She is a beaten bird, but maybe she'll make it?

A good question, March thought. Yet, two weeks before her thirty-third birthday she left the girls with her parents and flew to New York. There were good omens from the start. The plane did not crash. The sun was shining. When she called her friend Terry from the airport, he laughed.

You're here! I was afraid you'd cancel. Jump in a cab. I'm going out to buy champagne. And roasted almonds. Do you remember eating roasted almonds? And maybe we should have some of that Wisconsin cheese? That orange glop that comes in a jar and tastes like baby food? And some Jones sausage? What else can you think of? Never mind thinking. Come right over. La Rue. What could be funnier? I haven't talked to anyone from La Rue for years. It's terrible. I've been feeling deprived, and here you are! I'm hanging up now. I want to buy some decent glasses. The ones you see in the movies. Heavy as lead. You know them? I'll leave the door open. Four flights. Leave your bag at the bottom. Start remembering!

March hung up and called the editor she had not had the nerve to call before. The woman whose name was Margaret Cousins said this was all too good to be true. She had just been sitting there thinking about that poor beaten bird, and what was to become of her, and here she was, the creator of the bird, and would they ever be happy to meet her. How about Friday at four?

New York. That was the way things happened in New York. On Madison Avenue, on sidewalks under the pale trees. At Phoebe's Whamburger. At Orsini's. At El Morocco. Did those places still exist? Places she had gone to with her lover. With Max. What nonsense. She looked out from the taxi and noted how well people looked. She had forgotten. All dressed up. Not like La Rue. She straightened her shoulders, and sucked in her stomach.

Tell me everything, Terry said. They sat on the couch in his tiny living room, drinking champagne, eating cheese and roasted almonds. Dear March. Think how lucky you are! In La Rue. Right there, in the heart of it all. Your very own Peyton Place. Where

Grace Metallious would have given her last puff to have come from. You have the parade on the Fourth of July! The Wheatfield's picnic supper and Niagara Falls shooting over the lake! The New Year's Dance! The Country Club! Do you go there for dinner? Is that waitress still there? Evelyn, with the hair? Do you go to the hotel for lunch the way we used to at Christmas. Chicken salad under the fake palms? Is there still a hotel? Do you buy corn from the Pesey sisters? Does the old one still have a beard? Is Vernon Klupt still sneaking off on the three-thirteen to Chicago. Seeing the piano player? You didn't know? You must have. I can't help it if Vernon's married. The piano player was adorable.

March could not remember laughing so much.

La Rue, Terry said. La Rue. My old old life. I couldn't live there now, but I love every inch of it. People in New York just don't know what they've missed.

She fell asleep that night to the sound of television, and a radio playing in the living room; a record player somewhere, and all the lights on. It's the only way, love. You don't want the ghosts to find you.

The next day they went to the Russian Tea Room for lunch, then to the movies. To *Fahrenheit 451*, and after that to *Persona*, and finally to a Japanese film without subtitles. At ten they sat down for dinner at Maxwell's Plum.

Three movies, March said. Crazy.

They talked about Terry's decorating jobs and about her novel.

Of course you'll be famous, Terry said. I've always known. We'll both be famous. And live in New York. Or Paris. Or Marrakech. Another year, and I'll be THE decorator. I'm already doing showbiz people. Dick Cavett. You've heard of him. Never? But you must have. You are going to have to get yourself some televisions sets, darling. One for each room. And keep them on. Keep tuned in. And if you look right this minute you'll see Gary Merrill. Who? Oh, March. Dear, dear March. Gary Merrill. The ex-husband of Bette Davis. Who has recently befriended *me*. Who asks me to the country for weekends. I sit on the end of her bed and we gossip. Oh March, was anyone ever so out of it. But that's all right. That's what makes you special. Next year they'll be pointing at you.

They went the next day to F.A.O. Schwarz to buy presents for the girls, and to Design Research where Terry bought her a cotton shirt.

To give you the look of a beach child at St. Tropez. You will bring that little touch to La Rue. That's important. For them. For you. And a Lucite clipboard. For what? Oh, who knows. To carry around. To make lists for the cocktail parties you'll be giving at the country club. To keep your life in order.

They went to Tiffany's and shopped for glasses, and the clerk told them to please, please not touch. Those were sixty-five dollars. A dozen? No. Each. Oh well. They're very nice, Terry said. But I think we'd like something a little nicer. He frowned. But those would be lovely for the children's table.

They went to Bloomingdale's. For astringent lotion. Elizabeth Arden's best, March. You know what to do with it. You put it in the refrigerator with the champagne, and let it lead its own life. It will be very happy there.

They went to Yellow Fingers for lunch. No, darling. Not Goldfinger. Yellow. And drink some wine. Gives you iron. And there goes Truman Capote. Out the window. On your right. Do you think he looks like me? In fact, he did. March thought they could have been twins. I carry pencils with his name on them, Terry said. He took one from his pocket and handed it to March.

At four they stood in front of Doubleday's editorial offices on Park Avenue. And now you're on your own. If anything goes wrong, just take out the astringent and sniff it. That will stop them. Nobody does that. Yet. He put his arms around her for a minute, and then he was gone.

Waiting in the reception room, March thought of waiting in this exact spot years ago, looking for a job, straight out of Vassar, being told by an editor who was famous for her contempt, that March, like all the others, knew nothing. They all wanted to publish Tolstoy, Flaubert, Joyce. They knew nothing. Publishing was a business. They ought to get that through their fancy schmanzy heads. Now some other college graduate led her along a hallway and into a cubicle.

March Rivers Wright! The woman who introduced herself as Maggie Cousins took March's hands and folded them into her large, warm paws, and March had the sense of being eaten alive and blessed at the same time. Now if you don't look scared to death!

The woman was huge. A nice gold color. She went on talking in a deep, husky voice that reminded March of pecans and bourbon. Thanksgiving. Truman Capote. Where was she from. Before New York? March really wanted to know, but there was this kind, motherly woman, Maggie Cousins, going on about her book.

What was going to happen, she wanted to know. Something had to happen. Didn't much matter what. Just something. She's got to win or lose, this beaten bird. You've got to decide that, and get on with it. That's all. And then do another one. You've got lots of books in you. And you don't want to spend forever on this one. You do this, and get on to the next. A born storyteller, but you look a bit worn down right now. Life's been a little rough?

It had been that, March admitted.

Send me another fifty pages or so and an outline. We'll give you a contract. Just give us something to go on. And you ought to get out of Wisconsin. That doesn't sound too good. You want to be around people. Writing people. Book people. I have a friend who's looking for someone in Chicago. An editor. At *Playboy*. Fiction. A wonderful man. Brilliant man. Robie Macauley. You go to him, and you'll be back in the middle of things. In the mainstream.

March said that was certainly a possibility.

We just have to get you moving! She took March around the office, and introduced her to other editors, to one who looked like a movie star, who asked if March was the writer from Wisconsin, the new one. He told her he was expecting big things from her, and March nodded. Everyone was, it seemed. They weren't worried. They cared. And that was good.

And next time you're here, you let us know ahead of time and we'll take you to dinner. A little Texas hospitality for a change.

Texas. Of course. A big house, a porch, a warm kitchen, old aunts. Do you go back there, March wanted to know. To Texas?

I should hope. Last year, this year, and the good Lord willing, next. Those are my roots. My blood. Forty-two years I have lived in New York, but Texas is home.

Later, walking up Park Avenue, March imagined she was a girl who had come to New York from the sticks. Like Thomas Wolfe. A story of success and celebration. But a person would have to be awfully young to believe that. There was writing, and there could be success and fame, but as you got older, life intervened. Spring in New York, and you could dream for a while, but then you had to settle down again. You had to go back to the business of surviving. More than once in her life someone had believed in her, but it was still difficult for her to believe in herself, in her novel, in the future.

⁂

OUR HOUSE is somewhere north of that dome, March said. That gold dome is the thing. The capitol. We have to work our way out from there. Roads like rays emanate from that. A web is formed. Right now we are on the inner edge of the web. The problem is getting off this web and getting onto another outer one. She was peering at a map. Some place a little further from the hub. The nub.

I wish you'd stop talking like that, Littlemarch said. When you talk like that I don't know what you're talking about.

They drove around, and drove past a lake which was not their lake, but some other lake. There are many lakes here, but our lake is larger. There are many that are smaller than ours. Too damn many, March was thinking.

I thought you was here before, Alden said. You said you was here before. You said you knew all about Madison, Wisconsin.

I did say that. And we are definitely getting closer. There's the Oscar Mayer factory so we must be close. Count to a hundred, and look for a sign that says Oaknoll Village, and a street that says Sycamore Circle. And there it was, their circle, with the girls now fighting about who had spied the sign first. And there was the house. Their home.

What's known as a ranch, March said. Split-level with family room and wall to wall.

It looks like La Rue, Littlemarch said.

Yeah, La Rue for sure, Alden said.

La Rue, Mia chirped.

They were right. There were the familiar backyards and swing sets. No sidewalks. No trees. And something in the air, the smell of something spoiling, dead animals, and zero trees, just small saplings tied to stakes, all up one side of each street and all down the other. March turned into their drive, and led the way up the walk.

The words of the rental agent came back to her. Oversize family room. Unfinished basement, but real potential. A little paneling, some indoor-outdoor on the floor, and you're in business. A patio out back. You've got yourself a bargain.

A bargain was what she was looking for, March had assured him. Beggars can't be choosers. She who had, as usual, arranged for a loan from her family, had as usual dug herself into their debt, their generous, humiliating clutches, trying, once again, to convince herself that her indebtedness was only temporary.

Beggars can't be choosers, she had said, but Oaknoll was not a place for beggars, the agent shot back. A small, bald-headed man, in whose car March had toured the neighborhood until she, like the car, smelled of a sickly sweet air freshener, and in whose presence March had made an effort to be what she considered cheerful, optimistic, chatty. But she was no match for Mr. Nupples.

Believe you me, he announced. Believe you me, I would go so far as to label this a place for choosers! They don't deal with just anybody here. If you know what I mean. He raised an eyebrow. Here you had a high class home dweller. People who are basically savvy. People interested in keeping things up. Good school. All your branches at the shopping center. Easy access to downtown. Ten minutes and you're there. Parked and all! He snapped his fingers.

March had imagined a place in town. Something older. Near the university. You know what I mean? He knew, but those places went by word of mouth. Waiting lists a mile long.

In the living room Nupples removed a large piece of interlocking wooden squares from the front window. Here you can have a plain bay. He put the piece back. Or, presto, you've gone Colonial.

In the kitchen he spread his arms. Flexibility is the key. And in any case, here is the situation. Here you're all new. Spanking clean, if you read me. He was on his knees, patting the linoleum, and March saw that he had a rip in his trousers. She was terrified that the rip would spread if he insisted on staying down there, bent over, traversing the kitchen. You're not going to wake up some night and see rain pouring through this roof, he promised. You're not coming down some morning and finding the floor's buckled. He stood at last, and stamped hard, and the house seemed to shake. Here you have quality and ease. A community. Friends. A picnic on the Fourth of July, a tree lighting and the Christmas Sing, a spring dance with orchestra and cocktails and the works. Better yet, you might want to buy when the lease is up.

And the neighbors? Are they professors, March wondered. University people?

Instead of answering he took out a nickel and flipped it high into the air. Heads you take this and find happiness. Tails you settle later for a lemon. The coin hit the kitchen light fixture and landed on the linoleum. They both bent to see. Heads.

So, here we are, March said. Our home. She opened the front door. This is the living room and this is the kitchen. Up three steps to the bedrooms—yours—down three for the family room and my bedroom. Down three more to the basement. You can see most of it from here. And touch it, she thought. And I believe they left us this doormat. They looked down at the green rubber mat on the floor, with the outline of the state of Wisconsin, the helpful words, We Like It Here.

The movers were late, cheerful, clumsy. Other children from the neighborhood appeared, wandered through the rooms, demanded grape drinks, Hawaiian Punch, Fritos, popsicles. March gathered up Mia and her pocketbook, and drove to the shopping center, and bought what they had listed. They were future playmates. If only, she thought, driving back, if only she could find their street, their house. They would have to put out pots of flowers or something to remind them which one was theirs. And the strange smell again.

By midafternoon she was able to call the university and ask why she had not heard about her application. After many calls she was connected to a woman who said her application had been rejected.

Oh that's a riot, March said. Seeing as we just moved here for that very reason. So that I could go to graduate school. The woman said that was out of her realm.

Oh boy, March said to one of the movers. We might be going back. He laughed and went on unloading. She felt a little dizzy, but she was already working out a letter of appeal. She would write. They would take her. Whether they wanted her or not.

Dear Dean, she wrote that night. Here we are in our new house, and there is no turning back. We are here to stay. One mother, three children, a possible dog.

Where are you? Alden called from her room.

Right here. In the kitchen.

You're not going out.

No.

We're going to live here and get animals. Dogs and stuff.

Yes.

A cow?

No!

Rabbits.

Shhhh.

Pigs.

That's enough.

There was silence then, and since there were no light bulbs, she opened the refrigerator door in order to write and read for a while. She had given up *The Phenomenon of Man* and switched to Saul Bellow and *Herzog*. Herzog himself was as dear to her as anyone she had ever known. Dear Mr. Bellow, she began.

Dear Mr. Bellow. I take your Herzog everywhere. He is keeping me alive. I think. I heard you lecture this past spring in La Rue! I thought you seemed depressed, and tired, and bored, but you ought to have stayed for the reception. We had Maurice Lenell cookies and fruit punch in the basement of the student center, and though that would probably not inspire a man on a stormy night at a small Catholic college on the outskirts of town, there were alternatives. When Auden came they say there were lively hours over drinks at the house of one of the priests, and there is the Mosquito Inn, a farmer's bar, less than two miles down the road.

It did occur to me that you might have gone home with your friend, a friend of my father's, a man I once met on the train to Chicago. We had coffee in the dining car and talked about you, and it struck me that Louis—I forget the last name—was in worse shape than I was, or Moses Herzog for that matter. Talk about depression, and desperation, and hopelessness, and now I hear this friend, Louis, is seriously ill, and I think I know why. Brooders are the first to go. The heart clams up, organs panic, arteries pop. In the warm rain of grief, tumors bud.

From the kitchen she could hear Alden, or maybe it was Littlemarch muttering in her sleep. Haber low reaches nob lobo. Words that seemed to come from a foreign language. She heard a sigh, and from Mia's room, a slight bump against the wall behind her bed. Then it was quiet.

She went on with her letter. My husband also spreads rumors. Worse than the ones Moses' wife spreads about him. Equally embarrassing. And destructive. I too have lost my sexual confidence. I have no one. In June, in La Rue, I had dinner with a real estate agent who is also a flutist. He took me to a roadhouse where we had chicken in the basket and grasshoppers! To drink. Both of these stirred up old and unpleasant memories.

Later in the evening while we danced to organ music, he put his mouth on my ear, and bit off my earring and swallowed it! How's that for preliminaries, he said. I didn't know whether to laugh or cry, but I told him to cut it out. When we were driving home he said, the music of the spheres could be made with all kinds of instruments.

I also had a date with a heart surgeon who wanted to play tennis. I liked him right away, thinking that if I had the heart attack I had come to expect, he would be useful. But the tennis game went on and on. I began to hate him, and by the time we were back at the apartment my husband Warren—who had come from Chicago to see the children—was there (making himself at home as usual), and before I knew it we were having dinner together. The three of us.

The doctor told us about a sorry picture he came upon daily. The heart of a smoker! Not to mention the lungs. That morning he had examined the x-rays of a man who had come through the clinic for his company physical. A young man. In perfect health. Oh, but the x-rays told another story! The heart was enlarged. There was a tumor the size of a grapefruit on the left lung. There was no saving him.

The doctor looked at us smoking, and said it was only a matter of time. Warren did not seem downhearted, but that night, and for many days after that I found myself wondering about the man with the big heart and the grapefruit in his lung. Having learned the truth about him while he was still in the dark made me feel that we were responsible for him. I hope *you* don't smoke.

I sit here listening to my children talking in their sleep, listening to the hum of the refrigerator, wondering if you have ever felt filled up with words, have ever felt them rising and falling inside of you, and then, nothing. Does that make sense? In my case, the words are there, and they mean so much to me. In fact I feel a serious obligation to them. But there are few concrete results. Perhaps the problem lies in taking the obligation too seriously?

Dawn breaks. It always does, doesn't it. I wonder if there are many like me, pouring out their thoughts to you from kitchens around the country, telling you more than you want to know. I hope not. Please wish me luck. I am here, as I have read you were, once upon a time, to begin graduate work in English. As of this moment, I am not yet in, but I will be. And then. Well, thank you for keeping me going. Should you ever be in Madison . . . Very sincerely, March Rivers Wright.

She closed the refrigerator door, and closed her eyes and pictured Moses Herzog in his garden, at the height of summer, in the Berkshires.

ANOTHER YEAR. Another summer.

They celebrate their birthdays and the end of the school year; nursery school, grade school, graduate school.

March goes to summer school, but the courses are easy. They swim and plant mint. They walk to the beach. They go to La Rue and to the lake. To the Dells. To Spring Green. To Little Switzerland, Little Norway, Little Sweden. To Baraboo to the Ringling Brothers Circus World Museum. At the one-ring circus the glamour of the performance in an amphitheater, or under the big tent in La Rue is diminished. The dogs and ponies look scruffy, and it is impossible not to notice the aging performers' huge muscles and tired faces, their scars and drooping skin.

They drive around. They pick strawberries. They spend days on the Wisconsin River, floating on air mattresses above the golden sandbars.

On warm nights they sit on the front steps and listen to the crickets, and the northbound train, the sound of the siren when one of the patients is discovered missing at the mental hospital up in the hills.

We know our way around now, March thought. The names of the streets, the exact location of the shopping centers, the best place to buy fertilizer, how to use a drill, a screwdriver, a wrench. In the backyard there was a swing set, a plastic wading pool, a sandbox, a picnic table, a tipsy Weber grill. Two green and yellow chairs made of mesh or some material you could see through stood facing each other. A St. Bernard she had given Littlemarch for Christmas—once a puppy now the size of a small horse—wandered at the end of a rope. Flat Top and Motorboat, Alden's cats, and various kittens the cats had delivered in a shoe or in the living room of Alden's doll-house, tumbled in the flower bed. There were bicycles and roller-skates, towels and bathing suits drying on the line.

They had become shoppers. They had discovered shopping centers and discount stores and seasonal bargains where there was always something to buy, even if you didn't need it, or want it. There was always something because after a while you began to tell yourself you did need it. And there was no end to the choices. How about a brand new, super, seven-speed blender, or a four-way automatic vegetable chopper, a chance to wait at the counter with others for their own turn to drop a carrot down the hatch.

They wandered through aisles and ran their fingers over dog sweaters, and children's underwear, tasted miniature hot dogs on toothpicks, and stopped when a man with a yellow top hat waved to them.

Hello, Ladies! How about an electric apple peeler? Look at those peels! How about the portable merry-go-round! See her go! Pump with your feet. The man whose name—Mel—was pinned above his heart urged them on. Hang tight, missies! And they would laugh and whirl away, behaving as dopey shoppers were expected to behave, the children's eyes wide with excitement, March worrying they would break it, would be stuck with it.

And of course someone was always saying how easy it would be to assemble whatever they were looking at. All you need is a screwdriver. A simple screwdriver. Who in America does not have one of those! And you don't have to pay. So much a month. Nothing down. A bargain. It's practically free!

Things. Things to make them happy. Things to make them feel complete. To fill out long weekend hours. The momentary excitement of a possible purchase. Once they had bought a twelve-cup countertop immersion deep fryer. French fries, donuts, donut holes are now possible, March claimed. Who would have thought? Wouldn't you say, in all good faith, yes, now we have everything? Weeks would go by, and then they would find themselves examining a portable dry cleaner, mini television sets shaped like bowling balls, a sign announcing that not five minutes from Oaknoll, a twenty-four-hour store would open before Christmas, a place where it became possible to shop for a fake fur coat or a transistor radio inside of a toy lion at three o'clock in the morning.

In the fall of their second year Lynda had come to live with them. Lynda from La Rue who would not have been able to start college if March had not offered her a place to live. Lorraine Miller, a domineering, angry person March had met during their time in La Rue, had called to say March had to take this student. She was bringing her to Madison immediately. Driving her up on Saturday in her battered old car. You have no choice, Lorraine said on the phone. March had an easy life. Her parents were rich. She didn't have to live in the real world. This poor child's father had abused her, the child's brother had run away, the sister was already into drugs. March could take Lynda. Or she would stay in La Rue and study hairdressing.

When March said she had mentioned this to her parents, and they weren't crazy about the plan, Lorraine said, and whose house is it? Theirs, March had admitted, and offered to take her in anyway.

For March Lynda was company; someone who made her realize how lonely she had been, and the girls were in awe of her. Lynda had pools of white blonde hair that fell about her bare shoulders, like whipped cream, Alden said. And Lynda had delicious-smelling brown gunk she applied to her face. Leg makeup, she explained; and she had white goop she put on her lips. She had a radiant smile. She laughed. She played music. When she was home the house shook. The Stones, the Beatles, Otis Redding, Mama Cass, Aretha Franklin. You didn't know? Where have you all been?

The house came to life, and March saw that the dreariness of their lives had been interrupted. Lynda took the girls shopping on Saturdays, braided their hair with ribbons, put makeup on them so they looked like child hookers. She fried potatoes and baked bread. She brought home boyfriends who were busy organizing the Vietnam protests, black studies marches, Dow Chemical strikes. One night she rode up the drive with a dashing black warrior on a motorcycle, and one night she came in with a bearded teaching assistant who told March that when the revolution came she was not going to be living in this cute little ranch house in suburbia. When the revolution came he and his friends were going to be on top, man, and people like March were going to hit the dust before they had time to lick their fancy, rich lips. March listened. For all she knew he might be right.

Most nights, long after the girls were asleep, March and Lynda sat at the kitchen table, studying, eating Ritz crackers and drinking Cokes. It was what March had always liked best, sitting up late to study, talking about books and now making reading lists for Lynda, leading the way to books she had once devoured.

This you must have, she would say. This you cannot get through without. *In Our Time, The Sound and the Fury, Pale Fire, Tender Is the Night*. How can you have missed Fitzgerald? Hemingway? Then Lynda would want to know how March could have missed Jimi Hendrix? And why didn't March have boyfriends? True, March would acknowledge, but how could Lynda have so many. And did she worry when she slept with one of them and didn't hear from him again. Did that still matter? Yes, of course. You cared, and you worried, and you couldn't sleep. Couldn't eat. You called him up, and asked what's up. What's the matter. And he said, nothing. Like nothing. Like he'd never heard your name before. You took that chance. Sometimes it was a bummer. You know? And drugs? March wanted to know if mescaline was scary? Yes. And marijuana? Not scary. No big deal. Nice. You know? And clothes. Lynda wanted to know how March could wear those funny little dresses, and those shoes. She must be so uncomfortable. She looked like a mother. Well, yes, she was a mother, March would remind her. No, like *your* mother. And how could anyone wear a bra. Why did anyone wear a slip. A slip!

Soon, March said, I'll be going to class barefoot. And throwing out *my* underwear. In October she cut her hair and colored it. Dyed her eyelashes. Still, she felt so old.

❧

THEY WENT to La Rue for Thanksgiving. Her parents said she looked like a hippie. Because her father was now a regent of the university and had no patience with the campus unrest, March refused to discuss what was happening, the strikes that were ongoing, the marches, the students who had been beaten when Dow Chemical came to recruit, the police moving in, and on the news one night, the boy with his teeth in his hands, another student on the ground, bleeding and still being beaten, a cop's nightstick cracking coming down on a boy's skull, and near the curb a dog that had been trampled, its legs in the air, its neck twisted. And once, overnight, hundreds of white crosses that had appeared on Bascom Hill, the crosses making a strangely beautiful sight, row upon row, where there was usually winter mud and litter.

We won't tolerate these disturbances, her father would say, pounding his fist on the coffee table.

❧

CHRISTMAS, AND their little house was full of ribbons, tissue paper, pine boughs, cranberries, the smell of paste, bits of construction paper, glitter, ornaments made out of flour and some other ingredient that had resulted in dozens of angels with certain cranial deformities. They bought an ax, drove to a tree farm and cut down their own tree. They made Christmas cookies, gingerbread men, popcorn balls. Everything they touched was sticky. March bought a life-size stuffed lion for Alden and hid it in her closet. She was exhausted and worried about money. Did anything ever change?

In the late afternoon they lay on March's bed while she read to them. *The Love Song of J. Alfred Prufrock*, she said. T. S. Eliot.

We already know that, Mia said.

March read. Littlemarch snuggled up on one side of her, Mia on the other. Alden curled up near her feet, making soft clicking sounds with her tongue. Littlemarch told Alden to stop hogging the whole space, to *move over*. March hurried on. She wanted to somehow get these rhythms into their heads, to build memories of rhythms for them. Eliot, Auden, Yeats, Shakespeare. Words, names, sounds, a history. She watched them and smiled. She sped along, before the moment when Littlemarch and Mia would fall asleep, when Alden would say to stop, because it was all so complicated, and she did not understand and did not want to think about it.

Was it all right? Wanting them to grow the way she had wanted to grow. Wanting them to have her love of words. She could not look at them without seeing doubt and a longing for reassurance. They needed her to promise them a world she did not think she would ever be able to give them, a childhood that would be gone before she had managed to summon enough from what little she had to provide.

Sometimes as they all started off in the morning, Littlemarch and Alden with their hands in their pockets, shuffling along, Mia dragging her bear, she could not imagine them ever getting to the end of the street. Littlemarch would already be worrying about the stupid teacher who showed her math paper to the class and made fun of her mistakes. Alden would be talking about a lost book. On those mornings she wanted to stop them, to clutch them to her, to say, don't worry. And sometimes she did. Or, late at night she would go into their rooms, and think about waking them to tell them she loved them, to tell them she was sorry they were sometimes lonely or frightened. But sometimes on days when she came home from class and they were there on the steps, even the dog with his tongue hanging out, forming what she thought of as the lineup, all of them waiting, eager, pleased, anxious, she would wonder for a moment if she would even be able to get out of the car.

March went on reading. Listen, she said, and jiggled the sleepy girls. Oh this is so great. 'And indeed there will be time / For the yellow smoke that slides along the street / Rubbing its back upon the window-panes; / There will be time, there will be time / To prepare a face to meet the faces that you meet . . .' She smiled. Mia yawned and pressed closer. The door slammed. The dog barked. One of the cats leapt to the top of the lampshade. Lynda called out, I'm home. I'm home.

There was the thud of books on the kitchen table, the sound of the stereo going; and Lynda shouting over the throb of Jimi Hendrix, I'm in love, I'm in love! She came into the bedroom and looked at herself in the mirror. She smiled and turned to them. March the mom! She laughed and tossed a book in the air. This you will not believe. William Faulkner. My hero. She read the title. *Absalom, Absalom!* She plunked down on the edge of the bed, and took presents wrapped in red tissue paper from her book bag and handed one to each of the girls. In my book, you are all perfect, she said. All of you. Perfect. My family.

WARREN TOOK the girls for a weekend. When he brought them back he asked March to have dinner with him. I must be crazy, she thought pulling on a green dress and black leggings after the girls argued that she should not wear the black dress because she always wore black and black was so sad.

You shouldn't be sad, Littlemarch said. Because you are going with Daddo to the place where you know they have the red kiddy cocktails, and the organ player and the bear on the wall. Maybe they should go with her, Alden suggested. But March shook her head. She said they needed to talk.

Warren had news. He had fallen in love. People do, he said. And it was time. Time for them to fish or cut bait. And Mary Lou was getting itchy. She'd had her feet fixed.

March wanted to laugh. What's the matter with her feet?

Nothing. There was something, but now they're fine. But she had done this for him. Brave Mary Lou.

And we're not going anywhere, Warren was saying. We never were. We never will.

We had been, she wanted to say. Once. She studied the menu.

We're doing the apartment in all white.

Why?

With a zebra rug and a glass coffee table. All white. Very modern. He was lighting matches as though he had recently discovered fire. The woman at the organ was nodding and smiling in a grim sort of way.

Time flies, March. I'll be forty. You'll be thirty-five. Six. Sweet thirty-six?

Five.

Still, not exactly spring chickens, are we?

She thought how much she was able to hate him. In his plaid jacket. All those colors. The plaid jacket, and his green wool sweater, green the color of turtles, the small wet turtles that had crawled across their living room floor in Chicago and disappeared into the fireplace.

They were drinking chilled red wine, eating the roast beef, the baked potatoes with sour cream, the defiant wedge of iceberg lettuce with Roquefort dressing, the Wisconsin roadhouse food Warren loved.

We thought we'd have the wedding in Galena. In May. When the weather will be. Be. He shook his head. What would the weather be in May. In May? Pause. He lit another match. We were thinking about having the bunnies. Having them carry little baskets of flowers or something. Cute. But what would they do afterwards? And when you've already been married once. Not that Mary Lou's ever been married. Or just for a while.

Oh, for Christ's sake, Warren. For a while? How old is she?

Twenty-five. Six. In that neighborhood. I think you'd like her. The bunnies do.

They've only met her once. She's twenty-five or six so she'll want children. You know she'll want children.

She can't have children. Or she probably can't. She likes children, but that's up in the air. Having them.

Warren, once upon a time you said she had never been married. Once upon a time you said she lived above you. You would hear her up there in her apartment at night, so lonely, so sad. And you would call her up, and she would come down for a nightcap. And after a while she would go back up to her apartment, and you would think about her up there in her high heels, tap tapping away. Clomp, clomp, tip tap, even with her wounded feet, up there in her high heels, so alone. But then. It turned out she had never lived above you. She had always lived *with* you.

I wanted to ease you in. Keep her upstairs for a while. Then when you got used to the idea of her. Then I thought I'd say she was with me. I'd wait. Then I'd bring her down.

March shook her head.

Warren poured more wine. I've been thinking about your father a lot. How is old A.? How is old Noonie? God, I miss them. I do, March. I wish you'd give them my regards. Maybe I could pop in some day when I'm passing through La Rue. I don't suppose they'd like to meet Mary Lou. Maybe not. I want you to meet her though. You're practically related! Sort of stepsisters, aren't you? Hmmm? And if she should happen to have a baby at some point, you would be a kind of stepmother.

Warren, Mary Lou is not my stepsister or my anything. And I am never going to be this child's stepmother. In a million years.

Just a thought.

Well, have another thought.

You should get married, March. You should. Good for you. And for the bunnies. Mary Lou and I have a group of friends now. We play bridge. And golf. It's better to be married. You're not left out of things.

You want me to be married? After all of this. After everything. After trying to become someone. To matter. March could not breathe for a moment. How could he say these things. I think I'd die, she said. When I think about being married I think about that pink chair that didn't have any arms. And the bed, and the blue and white wallpaper, and all the coat hangers, and the window shades. It was so bleak. And cold. And we needed carpets. And there were too many light bulbs that didn't work. The lamps. The broken lamps. I loved you and I was so. So something. Bleak?

Warren said he was going to the gentlemen's room. Of course he would want to escape from her after that, March thought, but he even talked in a funny way now. Gentlemen's room? Where had that come from?

It seemed to her that he had become this person who never talked anymore about the books he would write, or going to Hollywood, or the beach at Malibu. Maybe just as well. But he had been someone who dreamed of becoming. Who cared about his life. Maybe she was just envious. But once he had been so handsome, desirable, strange, unlike other men. Funny. Very funny. And a troublemaker. And that had appealed to her. Making up stories about her father and mother, turning her parents into absurd movie stars. He had been someone whose struggle to understand his life had touched something in her, and she had understood his despair and his despairing struggle. She had been able to relate to his desperation. In him, had she only seen herself?

She had imagined him in another time. An explorer, a navigator, someone setting forth, believing in his destiny. She closed her eyes and saw Warren and his men on the shores of Santo Domingo. And then what? Then things had gone wrong. In the end there was a shipwreck. There was disgrace, poverty, bad health. And perhaps Warren knew all about that. Perhaps he knew quite well that he was not going there, knew that he wanted what most people wanted, and had it now, and was glad.

Now he played bridge and golf. He wore clothes to fit this jolly new arrangement. He wore shoes without laces, little boots, and a yellow turtleneck under his sweater. He wore a hideous sport coat, and a car coat. He had a mustache. A *mustache*. Suddenly she had wanted to hit him, and perhaps he had sensed that too. He was safe now in the men's room. With his mustache and his cigar. She could imagine him selling cars. He was forever going after his own car with a special whisk broom. She could picture him pulling the wool over someone's eyes. Hers. Once she had looked up the origin of that expression, and found there wasn't one. And his all white apartment. What did that mean, she had asked Alden, and Alden had said it just meant you had all your stuff white.

Then, did Warren still wake in the night, did he pull back from his soggy pillow, and rub the sweat from his forehead, did he go into the kitchen for quarts of ginger ale to put out the fire, sit in his leather chair, smoking and drinking Heaven Hill, and brooding? Did he come in on winter nights with his wet feet, with shoes all streaked with salt waves, his frozen gloves that stood on their own fingers, ready to do a cakewalk on the hall table where he had thrown them? Did he slosh and drift in a tub of hot water, did he still dream of inching his way up over the Rockies, did he still picture himself coming down into California, to the flat, gray edges of the Pacific. Did he break dishes. Did he hit Mary Lou. Did he have regrets. About her. About them?

No, because as he explained, installed once again across from her, with his cigar and another glass of wine in hand. No, because it was better this way. Because, he said, looking up, dabbing with his napkin at some spot on his sleeve. Because she loves me.

He said this again. She loves me. The few words were partly a challenge, partly a statement of something newly discovered.

What could she say. Oddly enough, in that moment, she felt happy for him. Full of absurd, moronic, warm affection, and relief. Warren was loved. He was not alone.

I'm glad, she said.

⟨⟩

IN JANUARY March took the Greyhound bus to Chicago. She stayed with an aunt, and went on a blind date her friends had arranged. A divorce present, they said. Like a wedding present.

The next day March stood with Leslie and Margo—from the old days—and her lawyer, and Warren's lawyer in a room smelling of wet wool. The judge asked about her name. Did she wish to keep that last name. The married name.

She did. After all. It was hers.

Very well then.

Divorce granted.

March and Leslie and Margo retreated to a coffee shop on La Salle Street, to celebrate, they said.

March is alive and well! Amazing. And Wisconsin? Tell us about Wisconsin. They spoke of it as a foreign country, and March knew it would always be that. Even in the Midwest. They really wanted to talk about their own lives. About Chicago. How it had changed. How the times had changed! How they had changed. How exciting life had become.

People who had been married were now divorced. Old best friends no longer spoke to each other. The Hoppers and the Livingstons? Divorced and then married to each other. Willy Livingston now with Alley Hopper. Sally Livingston with Bobo Hopper. Separations, love affairs, even nervous breakdowns were normal. Acceptable. Expected! You never had to worry about being pregnant anymore, not really; and if you were, and you weren't sure who the father was, and you told the pediatrician, the pediatrician would say, my dear, you have no idea how many times I've heard that.

Everyone is going to a shrink now, Margo said. Encounter groups are big. You get together with other people, and you tell about your feelings. You open up. Let it all out.

There's a fantastic man who comes from New York, Leslie said. He only does small groups. I don't mean he fucks them. He talks to them. He gets them to howl. Maybe throw themselves on the floor. On the carpet. He brings this carpet from New York. Maybe to encourage them. People love it. You have to sign up months in advance. People say they come out totally changed. Overnight.

Really, March said. And that's a good thing?

You start leading a new life. You're not a victim. You're in control. You control your own life.

You think of yourself as an onion. Then this man helps you peel off the layers of skin.

And what if there's nothing there, March said. Like Peer Gynt.

Oh, March. The bookworm. But you were the first. I envied you, Margo said.

You envied me?

Yes. You just went ahead. You said, fuck marriage. I'm out of here. We all envied you, Leslie said.

March had not thought of it in quite that way. When she considered Leslie and Margo, she thought she probably envied them. Leslie had been arrested in August during the protests before the convention. Her husband had been beaten by the police in Grant Park. Margo had gone to Italy to shoot a film on Van Gogh for the Art Institute. She had fallen in love with a man who picked her up on his motorcycle, and built perfect haystacks for her in Illinois when they couldn't find any in Italy. Leslie had briefly left her very dignified husband for a tennis pro who had been married twice, and had white rabbit teeth, and was said to have amazing ideas about sex.

March admired their energy and their optimism, their nerve and their love affairs. They didn't make everything sound so serious, so deadly. Margo kept saying fuck, and this shocked March, but maybe language was changing. And their clothes. They were dressed up. They wore boots up to their knees, and tiny skirts. And they looked so glamorous, while she looked, she thought, merely presentable.

Remember how we used to sit all day in that park, in Goudy Square, with the babies, Margo said, and suddenly they were talking about the old days when they gave dinner parties, when they made cheese soufflés and cherries jubilee, when people drank after-dinner drinks.

Stingers, Margo cried. And that stuff with the coffee beans floating around! When you woke up in the morning with a hangover and the baby propped with a bottle.

When we gave parties with themes, Leslie said. Remember, March, when you wrote the musical about Chicago, and we all had to take parts? When we made movies and had the film festival, when we taught in that school on the south side, and ran out of gas, and the time that guy held you up? When Warren gave the St. Valentine's Day Massacre party? When Warren got so drunk and turned the whole dinner table upside down. When Ronald Crip sailed all the dinner plates out our window into Lincoln Park, and the doorman collected them and brought them to the door. When Lou Lou what's her name threw her hamster down the incinerator and the same doorman brought it back up?

March, you had the blind date last night, Margo said. We forgot! You had that date with the ad man. With Buzzer Mills. How was it?

March shook her head. He said when he was divorced it was the happiest day of his life. I said I thought of it as the formal conclusion to a marriage that had failed and failed. They nodded.

He said he thought he wanted me. Did I know what he meant? I said I did, but I was going back to my aunt's for the night. He said, you're not much of a swinger, are you?

They laughed. They said good-bye. They hugged each other. Margo and Leslie climbed into a taxi. March walked to the Greyhound station, dawdling, kicking snow banks. She was early, and she took her copy of *The Lime Twig* from her knapsack. She felt she might always be sad, that this sadness might not leave her, was that perhaps a choice? Was that correct? That conclusion? Sadness was the path she had chosen, and the best she might be able to manage was a life that was not too sad most of the time.

She opened her book, and read until the Madison bus was called. She had left her overnight bag at the coffee shop. There had been time to go back, but she wasn't going back. She would buy a new bag, she decided; buy a nightgown, a toothbrush, toothpaste, lipstick, outrageous dental floss, the works, become extravagant, glamorous, flamboyant.

The bus left the city behind and took the O'Hare, Rockford exit, then north and west toward Madison. Then they were in the country, and it was already dark and she could not see to read. She could see the lights in the farmhouses, and in the little towns along the freeway, and she was grateful for the warmth, and the dark, the comforting knowledge that nothing could reach her for a while. She thought that being inside of the bus was like being inside of a person, the not yet born, someone floating in darkness. She smiled because it occurred to her that the lights never worked in either place.

SUDDENLY, WITH snow on the ground, there was a week of warm weather. Brave, pathetic white snow flowers appeared, and in the classrooms windows were opened. Because of a strike, and war protests, there was a general air of disarray on the campus. Many students stayed away, but graduate students like March felt they had too much at stake. An incomplete would kill them. They needed the credits. They needed to get on with their lives, to get out of here. So on a warm Wednesday afternoon March read her seminar paper, and the eight other students fiddled with notebooks, and pens, lit cigarettes, yawned, gazed with interest at the palms of their hands.

March cleared her throat.

Mr. Patchman peered over his glasses. Please. Go on, please.

She was reading from the William Dean Howells–Mark Twain letters. Two old men, friends for decades, now shoring each other up, consoling each other about the losses that came with age. March who had not cried for how long, months and months—as good as forever—felt the tears, not in her eyes but in her throat, and ground the toes of her boots into the loose floorboards under her chair, dug her fingers into the soft pockets of her jeans.

The bell rang and she hurried to finish as the others closed their notebooks, shot wads of paper cups and cigarette butts into the wastebasket, pushed back their chairs. Mr. Patchman blew his nose on a white handkerchief he took from his breast pocket. Very moving. A very moving story, I think. Indeed. Thank you.

March gathered her books into her book bag, and fastened the straps. Mr. Patchman had already closed his briefcase. In a moment he would be scuttling down the hall to his office where he would close the door and lock it, and go on with his examination of Washington Irving's papers. If anyone knocked it was assumed that he would hold his breath and pretend to be out. If a student with an appointment showed up he would open the door, and perch on the edge of his chair until the student had asked for approval of a seminar paper, and whether the answer was yes or no, he would rise, look at his watch, move toward the door. If the answer was no, he would explain that the list he had prepared would afford more interesting research possibilities than any a student might prepare on her own. If the student would be so kind as to review the list, examine it once again. You do have a copy? Thank you so much. The door would be closed, the lock would be turned.

March had known him since the fall, and loved his fussiness, his tidy ways, his impatience. He had, he said, one, at the most two, or three last tasks. March and the others had so much time, but he had so little. He did what he could. For Valentine's Day his wife baked cookies for these young people. Lovely, lacy oatmeal cookies. Like snowflakes. Packed in a round red tin, between layers of wax paper.

March followed him down the hall. Mr. Patchman. I can't tell you how much this class means to me. All that we've read.

Good. Good. Read. Read. The more the better. Everywhere. Always. Waiting for the bus, on the bus, at meals. No point in just looking into space. Waiting for the sun to rise and set.

What I wanted to say. I've been thinking more about the whole development of American literature. Carving out something new, a new voice. Daring to give form to what was just a longing, a rhythm in the air, in people's dreams, in the unspoken. She stopped for breath and sped on. I see now what courage it took, what daring. The need to break with tradition, to forge something new.

Quite, Mr. Patchman said. Extraordinary. A large bite indeed.

People say the novel is finished, but I believe in the possibility. Today, tomorrow, two, or three, or four writers who will have the courage and the power and the largeness of spirit to speak to us, to speak for us.

One must persist, he said. He was fumbling with his key now. It hung on a chain that stretched from some place inside his suit coat—from his suspenders? He was examining his watch with the cracked glass.

March went on. I have always thought of the artist as someone whose failure to participate was a failure to live. Someone locked away. A dreamer. I suppose that's because of my background. In my family they say, life is not a spectator sport. In my family the artist is not someone to emulate. The isolation and the solitude of a writer are not really acceptable when a person should be out doing something. God knows what. A writer's courage might never be recognized. Recognition, if it came, might come too late.

Mr. Patchman was at his desk, peering anxiously over the edge of the typewriter, a small battered manual that would have looked at home in a museum, but would never collect dust under his stained, tap taping fingers. Tell me, Mrs. Wright. You are a candidate for the PhD? Do you propose to teach? I wondered if you had ever thought of writing. Have you thought of that?

It had been a long time since someone had asked her about writing. Sometimes it was hard for her to think of herself as a writer. She had gone on with her novel, it had never occurred to her to stop, but she thought more and more about a way to earn money. With her degree she would find a teaching job.

I have part of a novel, she said. Sometimes though that seems like part of another life, a long time ago. I'll always be a writer. But now I sit at the kitchen table at night, translating Old English sermons, reading eighteenth-century plays, comedies! And I know that right here, on the hill, war protesters are being beaten. Black students are fighting for black studies. I feel I have to *do* something.

I have devoted forty-five years of my life to this university, Mr. Patchman said. Forty-five years. I have never had cause to regret those years. I feel my work has been of some value to the world. As you know, I have specialized in the nineteenth-century American writers for the most part. Some of them rather obscure, perhaps. But necessary. A part of the whole. Not without merit.

I realize that, March said. Your seminars have changed my life. They have made me care again. About so many things.

A bell rang, and she noticed that the hall had emptied once more. Well, I'm sorry to have taken so much time. I'd better be running.

I'll be needing someone to help with my research this semester. I don't suppose you would be interested?

Of course I would be. I would love to help, she said. I would be honored.

You'll be paid for your time, of course. On Friday then we'll speak about it. His chin was sinking into his collar, and he was reaching for his note cards, his thin fingers shuffling the corners as March said good-bye and started down the hall. Behind her she heard the door close and the lock turn.

She went down the steps thinking, now I'm an assistant, a paid assistant, for once. Instead of borrowing all the time, writing to ask if I could have just a bit extra this month, apologizing yet again, trying to get Warren to send his check on time, I'll have something of my own. And that is good. Pocket change, but still. Good to be asked, and who was she to be anything but grateful, but already she was worried about taking on more. She had the French cram course at seven-thirty in the morning, the dog to the vet, someone to fix the dryer, the exhaust pipe on the car dangling, someone at Alden's school to see about. Still, still, it was a step, a confirmation. She would manage.

She was coming down the hill when two girls stopped her and grabbed her coat collar.

There's a strike on. Nobody goes on the hill. Nobody goes to class.

The smaller of the two knocked her glasses off, and March said, Are you crazy. People have appointments. People have to work. She pulled a button from her coat pocket, something she had picked up months before, a stupid button. Kiss Don't Kill. She flashed it at them and they let her go. She tried to act as though she was accustomed to this kind of bullying, but truthfully they had terrified her. She retrieved her glasses, broken now, and went on.

Even in the library it was impossible to study, these days. She would settle down with her books and the fire alarm would be touched off. They would have to grab their books bags and get out. When she went to class she marched through rows of National Guard soldiers, their bayonets fixed, young men who might have been in Vietnam, so for the moment they might be called lucky. The signs of anger and violence had become ordinary. The day before, she had come out of the bookstore, and within minutes the street had filled with hundreds of students heading for the hill. She joined them, and as they moved along the crowd grew until she could look back and see thousands, curb to curb, block after block, and on and on until they curved out of sight. Sirens whined, cameras clicked and whirred, and whether they were marching against the war, or the federal government, or the state, or the university, or high prices, or stores that sold California grapes, or police repression, or against all authority was not the question. They were out there, making a statement. On that day they followed the leaders, and late in the day they got what they had wanted, a showdown. More arrests, tear gas, an enemy that was outraged, outwitted, outnumbered.

On some days the papers might report as many as eight or ten thousand on the move. Always there were students with armbands and walkie-talkies preparing for whatever would happen next, students with bandages, their badges of honor, and some who wore motorcycle helmets, the uniform of war. It was not only Vietnam, or the demand for black studies, there was an underlying rage any fool could feel. For March there was no question of which side she was on, but she did not like being ordered by any group. The students in charge of the strikes and the leaders under them made all sorts of demands, ran about flushed with new importance, and treated the followers like children. It seemed to March that there were enough restrictions on her life already. At night she sat at the kitchen table and conjugated verbs, and read about the war, read *The Making of a Quagmire*, and sensed that they were losing the war but would go on fighting it.

WITH SPRING came thunderstorms, and driving home one afternoon March thought what a serious storm would do to the neighborhood. Even on a sunny day the houses looked so small, so tentative, and because the development was new the houses were forever undergoing some sort of improvement. A patio would appear, then a split rail fence, another row of shrubs, a small tree tied to a small stake. So much work and time consumed in what might have been an attempt to make the houses take hold and settle in. She could imagine a straight wind or a tornado coming through and all the gold carpeting, and paneling, and artificial plants, the dinette sets, the flowered curtains in the kitchens, the bedroom sets, the bathroom carpeting and matching toilet seat covers, the portable tool sheds and barbeques shooting in one triumphant explosion up from their orderly arrangements, high into the sky. And when they settled down in one backyard or another, everything would look alike, and nobody would ever be able to tell what had belonged to whom.

On warm days the street hummed with radios playing, the blast of hoses turned on storm windows, and on hub caps that offered a tinny response. Gardeners were out in full force. In one backyard after another there were neat rows of buried treasure. Popsicle sticks with seed packages announced what might appear one day, strings formed straight lines through patches of dirt, a festival of orderly productivity that impressed March, and overwhelmed her. Why did she have her little collection of weeds, crabgrass, chewed-up bulbs. She rummaged around out there for an afternoon and thought she had probably made things worse.

All up and down the block there was action, but of a kind far removed from the chaos at the university. There would be no marches here. And not much of the neighborly camaraderie she had once imagined either.

When she asked to borrow a ladder her neighbor said, Good fences. He repeated this mantra again, in case she was hard of hearing. When March and the girls sat in the car listening to the radio after Martin Luther King's assassination the woman next door had said, King. King. That's all you hear anymore. When Alden said they had just been to the march for him, the woman, Mrs. Crandle, shook her head. Alden persisted. There were thousands of people at the march, Mrs. Crandle. The whole city was there. Mrs. Crandle went into her garage and lowered the door.

The neighborhood made March long for the city again, a bookstore, a coffee shop, something, anything, and then she would remember how lonely she had felt there too.

Actually she had two friends, Lutte and Myra, the two women who had asked her for coffee when she first moved into Oaknoll, women who had known each other for years, who no longer spoke to each other. Neither one would say what had happened. For years they had met for coffee, picked berries at the same farm, made jam together, fed each other's cats and dogs, but then. But then. Myra would stare across the street and shrug. That Lutte. And in her kitchen Lutte would take a cake from the oven and slam the door. That Myra.

For March, they were company, women she had come to care about and feel comfortable with. They had called on her on moving day, brought her pies, sent their husbands to help with the snow-blower, the assembling of the swing set. The other women in the neighborhood did not talk to her, mostly because, as Lutte explained, she was single, a potential troublemaker.

They're afraid you'll start something. They don't like anybody different here. Women who aren't married, your student who comes home on the motorcycle, who has the boyfriend with long hair. They like people who work on their lawns, who polish their cars, keep them all shiny so the street looks good.

Lutte's life in Germany as a child during the war years, when she had been forced to work on a farm, to live on onions, to lose her toes to frostbite, had made her permanently needy. You want something so bad, and you finally get it, and it runs your life, she said. You want your house to look nice, but it's never nice enough. There's always something. New stones for the patio. More roses over there. A new hedge behind the roses. Maybe a fence. And gravel. White gravel on the walk. At three o'clock in the morning you lie awake. You think, gravel.

Lutte and her husband worked separate twelve-hour shifts packaging bacon and sausages at the Oscar Meyer plant, and rarely saw each other. When Lutte had the night shift she claimed she could not sleep during the day. And if she did sleep, who would keep the house clean. Who would bake, and can, and freeze, and sew if she didn't. Who would make sure the kids stayed out of trouble, got into the university, and stayed in. Got educated. So they didn't end up like her, going to work in the summer in a winter coat, working in a freezing room, getting wet feet, getting pneumonia. What if they end up like me, she said. I still can't speak English. Right?

March and the girls would sit in her spotless kitchen, and stuff themselves on lasagna, strawberry shortcake, apple pies. They had worked their way through hundreds of Christmas cookies, Lincoln logs and cherry tarts. On the Fourth of July they ate potato salad, fried chicken, baking powder biscuits, meringues with ice cream and strawberries.

Eat more, Lutte would say, and they would try. You don't like it, she would say, and they would keep trying.

In the summer they would go with her to pick strawberries, or raspberries, or green beans, or whatever she was after that week. March loved the mornings when they would go out to a farm, bouncing in the back of Lutte's blue pickup, watching the sun come over the fields, spotting an octagonal barn, a colt leaping, sharing the adventure of being up and out so early. The country mornings reminded her of her childhood, of the farms beyond La Rue where they would go to the roadside stands for corn and tomatoes in the summer.

Myra did not work, and her daughter Hester was Alden's age; and the two played together every day with an obsessive commitment to many small, rubber kittle dolls that frequently exchanged rubber heads. They played, and March and Myra talked. Myra said her life was depressing, and to underline this she always wore brown. Her house was brown too. The furniture and the carpeting were brown. Even the kitchen. Also, March noticed, she would cut the paper napkins in half before she used them, just as she would give the girls a half of a sandwich, half of a banana, not so much to save money March had decided, as to cut down, to make everything in life smaller, lesser, least. But she was smart and funny. She hated Madison, hated the neighborhood, dreamed of escape. She swore she had never been anywhere but the Dells, to Florida fifteen years ago. Then she would tell about these trips and make them sound quite hilarious.

Myra would drop by for a glass of wine, a cigarette, a Valium, and they would talk about books. She was a reader, and March would hand over her own lists, writers she had discovered, writers neither of them had heard of before, Barthelme, Robbe-Grillet, Gaddis, Queneau. Then Myra would look through March's notes and sometimes she would talk about going back to college; but when the time came to register, she would say she was too old. Thirty-four. Not exactly ancient, March would argue, but she knew that sometimes she too felt old, that life might already have passed her by.

Myra's latest excuse was a figure skating test. She said, I got up to the test, and I flubbed.

Figure skating, March cried. Figure skating! I went to that place and I had to skate with a goddamned chair! I will go with you to register. You are smart. They need you. Students are dropping out like flies. Everyone is in Vietnam. Or running away. Going to Canada. Or trying to blow the place up. Go now before they do.

No. It's easy for you, Myra said. You're strong.

Myra, I am a disaster. A walking nut case. If I can manage, anyone can.

No. It's not going to happen. But you'll get out of here. One day you'll be gone.

Myra and her husband, dark-eyed Juley, had separated after Christmas, and in some ways the two of them reminded March of her years with Warren. They could not live together. They could not be rid of each other. Juley had moved to an apartment near the university, but he was often back at the house. March would see him cutting the grass, washing his car, throwing a ball for their dog. She would wave and he would wander up the street to talk.

Myra was sick, Juley would say. She needed help. March told him that she had been that way. For a long time. I'm better, she told him. But it happens so slowly. You start with the smallest step you can imagine, and sometimes that's too much. She spoke with assurance, but she felt that her own existence was still tenuous. What made her think she could offer advice?

You're alive, March, Juley said. You won't stay here. You'll leave. He asked her to come away with him for a day on the river, just the two of them. In another month the weather would be warm and they would float from one sandbar to another, letting the current carry them. March remembered doing that the year before. She often thought of the lovely gold color of the sand, the way the current had moved them along, the lazy beauty of that day when she and the girls and Myra and Juley and their daughter had gone together. Now on a warm night she and Juley walked down to the lake at the end of the street and sat on the dock. When she kissed him she thought how young he seemed, like a boy, his face already almost black from the sun. She wanted to go away with him, but she knew she wouldn't.

And Myra was no fool. When March was studying that night there was a knock on the door and Myra came into the kitchen. Please, she said, standing there for a moment, looking down at the paper March was writing. Please, March. Don't.

❧

MARCH DID think about getting out. She dreamed about it, dreamed about beating it down unfamiliar station steps for an outbound train. Her suitcase would open as she ran, her clothes and papers would scatter, the bits of her novel would go up into the sky and disappear, she would call out. Wait. Wait! Sometimes the train was on its way to La Rue. Sometimes the train was just on its way to somewhere else. Always, she was desperate to be on it. She would open her eyes.

She no longer woke suddenly, or saw her other self on the ceiling, gazing down at her, threatening a permanent separation. Now and then her heart pounded, hammered away in there to remind her that no, she was not exactly home free, but this did not happen often. She went to class. She studied. She took care of the girls. The days were predictable. They had come here full of hope and plenty of doubt; shabby, worn-out souls from just down the interstate, and they had found a safe haven. And rewards. Academia, green grass, frozen custard, kitty litter, birthday parties, the Beatles, Lynda and her boyfriends. It wasn't perfect, but it was bearable and she should be grateful. She *was* grateful. But she could not be grateful indefinitely.

During the winter she had written to the fiction editor at *Playboy* magazine, asking him to let her know of any editorial jobs there, telling him about whatever it was she was reading. We are doing Melville now, she wrote. *Moby Dick* again and *Clarel* which I had not read before. He would write back. He was actually interested in what she was reading. What had she thought of *Typee*. And *Bartleby*. He was also interested in Warren. He had published one of his hideous stories in *Playboy*. He urged her to come to Chicago.

The thought of making the trip to Chicago, of actually sitting down with this man, of trying to think of something to say kept her awake most nights for a week. Finally, on a Friday in June she took the bus into the city, and walked up Michigan Avenue to the Playboy building. On the floor where the fiction and editorial offices were crammed together, young men in blue jeans and women in miniskirts flew past her and she caught the feeling of energy in the air—though Robie's secretary who came to meet her and take her to his office was a sweet plump woman in a navy blue suit. It all reminded March of years ago at Doubleday. Not necessarily a good omen, but then they were in the fancy corner office and Robie was stepping out from behind his desk, straightening his tie, bowing slightly, reminding her of her father.

He introduced her to his assistant, a young man with a beard who looked very much like the rest of the young men, and said they would go immediately to lunch at the Cape Cod Room. He took her arm as they crossed the street to the Drake, and as soon as they were seated in the restaurant ordered each of them a martini, again reminding her of her father.

He wanted to know what she thought of the fiction he published and she was ready to talk about it all night if necessary. What did she think? Of Saul Bellow. Of Nadine Gordimer. Bruce Jay Friedman. Alberto Moravia. Joyce Carol Oates, Carlos Fuentes. March laughed. What would anyone think. The list was extraordinary. She had read them all. She liked a story by someone she had never heard of. Paul Theroux. A new one, Robie said, his latest discovery, and she must meet him. And she would like meeting Saul Bellow. And Nelson Algren. Of course she was a writer too, he said. Yes. And she knew *he* was. She had read his novel. He smiled and lit a cigar. Was March considering leaving Madison. Not working toward her PhD, but looking for something away from the academic world? But then would she be afraid to move her family back to Chicago. How would it seem for her to be here, near Warren again. March was careful. She knew he found Warren amusing, wonderful company. Warren the mystery writer, the cheery survivor of the March Wars. Old Warren pouring himself another Heaven Hill, lighting *his* cigar, summing up the plot line for *Blood on the Dining Room Table*.

The children miss him, she said. I think he misses them.

I hear Mary Lou is pregnant, he said.

March nodded. Mary Lou who could not have children could in fact have children. Then again, why should this matter to her?

I may be making changes in the office, Robie said. Sooner than I might have. My assistant. We'll see. In any case, would you be interested?

They were finishing lunch, and March said she would certainly be interested. She was through with classes, and she was definitely looking for a job. She had sent her resume to a few small presses and to private schools in the Chicago area.

He would like to read the novel she was working on. Would that be something she might let him see, he wondered. Oh yes. What there was of it. They stood on the windy corner of Michigan and Walton. Down one block was the first apartment she and Warren had rented when they arrived in Chicago. Next to a hangout for the Mafia, above Elizabeth Arden's salon. Ten years. Blue and white striped wallpaper in the bedroom. Summer. Littlemarch spitting up on Warren's new suit. Someone coming for dinner. Warren mopping up the suit with the fancy Marghab cocktail napkins, throwing the napkins out the window onto the roof of the Chinese restaurant.

Robie signaled for a taxi and kissed her on the cheek. We'll be in touch.

All the way back to Madison she wondered if she would have the nerve, the determination and ambition to get rid of the house, move the girls, go back. She honestly didn't know yet. She thought about what the move would be like for them. And about what it might mean for her, for her future, her writing. Once after her trip to New York she had written to Maggie Cousins at Doubleday, but she had never produced the outline, the promised pages. What there was of the novel was in a box on her desk, more precisely in her desk, in the bottom drawer. The paper had become thin, and faintly colored, not exactly yellow, more a pale biscuit color, and the older pages tore easily at the corners. Once in a while she would take them out and hold them, carefully, like a newborn.

Would it, would they, the pages, ever become something. She read Robert Walser. 'Just wait,' he wrote. 'The good will come. Goodness is always closer to us than we think. Patience brings roses.' She copied the words on a note card and stuck the card in her mirror. She cheered herself by telling herself that as the girls grew older she would have more time, as the family changed in ways, over time, she too would change.

❧❧

THE FAMILY—her other family—was falling apart, and strangely enough she was needed. Will you do me a favor, her father said in July. He had decided to have neurosurgery for a nerve condition known as tic douloureux, something that caused sudden stabbing pain on one side of his face. At the Mayo Clinic they would operate and move the blood vessels pressing on the nerves at the base of his skull. A family member was needed, someone to be there for him.

For much of her life March had known people from La Rue who traveled to Rochester, to the Mayo Clinic to see what terrible fate might be awaiting them. Now, her mother was in bed in La Rue with her leg in a cast after a knee operation. Her brother and sister were away. March was in charge of three children and two invalids.

She flew to Rochester, in some ways a typical Midwestern city. The wide tree-lined streets and mansions crumbling, the neighborhoods pushing out to flat lands on the edges. The terrible bareness. And yet, a place where she felt very much at home. It was like La Rue turned into a hospital town. People in wheelchairs whizzed along; people at the hotel cafeteria discussed diseases, their tests, their diets. Jell-O for me, a woman would say with a hearty chuckle. I'll be doing toast no butter, her companion would chirp.

March sat with her father after he was settled in his room at St. Mary's hospital, and later had dinner at the restaurant on the hotel roof. At the next table were friends of her family from Oshkosh. We come every year, they announced. Mayo's is the only place. We always stay here at the Kahler. It's the only hotel. They looked very pleased.

The next day during the operation March paced around the streets near the hospital, ducked into a chapel to say a prayer, feeling every bit a fraud, but pleading anyway. Let the operation be a success, let all be well. Finally, sometime late in the afternoon she was allowed into the intensive care unit. Now and then her father opened his eyes and smiled from beneath layers of bandages that covered his head. With the first two fingers of his hand he formed a V. March put her hand over his, gently, gently, a wing touching. I am here. I am here. When they moved him to his room, she sat with him through the night, anxious that something might happen if she left him alone.

Early the next morning, she walked back to the hotel through empty streets that were already sticky from the heat. The heels of her sandals settled into the soft tar in places, and she imagined a shower, coffee, clean clothes. Instead, she opened the door to her room and it was bare. The bed was made. Her suitcase was gone.

Was she losing her mind? I have no things, no things, she said. Where are my things? She wept like a fool at the manager's desk. The manager seemed at ease. Yes. Yes. Guests went off to the hospital and did not return. Ever. In some cases. He smiled and raised an eyebrow. But her reservation was for three days! The man nodded. There was much commotion in the hotel these days. A head of state was present. A certain foreign dignitary, a well-known monarch, and of course his retinue. Special meals. Bodyguards. March raised her eyebrow. So? Her suitcase would be retrieved. The housekeeper on her floor would attend. My father, she told him, is a well-known monarch also. Not yet deposed. The man laughed out loud. We must all do our best.

She stayed on for an extra day until her father's fever that had troubled the doctor went down. He is no longer anxious, the nurse reported. He is cheerful now. A darling. March flew to Madison, picked up the girls and drove to La Rue.

Her mother lay on a hospital bed in the library. The doors to the terrace were open, and there were roses in a vase on the table, a glass of ice tea on a tray, new books, new magazines, white sheets with monograms, a blue silk blanket cover. Her leg, in a cast, was propped on a stack of small pillows in linen cases, blue and pink and white with her monogram. Her mother was wearing a bathing suit with a flowered skirt.

You look glamorous, March said.

Don't be silly.

You can be glad you're not in Rochester. The whole town is on morphine. Gulf Arabs pacing the halls. Out on the streets, the trees are baking. There are chapels everywhere, dark and cool, but frightening, considering. If you don't check out of the hotel on time, they assume you've checked out for good.

I'm ready to, her mother said. I can't move. My leg itches. It takes me all day to get upstairs for a sponge bath. As far as I'm concerned they can have the damn leg.

You don't mean it. But she suspected she did.

I've been lying here for three weeks and the garden's going to the dogs.

The garden looks perfect.

I'm sure.

It does.

The rabbits have picked the place clean.

March tried to think of what her father would say. He would say, cheer up. You'll be out of here in no time. I'll help you.

Cheer up. You'll be out of here in no time.

You sound like your father.

I know.

They can take the leg and keep it. At my age bones don't heal properly. There's no point in pretending they do. They don't. I've been lying here for weeks, and all I've gotten is fatter. I've read three books, and I wouldn't give you a dime for any one of them. You can say what you like about American writers, but as far as I can see they're all obsessed with sex. She tapped her finger on her copy of *Couples*. John Updike is not a person you would want to have for dinner. People we know do not behave like that.

But she was reading it, March noted. The phone rang then, and she could tell it was her father on the line, planning to come home sooner than expected.

The doctors at Mayo's must be out of their minds, her mother was saying. They ought to keep you right where you are. I know you. You'll be running to the office, racing around town, going out for dinner, pacing up and down. A caged lion, and then it will catch up with you. You'll be flat on your back. The doctors don't know who they're dealing with. Someone who has not one ounce of common sense.

A pause, and then, I'm sure they just need the bed.

Then, No I'm not fine. I couldn't be worse. March is here. And the children. They're getting ready to swim. It's ninety-five, but it's going to rain. I heard the weather forecast, and it's going to pour. I have no idea what they'll do then. I'm sure I'm in no position to entertain them. I can't imagine they'll be happy. I can't imagine why they came.

Then, the hospitals are like the airlines. They overbook. No. There is nothing anyone can do for me. I've had enough ice tea to sink a ship. I've watched more television programs than God. War, violence, some woman in Tennessee setting fire to a nightclub. Veronica Lake and Betty Grable are dead. What am I to do about that?

Her mother hung up. He can't wait to start running around. Everyone we know has retired. Your father still thinks he has to run the world. The world ought to try organizing itself for a change. We have been on every committee in this state, and as far as I can tell it has not done one damn thing. The world is intent on going to the dogs.

She helped her mother from the bed, and from there to the terrace, her mother swaying along on her crutches; March walked beside her with cigarettes, dark glasses, a straw hat, sun lotion. Then she went off to find the girls and change into her own bathing suit. In the pool March held out her arms so that Mia could swim to her, and Littlemarch and Alden dove for toy ducks, slid backwards down the slide, did tricks off the diving board, and finally lay on the warm stones and closed their eyes. There was a breeze off the lake and the leaves on the chestnut trees rustled. The water in the pool was still. A blue raft floated toward the filter, a jet headed out over the lake, her mother lit a cigarette, March rubbed lotion on her shoulders. She thought she could have stayed here, in this place, so still, forever.

When they started into the house her mother's crutch slipped, and she tilted against March who tilted against Littlemarch and then they all fell, so slowly that nothing seemed to have happened. They might have been leaves coming to rest on the dirt at the edge of the rose beds.

Oh, God, are you all right? March said.

But her mother was laughing. Poor Littlemarch, she said. Squashed.

Imagine *you falling on me!* Littlemarch said.

I just sit here on the chair, her mother said when they had climbed the stairs to her bathroom. I keep my leg out of the shower, and the rest of me in. Her mother had always seemed fresh, clean smelling, elegant. It was something she remembered about her mother from childhood. Her perfume, her pearls, her rings and her white gloves.

Her navy blue suit, her navy blue coat, her hat with the birds, her pocketbook. Her pocketbook with the clasp snapping.

How to bathe her, she was thinking, but her mother was already slipping the straps from her bathing suit; slipping the suit down over her breasts, over her stomach and hips. No, she said, she did not wish to take the suit all the way off. Certainly not. She had put the shower cap on her head; she was already adjusting the water, handing March the sponge and soap, waiting for her to begin.

March soaped her shoulders, her back, her arms, hesitant at first, waiting for complaints, but there were none, and then it began to seem the easiest of chores, the most natural act, to bathe her mother as she had bathed her children for so many years; standing there under the water, wet and soppy in her bathing suit, rinsing the suds away, making narrow rivers along her mother's back, washing the toes on her good foot, the soles of the foot, the high arch. She concentrated. She took her time, thinking of what she was doing as an act of love. What else could it be?

She came out from the shower, and her mother steadied herself on her arm, rested one hand on the sink, reached for the towel, removed the bathing suit at last, let it fall to the floor.

I can manage now, she said.

In her dressing room March lifted a clean nightgown from a stack, and heard her mother calling. Bring the comb and brush. My hair is a rat's nest.

In August March stood in the family room looking out toward the backyard where the small rose bushes continued against numerous odds to give up an occasional rosebud. The family room was a place they mostly avoided, because as Mia had said, it was creepy. In spite of the picture window it was dark and filled with the furniture they had dragged from one apartment to another. The lumpy couch, the fake oriental rug, the Turkish puff they had stuffed with newspaper where the dog now lay groaning in his own sweet dream. She would take him for a walk, she would wash the smudged picture window.

She would pick the iris, put them in the kitchen. In a mason jar. She would do that, and then she would dress up and call on Alan Stein. She would pick up the paper she had written for his course, and perhaps they would have a drink. A glass of wine. She watched as the man who lived in the house behind them came across his lawn toward her door. Ray with the two boys and the wife who had once brought her a jelly donut. Welcome to the neighborhood. Ray was carrying a package and knocking now, rapping his knuckles in a manner that seemed to rule out another donut.

He held out his newspaper offering.

In the sandbox, he announced. Our sandbox. Your cat. Made.

March shook her head. Made.

Doodoo. I have it here. He offered his gift, thrust it at her. Zachy and Kiley need clean sand. They have a right to expect that in life.

He spoke in a low, shaky, furious voice. His face was purple. March could see right through his crew cut to his scalp which had a sort of purple sheen. He was shiny and ominous. Suddenly he brought his leg up and stamped it down, and she could see his calf muscles swell above his neatly shined shoe and black ankle sock, and she imagined the blood rushing up into his thigh inside the tight corset of his Bermuda shorts, pausing and shooting upward. She imagined him having a stroke.

Oh Ray, she said. Ray. Ray.

Stop calling me Ray. My name is Rob.

All this time, March said. I thought it was Ray. But it's Rob. Rob. Right.

The doodoo isn't the only thing. People here don't like you. People know you're a radical.

Rob, I have to tell you. I think the little one. Zachy? Zachy should not have to stay in the pen you built. The wire pen? It seems so sad. And Kelly?

Kiley, he shouted. Kiley!

Kiley should not go on with the baseball lessons. He is out there with you every night. He has to throw, and hit, and run around to imaginary bases, and he looks so worried. He is probably thinking about Little League, and how will he make it, and his little shoulders droop. Also, the badminton bird? He can't get it over the net. He feels defeated. You have to try to let up. To relax.

Don't tell me what to do! You're getting out of Oaknoll. Oaknoll doesn't need you. Your dog is a menace. He's dangerous. We see him out there. He roams around. Your cat. Other things. I've noticed things. People here notice. I'm taking you up with the board. People don't want you here.

Rob.

Stop calling me Rob.

That's your name. Your name is Rob.

I know my name is Rob.

We're not going to stay forever, Rob. Trust me.

I'll tell you something, he said. I'll tell you.

He shook his shiny head, and his fists, and struck the edge of the screen leaving the slightest dent. Then he was off, fists still pumping, jogging across the grass until he disappeared around the corner of his house while March stood in the doorway, the small newspaper bundle in her hands.

But the day was young, and she had plans. Before midafternoon, before the girls came home from day camp, before Lynda came home from class to take charge. She washed her hair, curled it on Lynda's huge red rollers, borrowed, no stole, well, helped herself to Lynda's makeup; dipped into the pots of gloppy face stuff, eye shadow, mascara; and the stacks of little sticks and tubes she had practiced with when Lynda was out on dates with teaching assistants, boys in March's own classes who called Lynda all the time, boys who made Lynda laugh and say to March, They're sort of old, don't you think? For me? I mean, like *you* should be dating them.

She put on sandals and a very short skirt and t-shirt, and drove down to the street where Mr. Stein—Alan Stein—lived. She knocked on his door, feeling like a teenager. She waited, heard music, someone talking, and knocked again. She was half anxious not to disturb him, half determined to do just that. She thought about brushing her hair again, putting on more lip gloss. Then he opened the door and stood there, in his bare feet, looking startled. What on earth? Yes? Yes?

March looked past him, and saw the phone off the hook, the table covered with ashtrays and coffee cups, a bottle of scotch, a record player, newspapers.

He saw her looking and threw up his hands. Then he put his hands over his face, and went back to the telephone. Don't hang up. I'm still here.

His life was a mess, he was not getting tenure. March knew that. Everyone knew that. She had signed a petition. Allow this man to go on teaching here. He lights fires. This charming, undernourished, crazed man who ran around the lecture platform, and shouted into a disconnected microphone about Roethke, Hawkes, Nabokov, Faulkner, who stalked, wrung his hands, shouted, collapsed, lay on his back, who got up, came to the edge of the platform, sat with his legs hanging over, like Judy Garland, saying, listen, my children. Listen. And then he would read to them. Page after page from *Pale Fire*. From *Absalom, Absalom!* On and on. And they would listen. Still as the mice of their childhood bedtime stories.

He picked up his socks and came back to the door.

The paper. You said to pick it up, March said.

Yes. But I meant in my box. In fact, I did put your paper there. I think. I think. You are.

March Wright.

Wright. Right. Having said this, he began to laugh. I put your paper there. It was extremely clever. Brilliant at times. I wrote all that on the paper. He put his hands in his socks, and began to wave them.

March would not leave. I'm sorry you're not getting tenure. You should have it. Everyone thinks so. You can't teach *and* write. Not the way you do. Which is what the shouting is about. Shutting the university down. It isn't just the war. It's more than that. Students want more. Teachers like you. She thought how she longed to comfort him. The bottle of scotch on the table behind him beckoned. Why not share. Why not have a drink together? She smiled, hoping to encourage what was not yet a promise of sharing anything at all.

What can you do, he said. I'll find a place. Australia. Africa. Out West. There are agricultural colleges. A new life. Look at Malamud.

Out in Oregon for years. Eating onions and making art. *A New Life.*
I read Malamud and I weep. For myself too.

You can't go to Oregon, March said. I know Oregon. She had
never been to Oregon. There is nothing there. Trust me. Rain, grapes,
fish. More rain.

She could hear the person on the phone shouting. Alan. Donde
esta? What the fuck Alan.

I'm on the phone, he said. He put a hand out and March put
a hand out. Oh Christ, he said. Look at me. Socks. I'm a wreck. I
have socks on my hands. Well. Good-bye. Good night. I'm sorry. I
can't talk. I'm on the phone.

He started to close the door, but March would not go gently. It
would be nice if we could have a drink, she said. Of course you're
on the phone. But. She shrugged.

He looked appalled. He held up the socks. Right, he said. Very
soon. A drink. We should have a drink. Though. I'm on the phone.

Yes. Yes. You're on the phone. We could have a drink some other
time. When you're not on the phone.

Yes.

She withdrew her foot, defeated at last. He closed the door. She
leaned against it. Her grandfather who had taught her to play gin
rummy would have said, I smell defeat! She had no sense. No real
seductive force. No charm? Was that it? But at least she had finally,
at long last, stuck her neck out, more to the point, her foot. She had
gotten herself all tarted up. She had been pushy, and risked complete
humiliation. But she did not feel humiliated. That was a good sign?
It was. She was not offended at all. She was inexplicably pleased and
she wanted to laugh. What must the poor man have thought?

She drove home in the rain, more a warm misting, an English
afternoon, and everywhere the heaviness of summer past its prime,
so much more calming than spring with its insistent reminders of
birth, rebirth, buds bursting, innocent fragile bits of life appearing.
The fact of spring, with its determined air of exuberance, had always
made her feel lethargic. Not up to the challenge, the Chicago shrink
had said once, gloating, she thought, before she left him, and threw
his bills in the incinerator. She wondered if he was still alive. She

remembered the shirt he had worn the last time she had seen him, puffing out his chest like a spring robin. Well, he had probably needed a spiffy shirt to cheer him on with a nightmare patient like her. She passed the park where small boys were playing baseball, the lagoon where they skated in the winter, the neighborhood school, the Dairy Queen, the donut shop where she had taken the girls on April Fool's day; the school had burned down, she explained, and they would go to Mister Donut instead. (Oh Mom!) She drove past the Oscar Meyer plant, left again and down the hill, into old Oaknoll, where life tumbled on.

Mom! Mom! Their faces shone, and their pale, hairy legs sticking out of last year's shorts pounded the turf. Littlemarch and Alden raced to beat each other to the driveway, and Mia came forward on her tricycle, banging down the walk, cheerful as a drunk driver.

Daddo's married, Littlemarch cried.

He sent us a telegram, Alden shouted. He's married to Mary Lou! Mary Lou and Daddo! They hugged her, and looked at her for support, for confirmation. Then, Mom, you look so pretty. All dressed up. They were excited, and she could see them searching her face for an explanation.

Lynda, at the kitchen sink, came out with a sweater dripping with suds. Well, well. Look at *you!* You could have someone too, you know.

Warren had been folded into another life, and this fact served March as a kind of passport out from her own past. Although she had known this for a while, she had somehow failed to notice that the prison that was the failed marriage no longer required her presence. She put her hand there where she felt the center of herself to be. Not on her heart, but not far from it, a sort of core. A place that would slip around, and when that happened she had to stop, get hold of it. She felt it there, now, where it belonged.

We are going out for dinner, she said.

To celebrate? The wedding? they asked. Looking to her for confirmation. It was all right then?

Yes, March said. The wedding.

            ❧✕☙

A BALD eagle soared above them, circled, dove, rose and disappeared toward the far shore. Its nest was high and wide, the fixed abode of a pair of noble homebodies, a diligent, resourceful couple, keeping at their ancient pile of twigs and mud and pine needles, season after season.

Often when they were at Blue Lake they would look for the nest, hidden away in the tops of the trees, behind masses of branches, one tree looking like another. Late in the afternoon they would take the boat across the bay, cutting the motor, floating over the rocks where the water was low at the narrows, then drifting while they searched. Waiting for someone to say, there it is! Right between the two highest pines. At the end of my hand. Over there. Where? Which hand? Which pines. Those pines!

In Vietnam people were setting skin and land on fire. In Madison the unrest had increased. A camera March had been using at a rally had been smashed. A friend of Lynda's was in the hospital with a head injury. At Blue Lake the days were quiet. This was the one constant in their peripatetic lives, the place where March had been coming since childhood, in the years when she and her brother had climbed the steps to the North Woods Fisherman's Special in their pajamas, waking at the Blue Lake station where the sleeping car had been sidetracked before dawn.

For the last week they had played cards, fished, canoed down the Namekagon River, gone into town for groceries, stopped at the log cabin library, bought leeches for bait at the gas station, wandered through the small farmers market where they bought bread and butter pickles and honey. They held up the jars of honey, and looked through the gold glass at the fields, now a burnt brown, and drove slowly down the road that wound past Mt. Telemark, stopping for raspberries at Helen Jaloliwitz's, stopping for a chicken at the chicken lady's where they waited on the front steps, drinking lemonade under a pale skin-colored sky.

They went for a last swim. Littlemarch and Alden swam to the raft and March and Mia drifted along the shore, under the roots of giant spruces that had been torn out by a straight wind and now hung over the banks, their smashed tree bottoms pushing out, high above their heads, presenting mangled root systems that had taken on the appearance of something challenging, defiant. Afterward, lying on the dock, they wrapped themselves in towels. By mid-August, the water was cool, but the wood on the dock was still warm. March said it was what she remembered during the rest of the year. The warmth of the wood and the quiet.

Tomorrow they would drive back to Madison. Next week they would follow the moving van to Chicago, travelers wending their way home, or what had been home, and would become home once again, where they would hunker down, build their new nest, and take on the city from which they had fled three years before. The editorial job at *Playboy*, a new school for the girls; it was a gamble, maybe too much of a gamble, but they had come this far, and why not hope their return would lift them up in some way, offer them choices they had not even considered. They were in this together, March thought, but it was up to her to pull it off, to pull them through.

The sun was already setting behind Loon Island when she got up to check the boathouse. She picked up a fishing rod that had fallen from the rack, straightened the kayak paddles and slid the boat door down and locked it. In a while the sky would be black and blue and shot with stars. The mosquitoes would swarm. The owl would hoot. The wolves would howl. Time to get a move on.

In October March stood in their apartment on Lakeview Avenue, and surveyed the land. Beyond was the park, the zoo, the botanical gardens, Lake Shore Drive, Lake Michigan. Home, she said. Forever. For better for worse? Roots. Commitments.

The apartment was small, but on clear days they felt they were living in a sun-dazzled tree house. And this tree house is going down, Mia said. At night when the wind came up, and it did often, the building swayed, the water in the toilet bowl sloshed, and the conviction that they would come to the end of their days somewhere along the Lake Michigan shore was something March did not admit to.

We's a gonner, Alden said, continuing to speak with her interesting take on the language.

She knew she had come up short when she thought about their school, but they did not seem to mind. They could barely remember friends from the old days, and they liked the chaos of this new school, a progressive dump in an old house up the street, a cheerful experiment in learning creatively, or probably not at all, March thought. Before their return she had written to the school where the girls had started out, but the school had expressed no interest, saying there was no room, but March suspected otherwise. No room for a divorced mother with the reputation of a dingbat, and no big-time connections.

Late at night she scribbled messages. Let us consider. Let us *recon-sider.* She would describe the girls in detail. Tiny geniuses, amazing artists, storytellers, charmers. Who could resist. As for myself. I have a job now, a fiction editor (assistant, really, but never mind) at *Playboy* magazine. In each issue we publish the work of extraordinary writers. John Updike, Joyce Carol Oates, John Cheever, Nadine Gordimer with whom I recently had cocktails at the Pump Room. She had just bought a long black winter coat and wondered if this had been a good choice. I reassured her. Last week I had dinner with Saul Bellow who admired my ankle-length boots, among other things. On my first day at the office I took Carlos Fuentes, the Mexican writer and statesman to lunch at the top of the John Hancock building. Crabmeat salad while looking down on the clouds. Astonishing and disorienting! We had an extremely interesting chat!

As a family, I want to add that we have settled for good this time. I see us, the girls and myself, as a force in the neighborhood, the community, the city! Chicagoans with serious interests in education, politics, air pollution, better parks, safer streets. You name it. If it is positive, we're behind it. Here we are, taking risks, exploring new territory, living by our wits. Memories of Wisconsin are fading even as I write, and what I see are four people busy uncovering the selves we know are within us. So alive, so warm, so fierce with life, I sometimes suspect we have permanent fevers. Our cheeks burn. I think of you as our refuge, our second home. She scribbled on.

The notion of the school obsessed her, causing her to write a long magazine piece about the school for the *Chicago Sun-Times*, work that resulted in no success with the admissions office. Finally, a friend who was having an affair with one of the trustees convinced her it was not to be. Tell your pal to forget it, the trustee had said. They're looking for married people, African Americans, big spenders. Your pal gets a zero.

So the girls went to their school and March went to her office. A small, rosy-cheeked woman, an industrious apple with a kind soul named Alice collected the girls from school, shrunk their clothes, cooked fish sticks and charmed them all by exclaiming over the birch trees when they went to Blue Lake one weekend. I mean, painting all those trees white! Will you have a look now!

⁕

MARCH THE mother, March the editor, the would-be writer, the would-be hot-lipped hotsy-totsy lover.

March the editor sat behind her desk and counted her blessings. Free plants and paper clips, more pens that she had ever had her hands on before, a thousand memo pads with her name on each, a typewriter that worked, thick rich bond paper, a hot line to New York, health insurance, a secretary who worried about her, brought her coffee, vitamins, foods made out of pressed vegetables and sea-weed. A title, status, money. Now, when people asked, what do you do, she had an answer, and her answer gave her confidence and a certain cachet she found odd. People invited her to dinner, seated her next to hosts she barely knew, introduced her to artists, took her off to gallery openings and dances, to Maxim's, the new disco-theque. Pursued, March flirted, conveyed a sort of protected reckless-ness, occasionally slept with some man she barely knew, sometimes had a brief affair—thinking why not—wore the lively clothes of the moment to amuse herself and cover her anxiety. A black suede suit with a silver belt, leather pants with yellow bull's eyes on the back side, a dress made of paper, a black dress the girls called her Kleenex dress, red suede hot pants with edges like torn tin cans and black boots that laced to the knee. Like the Jolly Green Giant, Littlemarch, or March, as she now called herself, observed.

The days at *Playboy*. Manuscripts, stacks of manuscripts, long lunches, a steady stream of writers from around the world. Robie, whose office was next to hers, was kind, attentive, proper—unlike the young men in jeans and boots who put their feet on their desks, played the pinball machine, worked late into the night—a shy, proper soul, apt to quote obscure nineteenth-century poets, a formal professorial man who wore a suit and tie and only lay on his leather sofa when he had a migraine. His wife had died of cancer not long after March arrived, and she often had dinner with him at restaurants near his town house where he would talk about writers he had known. Robert Lowell, Cal, he would say; Lizzy, Elizabeth Hardwick; Ford Maddox Ford for whom he had been the literary executor; Flannery O'Connor whom he had known at Iowa. At the end of the evening he would hail a cab for March and kiss her goodnight. She would look back to see him on a corner, in his overcoat, pulling on his gloves, adjusting his felt hat.

He would stride into the office in the morning as though on a deadly mission, wearing a black suit, a black hat, carrying a black umbrella, encouraging Darius, the other editor in their department, to call him Mr. Death. Through Robie she met writers who gathered around him. Saul Bellow, Alberto Moravia, Paul Theroux, Stephen Spender, David Halberstam, Murray Kempton, Marshall Frady, Larry King. She sensed that he might have liked a more serious relationship with her, but she had no interest in settling down with anyone. Long after those heady days she wondered, and why not? One looked for someone to share a life with, to perhaps find happiness with, to grow old with. Wasn't that how it worked, life. Wasn't it? The possibility made her shudder.

Darius, whose office was next to March's, who never appeared to do any work at all and was usually on the phone to friends in New York, would lie on her office windowsill, nibbling French pastries, spreading crumbs over his fabulously expensive clothes, his splendid deep purple shirts and bow ties, entertaining her with gossip about New Yorkers in the publishing world (Brendan Gill will be here on

Saturday. And John Lahr next week. I have no time for anything but planning the party). He brought her onto the board of the Modern Poetry Association, encouraged her to work on her novel and entertained the girls who thought of him as their friend. He's just like us, they said. And like March he found the *Playboy* world outside their own small fiction department unfathomable. He was only here for a moment, Darius would explain. Then it would be back to New York where he belonged.

One winter weekend they invited Nelson Algren and Studs Terkel, whom they had never met, to a party that went on until morning. Later, as Nelson became a part of their lives, there were many afternoons at the race track, parties on Nelson's back porch where Christmas tree lights were plugged into an electric coffeepot, where the cook fried chicken and opened champagne, trips to the south side for elegant dinners given by African American writers, outings for the girls, afternoons at the Goodman Theatre and the circus; a dinner with Marcel Marceau whom Alden reported did talk. A lot.

On Sunday nights March and Darius and Robie would go along to the buffet supper and movie at the Playboy Mansion, a place they agreed was just plain creepy. It was huge, dark, baronial, with bunnies dashing about; a bar built over a pool where swimmers could retreat into the dark of a grotto—the pervasive air of sexual adventures, the assumption that up the grand staircase monkey business was going on. Editors were expected to appear, and there were the usual visiting writers and the women they brought along, and the bunnies who seemed enchanted by the possibilities for supper, ordering hot fudge sundaes, banana splits, daiquiris, anything at all. Young women hoping for whatever: city life, perhaps, money, fame—anything but small-town America. When the lights went down for the movie of the week, Hef in his maroon robe, his Barbie by his side, would enter and settle onto a kind of pillow-strewn daybed, creating a bit of a flutter. There they are! Imagine!

In the spring of her second year at the magazine a writer arrived who wanted a glimpse of such goings-on, and March was told to take him to dinner. She did, and half way through the frog's legs it dawned on her that she would far rather be done with the dinner and far above the Cape Cod Room in bed with this funny, smart man. Later she swore she had almost forgotten about meeting someone, out of the blue, just like that, on a spring night, midweek. Such feelings she thought had deserted her for good. But no, she thought as they finished their wine. Not at all.

He breezed into her life, claimed her, let March take him everywhere and departed. March's friends who had met him asked about him. Was he married. Oh yes he was married. And where was the wife. The wife was far away, in Rome, where they lived. And would he return for our dear March? That was hard to say. She hoped for more than the letters and charming promises. Your last letter gave me a cheery feeling in my loins, he wrote from Bombay. You do recall them, don't you, my loins? Indeed. From Santiago, do not leave me, you will recognize yourself in my next novel, and from London, do you suppose when we are very old we will spend our days together in a far-off tropical town? March did not rule this out. She wrote a story in which lovers came together after years apart. When the story was published in a little magazine she was amused, somewhat, by how she had treated herself with her usual black humor:

> *In the courtyard of the old hotel where a recent hurricane had blown out the windows, and yellow curtains fluttered, and the sign on the desk said,* Trips to the Interior, *the aged lover waited, in a white suit, looking young, splendid, delicious, at eighty! The woman, not so. Dressed in black, as though she had been in mourning for decades, she seemed to have very little hair, wisps here and there, and a small piece attached to the top of her skull, to cover the bald bit, something like a tipsy antimacassar made of hair, or wool, or perhaps nylon?*

She put to rest her marvelous fantasies when a letter came from the writer's brother, claiming he too was a writer, and wanted to spend time with her, wanted to see someone his brother claimed was amazing. Dear God, what had brother number one said. She did not encourage any such visit.

She tended to her own corner of the world, went out with men she had known years before who were now single, bankers, lawyers, stockbrokers with whom she could not imagine a weekend, much less a life. Then, after many lunches and dinners she began an affair with an architect who was notorious for his philandering, someone she grew to care about, whose letters she kept, whose Matisse lithograph hung on the wall of her kitchen, the invitation to his memorial service in her desk drawer. When she thought of him she realized how few men she had ever shared her thoughts with, loved. Because the ones you cared about were not available, a therapist suggested, and she thought that was the truth. During those years when so many of her friends chose to divorce and remarry, when she too had been offered the possibility of marriage, she had backed away. She would say, later, yes, of course I'll marry again, and mean it; until one day when the girls were already in college and she was working in New York someone asked exactly how long she had been alone, and she answered, half surprised, oh my god, twenty-five years.

IN FACT, with little free time, she hardly noticed the years going by. She was always pressed, often worried, taking up nights and some weekends to finish book reviews, a short story, articles for *Cosmopolitan* where she was a contributing editor, introductions for a *Playboy* collection of writers whose work would appear in a twentieth anniversary book. And day by day, hour after numbing hour, she poured over the manuscript pile that never seemed to shrink, the stories, novels, essays, poems, a slice of life, dear lady, which found their way from kitchens and offices, and prisons, and truck stops and hospital rooms from one country or another to the stacks that rose from her windowsill.

Dear Editor, thinking of a career in fiction. Please advise. Dear Ed. I am involved with cosmetic dentistry, and have stories you will not believe. Enc. are seven. My price is negotiable. Dear Mr. Mrs. Miss Ms. Who are you? I am a spy, and have information on the F.B.I. that could blow lids in high places you are no doubt not aware of. For obvious reasons I am not sending material but can be reached at this number in Texas. Dear Sir. What is this crap on my novel? Bacon? Coffee? You say your mag reads everything, but pages 211, 385, 607 and 687 are still upside down. Don't expect a second chance. I hope you have a crappy love life. The offerings affected her like sedatives, and some afternoons she could not keep her eyes open, but the letters also touched her. The awful desire to be heard, to be recognized.

At night there was the comforting buzz of radios playing, a stereo down the hall, country and western, a shout, a cork popping, the sight of businessmen from the hotel next door peering from their windows, an editor dropping by to tell about an underwater orgasm. I was ninety feet down. Ninety feet! Jeffrey from upstairs coming to tell her about the guy in his office. You have to come up and meet him. This guy. Hawkes. In my office. And March saying, oh my God, John Hawkes. *The Lime Twig*. You're kidding. I loved that novel. And Jeffrey saying, no kidding, the guy has a fourteen-inch penis.

Her Hawkes and their Hawkes; the wondrous meshing of many worlds. Journalists who wanted to meet fiction writers, the writers who wanted to meet journalists. Photographers, artists, sociologists, psychologists, freaks, addicts, bisexuals, homosexuals, transvestites, everyone wanted to meet someone. And March was no exception. There was James Dickey having an early morning nip at the lobby bar. A dinner at the Pump Room with one of their editors and Gay Talese coming along to join them in his splendid attire. Alberto Moravia complaining about his lost luggage. Alex Haley in a bar at midnight telling about a book he was working on, a history of African Americans that would become *Roots*. Bruce Jay Friedman at a supper arranged by Nelson at Riccardo's. Dan Greenburg and his then wife Nora Ephron and Beverly and Murray Kempton at a late night dinner. John Cheever pelting the conference table with spitballs. Heady stuff, March's friends thought, and when she looked back on those days she thought they were probably right.

March the editor, March the lover, yes, but more often than not, at six o'clock, on certain winter nights she would never forget, she would huddle in her father's old raccoon coat, hang onto the rope on Michigan Avenue, board the bus to the Fullerton stop, then through the park and into the lobby, into the elevator, up and away. Grocery bags, dry cleaning, mail in hand, she would beat it down the hall, her net shopping bag swishing along beside her, over the blue hall carpet like a bright fresh fish. She would kneel at the door and spread the contents of her bag on the folds of her coat, extract the key and slip it into the lock. And there they would be.

Mom! Mom!

We were waiting.

Are you going out? You better not be.

The phone's broke. Mia broke the dialer.

Alden said shit again. You should discipline her. You should do something about her.

Alice had to go. She has a boil. She can't sit down.

We had fish sticks. And Jell-O. Alice made it blue.

How come you're late? I bet you went out with your lover boy and kissed!

That's all you ever think about Mia.

Oh I love you so much. Oh my darling. Oh I am going to *marry* you.

That's all you ever talk about, Mia. And you lie about washing your hands before you eat. You never wash your hands.

You never brush your teeth.

You have breath like a owl.

Look at me, Littlemarch would cry, tears sliding down her face, so slowly, one by one, LOOK AT ME!

March would fold all of them into her arms, and they would tumble onto the couch, and after a while slip to the floor and lie in a heap. Through crossed arms and a tangle of limbs she would look out and see their legs poking up like flowers from the snow, making shadows on the white wall.

Mom. You won't ever die will you.

No.

You won't.

You promise.

You have to promise.

I promise.

What if you break your promise?

I won't.

What if you get married.

I won't.

What if you die.

I won't.

How come you know?

I know.

I'll live forever, you goofs. You'll have lives of your own, and I'll still be hanging around. A little bundle. Wrinkled and worn. A writer. A monkey. One hundred and one. Look see what we have here, you'll say. The dear mum. Mamacita! A piece of peanut brittle on a soft white handkerchief. Splendid! Amazing! She talks! She sings!

And you'll take turns wheeling me in a buggy through the park. I'll tweet like a bird on a leaf. My darlings. My darlings. You are my life.

And you will say, Oh hush. You'll wake the world.

EPILOGUE

The Attic, she had written on the side of the same leather suitcase she had once imagined stuffed with dollar bills, bursting onto the train platform as her father wended his way toward Montreal or Denver. The train platform where she had once stood beside her father with her own small bag.

The Attic had moved with them, from Chicago, to New York, to the tip of Long Island, from one apartment to another, one house to another, twelve moves in all (not including a stay at the Chelsea Hotel in New York, where the manager had assured March that the sheets were clean, they just looked dirty). The Attic was packed with the stuff of their lives. Photographs, letters, postcards, stories, a tiny pair of pink ballet slippers—her first grandchild's—a white leather wedding album—hers and Warren's—a cocktail napkin with Marlon Brando's telephone number, a photograph of her mother and father at a hunting party in Wisconsin when they were probably in their thirties, the only photograph she had of them when they looked happy, a *People* magazine photograph of a doctor she had met in La Paz where she had arrived after a hurricane, the doctor saying, you must be the new nurse, then taking her promptly to bed. Life was full of surprises in those days, when she was thirty-five, then forty, forty-five, new people, love affairs, not a few mistakes. A sense that the magic moments of the times would continue, mixed in with her anxiety, her fear, ever present, that she might fail the girls, that she might have let them down in ways she had not known; then, much later the conviction that she had failed them in ways she regretted, but could live with. They had come through. More credit to them, she thought.

Here were essays and short stories she had published, stacks of her magazine pieces and book reviews, a clipping covering the crash of an American Airlines DC-10, killing all passengers, including many *Playboy* friends on their way to a meeting in L.A.—among them the woman who had taken her place at the magazine. By that time the fiction department at *Playboy* had shrunk to almost nothing, and both she and Robie had moved on, he to Boston and Houghton Mifflin, she to New York to freelance, a life she had found tougher and lonelier than she could have imagined.

Here was a paper she had written at Vassar, "The Influence of Freud and Nietzsche on Eugene O'Neill"—what *had* she been thinking. A photograph of Max in Newport, torn not so long ago from the *New York Times*, looking, as she said to Mia, so old, and Mia saying, he *is* old, not adding, and so are you, only suggesting it was time for March to join a church and get a dog. March saying, she thought she had better start with a dog and so she had. Gus. Letters from the lover whose obituary she kept, the one she still thought about, a few photographs from their time in Port-au-Prince, one of her dancing with the new Minister of Culture, Graham Greene's small, wicked gossip columnist, those absurd days and nights at the famous and infamous Grand Hotel Oloffson in the time of Baby Doc, actors and journalists, con artists, senators, and musicians crowding the bar, the palace like a ghastly wedding cake glowing far below them, the Tonton Macoutes in their dark glasses, Mercedes wa-wa-wa-ing through the empty streets, the roosters crowing at dawn, the nuns in their slap slapping sandals walking up the hill to church. A photograph of Dr. Mellon and his wife whose work she had written about at their clinic in Haiti, a story about the women who worked in the baseball factory in Port-au-Prince, the goat farm where she had stayed, where she had developed Dengue fever. A sonnet from the traveling writer who had swept into her life and out, sending letters from Timbuktu and Ulaanbaatar, the one about the cheery feeling in his loins, you do recall them, only the word, smeared with something sticky, now appeared to be loons.

The present. An afternoon in late September. On the deck of the house March had bought in Sag Harbor, two hundred years old, charming and impractical in every way, bought when houses were cheap, and the Black Buoy was lively, and the Paradise was where people stopped for breakfast. They had come here years before to spend time with Nelson, who had died of a heart attack just before she and the girls rolled into town in a purple Chevrolet rent-a-wreck. Our godfather, the girls said. (Well, yes, in his way.) On her desk she kept a framed formal photograph he'd sent, a letter, so bitter, about the years in Chicago, when he felt he'd been ignored, and a letter from a filmmaker asking her to be part of a documentary about him.

Here was a note from her mother, sent from a retirement home, beginning Dear Mother, What is to become of me? I am lost. A photograph of Warren, at his typewriter, smoking a cigar; Warren who had died in San Francisco, high up in his apartment looking toward the Golden Gate Bridge, having lunches with old girlfriends, on his own, single again, a diabetic, sipping Heaven Hill, home at last, then nothing. Gone. Warren at fifty-four. She and Mia had been traveling across Eastern Europe before Mia's junior year in London, when the phone rang at three in the morning, in their hotel room in Warsaw, with March calling from New York, saying over and over, Dad. Dad. Dad is dead. She could still remember how the words had sounded as though her daughter was asking a question. Warren who would never know that his daughters had become women who would have made him proud, would never see his grandchildren who would have charmed him. He could still touch her heart.

Warren, who did not go gently, whom March and the girls had ended up taking care of when he lived alone in New York. In and out of hospitals, staying in a walk-up on 23rd Street, sweating out the morning the movers arrived to take his belongings back to California, March on hand to apply bandages to a staph infection on his foot that would not heal, Warren on the phone to the hospital in San Francisco, insisting on an emergency room appointment, the Fourth of July, the thermometer at ninety-five, the city mostly empty; the Spanish four-poster bed inherited from the rich grandmother heading down the stairs, boxes of books, two cases of wine, frozen Omaha steaks, out the door; and farewell to the movers, one of whom was a dwarf, both of whom were on something; then a taxi, and let's have a last lunch at the charming French spot up the street, but of course the French spot was closed for the holiday, and they ended up at the hot dog stand on Broadway where March got out and waved good-bye, and Warren did not look back and March went on waving, waving, the way she had once years before when he had left them in La Rue.

Here were boxes of thirty-five-millimeter slides for which she no longer had a viewer, the one she had ordered on eBay having arrived with a crack. An invitation to a showing of the old house in La Rue, moved, along with her grandparents' house, to another part of town, preserved as historic. A photograph of the house beside the lighthouse, sold years ago, the light no longer flashing over the shoreline, the foghorn no longer droning in the night, the last of the family having moved away, and so after six generations, only the dead in the cemetery on the hill. Contact sheets from her attempt to photograph the old haunts decades earlier. The Venetian Theater, Green Meadows, the Red Cross Drug Store, an attempt to somehow steal part of her past, freeze it, keep it.

Alden's wedding invitation in red Chinese characters, following a journey through China, with her boxer husband, her first, the feisty Serb; a wedding picture of Littlemarch and her husband in front of the Church of the Heavenly Rest in New York, one of her with her husband and children skiing in Vermont, a photograph of Mia and her husband leaving their wedding reception on a December night, one of them with their children and a small white dog, in the garden of their house in San Francisco, Alden and her daughter and her second husband on their wedding day, on the steps of a porch overlooking summer fields on Long Island, their bear of a dog pushing his way between them. Photographs of summers at Blue Lake, her oldest grandson waterskiing, barefoot, and the stunning touch of a bear moving from the shore toward his wake, March at the wheel of the boat with her youngest grandson flying behind, two granddaughters in kayaks heading toward a picnic on Red Rock Island, her older granddaughters in bikinis sailing toward Loon Island, a Fourth of July picnic at her cousin Annie's house down the road, fireworks on the dock, a dog show on the tennis court which she had judged and been accused of favoritism. True.

A family. Her family. When people asked why she had never remarried she said that what she had was what she had always wanted.

She thumbed through a much treasured review of her collection of stories, many written when she had spent time in Gordon Lish's famous writer's workshop, Gordon, brilliant, eccentric, a trouble-maker toward whom she continued to feel a certain affection. News clippings: President Kennedy's assassination, Martin Luther King's, Bobby Kennedy's, her father's obituary, her mother's, programs for memorial services, one for Penny and David, close friends whose car had slid off a cliff in Albania while they were on a rescue mission for Refugees International, a photograph of the three of them a few years before, a post-Christmas week they had treated her to in Venice, on the terrace of the Gritti, sipping Prosecco. A program from David Halberstam's funeral, in the same Riverside Chapel where he had been married, so many years before, where she had stood as a matron of honor for Jean, whom she had first known in Chicago, then for years in New York where they had shared a thousand dinners; but on that funeral afternoon, a lily placed on each chair, the casket, born by old friends, the gloom of the hour, the wind coming through the chapel doors, an awful low howl, the doors closing and silence, and the lonely heartbreaking sound of the flute. 'When Johnny comes marching home again. Hurrah! Hurrah!'

Finally, packed in a box, the draft of her novel. The novel with its absurd history. It had come close to acceptance, had then, to her mind, fallen down a dark hole; landing last on the steps of the brownstone on 90th Street where her small Albino neighbor had handed her the package, saying as he always did, pretty lady, pretty lady, which did something to soften the blow, but not much. When asked about the novel March said she had shot it with a gun she had brought from Chicago.

A novel too long, too long, four hundred pages, rambling, a real mess, she thought, but in fact it seemed better than she had remem-bered. The business of coming face to face with this work was the reason for delving into the suitcase. To have a look. To consider, to reconsider. She was more patient now, more confident, a writer who had learned from so many others, from Jane Bowles and Christina Stead, from Beckett, from Gertrude Stein and Harold Pinter, from Kafka. From Robert Lowell's widow Caroline with whom she had found a friend to share work with when they became neighbors in Sag Harbor, Caroline whose Irish aunt Oonagh March had known in Haiti, and who had to their great amusement turned up in one of March's short stories. Strange to make a friend at this age, Caroline had said, and March had agreed. But Caroline was gone now too. Best of friends, slipping off.

The Indian summer days soon coming to an end, the long winter months ahead, the monotonous gray afternoons, the early dark clamping down on them, Gus waiting for walks at the ocean. Blessed with good health, friends, her family, some loneliness, but not too much, stacks of new books waiting, firewood, the garden soon to be put to bed. Time to finish what she had begun.

She took the pages from the box, read the words for the first time in many years, words she could have spoken from memory anywhere at any time, words written shortly before the end of her marriage. *Even before she is born, March Rivers hears all about it. She rocks down there in that dark, warm river, listens to the music, the enchanting soap operas, bits of chatter, and tells herself, oh you're going to love it out there. Life. Yes you are, March.*